D1625335

# THE
# BONE
# CAY

**Also available by Eliza Nellums**

*All That's Bright and Gone*

# THE BONE CAY

## A NOVEL

### ELIZA NELLUMS

CROOKED
LANE

NEW YORK

This is a work of fiction. All of the names, characters, organizations, places and events portrayed in this novel are either products of the author's imagination or are used fictitiously. Any resemblance to real or actual events, locales, or persons, living or dead, is entirely coincidental.

Copyright © 2021 by Eliza Nellums

All rights reserved.

Published in the United States by Crooked Lane Books, an imprint of The Quick Brown Fox & Company LLC.

Crooked Lane Books and its logo are trademarks of The Quick Brown Fox & Company LLC.

Library of Congress Catalog-in-Publication data available upon request.

ISBN (hardcover): 978-1-64385-844-9
ISBN (ebook): 978-1-64385-845-6

Cover design by Melanie Sun

Printed in the United States.

www.crookedlanebooks.com

Crooked Lane Books
34 West 27th St., 10th Floor
New York, NY 10001

First Edition: December 2021

10 9 8 7 6 5 4 3 2 1

To Karen and Richard Nellums, always

Monday, October 7<sup>th</sup>
8:00 AM

*Day One*

FROM THE EDGE of the shore Magda paused to look left, where the roots might catch on hair or clothing. The branches ticked against each other in the breeze, like tittering laughter. She bent down to get a better view to the right.

Sometimes the bodies got tangled in the mangroves.

The ocean seemed lower than usual, even for low tide, but despite the dire forecast the morning was mild. There was a rowboat about thirty yards out, fishing the drop-off for grouper.

She was running late to set up for the meeting, but Magda never opened Whimbrel House without checking the dock first. Not after the first time.

She straightened up and stepped out onto the dock. There were people who refused to set foot here—as if Isobel herself might reach up out of the water and grab them.

A radio blared suddenly offshore as the man in the rowboat cast about for a station.

> *Hurricane Myra continues to gain strength and size as it closes in 100 miles south of Havana. The storm's final trajectory is still uncertain, and all of South Florida should be expecting evacuation orders within the next few hours.*

The dial was switched over to merengue music.

Magda sighed. *"Like being stalked by a turtle,"* Bryce had called the threat of hurricanes. This one had been on the radar since it had formed a week ago. It was the twin of one they'd been tracking last week, which had died out in the Gulf. It had already been a long and tedious season of near misses, and Magda didn't have time for the annual drama, not with having been unexpectedly obliged to close the garden for the whole weekend after the last suicide. The Cultural Landmark application wasn't going to complete itself. This was the year for greater national recognition; Magda could feel it. Also, they needed the funds. Characteristically, the estate was just barely breaking even despite the two big donations she had brought in back in August. And wedding season, the most lucrative time of year, was over.

She walked all the way out to the end of the dock and then got down on her hands and knees to peer underneath it, her face inches from the water's surface. She squinted, but there was nothing in the dim corners, nothing caught up against the pilings.

This was how she'd found the last one, three days prior.

Thank goodness she *had* found him, before a school group scheduled for that afternoon experienced a far more memorable tour than she'd planned. The high tide would have flushed him out just in time for the kids to be afforded the sight of his green and bloated face.

Back in Isobel's day there had been deep water right at the end of the dock, with a strong current. Nowadays you had to get out almost ten feet before the trench dropped out below you, a much more difficult proposition. You would still drown with a weight belt and enough alcohol, but instead of being quickly swept out to sea, you'd be washed back in by the waves.

In her first year as caretaker of the estate, Magda had found bodies twice—one a naked torso the scavengers had gotten to, the other still immaculately dressed. They had reinforced the lock on the gate after that. The next one climbed down the kapok tree from the apartment side. Magda, trained as a botanist, had overseen the trimming of all the branches low enough to reach. The next one had apparently swum down from the hotel up the beach. The Foundation hired a night guard, who had stopped two more in the attempt, and missed one. There was at least one other suspected, based on a letter, but never found. Maybe, like Isobel, she had reached the current further out.

Then, on the hundred-year anniversary of Isobel's death, there were three in a row, each two days apart.

A *hotspot*, they called it—like the bridge in San Francisco, or the forest in Japan. People were still drawn to the place Isobel Reyes had died. Magda couldn't blame them for their fascination, but she wished they could find a way to express it that didn't result in closing the Estate.

Today there was nothing. The police still hadn't given permission to reopen, but Magda had an important meeting with the application consultant in—she checked her watch—only ten minutes.

As she started to rise, one of the big snowy herons appeared behind her, silent as a ghost. Startled, she bit back a curse. *How is it possible,* she thought irritably, *for such a big bird to move so* quietly?

"Oh, you," she scolded. "Sneaking up on me again?"

The bird watched her with bright, inquisitive eyes, moving closer. "You could show a little fear, you know," she muttered, waving it off. Someone had probably been feeding it. "Shoo. I don't have any frogs or whatever for you. Go."

Whimbrel House had been declined as a Cultural Landmark the year prior, but the awards committee had been encouraging. Magda had been planning the new application for the past six months. This was her chance to prove that Isobel was not just a cultural icon here in South Florida—her poetry had truly changed the course of American literature.

Or wait, "truly *altered* the course"? That was more atmospheric, surely?

Still revising her opening, Magda followed the garden path up to the house and let herself in through the back door. As always, even her quiet footfalls seemed disrespectful in the waiting silence of the house. She made a quick circuit: everything was exactly where it should be, not a folded drapery out of place or a speck of sand on the hardwood floors. These were Magda's favorite moments, when the house was peaceful and Isobel seemed just barely out of reach.

Her phone chirped. The consultant for the Cultural Landmark application had cancelled because of the threat of being caught on Route 1 during an evacuation.

Magda sighed, and offered three dates to reschedule.

\* \* \*

The mansion, although right on the water, was built on an upwelling of rock that raised it above most of low-lying Key West. The houses inland were much closer to sea level and prone to flooding when the rainwater came in a torrent down the streets.

Still, it was a lot of work to brace for even a near miss. Magda decided she might as well start the preparations. There was a handyman from up the Keys who had agreed to drive over and look at the shutters on the ground floor, but she wasn't sure he'd be willing to come out given the forecast. She shot him a quick text just in case.

She was sorting through the emergency supplies in the kitchen when she heard Starla's old Camry grinding its way down the drive. Starla was a part-time employee who usually worked the gift shop and led the tours if Magda wasn't available.

"I heard you came in today, Magda," she said, leaning out the window. "You want the shop open?"

Of course she had heard; Key West was really just a small town.

"I doubt anyone else will come, with this forecast, but you can certainly help me get the house ready for wind. I've hardly done a thing since last time. That handyman was supposed to be coming today, but I'm sure he's got plenty of other people needing him now."

Starla popped her gum and rummaged around in her purse. "I think they're going to call the evacuations early this time. They're saying now it may be all the way up to the panhandle. Lord, that's gonna be a mess."

"I didn't think it was even supposed to hit Cuba before tonight," said Magda.

"Oh no, you haven't heard! They moved up the timetable. This is already the outer edge of it, these clouds and rain. It's getting real big."

Magda glanced out the window. It was true that the sky had clouded over, but if this weather was the harbinger of things to come, it wasn't much to write home about. Some mist, some gray clouds—a pretty common fall afternoon.

"I haven't been checking my phone. Are they still saying it'll hit here?"

"Dead on."

"I guess we'll see," said Magda. "You seen the last pictures? Jee-sus, that thing looks like God's own asshole, stretching halfway across the Atlantic." Starla extracted her phone and flicked through a few screens before holding it out.

Magda studied the image. The storm looked like all of them did—like a galaxy, broad and flat, with its arms stretching out. It took her a moment to find the scale, and then she saw what Starla was saying: it had been big the last time she'd seen an update, but now it was huge, practically spanning the Gulf, and the little divot of Cuba was barely visible.

"Wow, that is massive," she said. "Well, surely that just means it'll overextend itself like the last one. It's still only a category three, right?"

"Yep, just a three. I never think of leaving for less than a four, myself. And you know it's gonna turn," said Starla. "They always do. They keep you guessing and guessing, but then they hit this shallow water and they think, 'Nope, I'm not doin' it.' And by then we're all squatting up in Orlando for no reason."

"I guess we'll find out in the next day or so," said Magda. In her eleven years in the Keys, with at least a few threatening storms every season, she had never actually had a hurricane hit Key West directly. The island was a tiny target in a huge ocean—plenty of room for them to miss.

"I figure I stayed through Wilma, I can stay through anything," said Starla.

"Well, Jose didn't hit, Katie blew herself out, Lawrence turned out over the ocean at the last minute . . ." There were so many storms already this season. Experts suspected climate change was a factor. "Hopefully Myra will follow her brothers and sisters gently into that good night."

"I think that's the wrong poet," said Starla, taking off her ball cap to scratch her forehead.

"Very wrong," said Magda, smiling. "I guess Isobel would have said, *"Smooth Hands not waving off / but calling into safer Harbor."* Dylan Thomas was probably being born when that line was written."

"Is that from the shark one?"

Sometimes Magda wondered about the quality of Starla's tours. "That's *'Undine.'"*

"I knew it was one of them watery jobs. Well, what do you want to start in on first?"

Each of the big double doors had fitted hurricane shutters that fastened over the glass. The upper floor still had the originals that took two people to bolt into place: both women had done it many times, and they started there.

The handyman, Hank, finally puttered up in a shiny pickup as Magda was dragging the big cement planters—which in a strong wind could become projectiles—up from the front steps.

"Whoa, hold up—that looks heavy," he said, jogging over. Magda was stronger than she looked, but was grateful for his help, as any scuffing would damage the wood floors.

"They're just going over here," she said, lifting with a grunt as he took the other side. There was plastic sheeting set up in the hallway so that the dirt wouldn't cause a stain. "Thanks."

"Happy to help." Hank was deeply tanned the way people who spent a lot of time on the water tended to be; Magda could make out the shape of sunglasses in the ruddy skin around his eyes.

"I'm glad you could make it out," she said when they'd got the planters in place. "I'm sure a lot of people are calling today."

"Should have seen it yesterday." He turned back to his truck. "Haven't had hardly a minute's peace. Would have been here sooner today, but I had to borrow my buddy's pickup."

"Do you need help unloading?" she asked, surveying the stacks of plywood roped together and tied down to the bed of the pickup with jaunty blue rope.

"Oh, I think I can handle my own wood." He winked; Magda rolled her eyes.

"Alright, well, all the windows on the ground floor still need to be covered. I'll just be inside, packing up what's fragile."

"Remind me, what is this place again?" asked Hank, untangling the rope. "Some kind of museum?"

"It's the family estate of Isobel Reyes. The poet?"

"Oh yeah, I've heard of her, I think. Sorry, I'm docked in Key Largo—I don't know all the sights down here. And I was never one for literary stuff."

"She wrote a lot of famous poems," said Magda. "'Antigone,' 'Wake-Robin'? 'Showman's Rest'?"

"Like I said, not a big poetry guy," said Hank. "My little girl probably knows her. I'll ask when I get home."

Magda decided not to debate the gendered nature of poetry right at that moment. "I'll let you get to these windows." she said. "All the ones on the ground floor could be reinforced, but the worst ones are near the front door."

"On it. They'll be good as new."

Magda, who actually hoped they'd be as good as *old*, decided to head back inside and shoot a quick email to their intern, a student at University of Miami, about sending some tweets with their donation link. It wouldn't do to miss out on the potential of a disaster.

The slam of a car door had her looking up next: a family of four made their way down the drive: mom, dad, and two little kids, maybe eight and twelve. Magda pushed open the wooden blinds so they would see her in the window, and waved.

"Are y'all closed?" asked the mother, coming up onto the porch. "They said in town you might be closed."

Technically they were, but between the investigation and the forecast, there weren't likely to be any other visitors. And tours paid some of the bills.

"I'd be happy to show you around," she said, double-checking that her laptop and her notes were hidden under the tambour of the rolltop desk. It was a point of personal pride—and the result of a decade of labor—that not a single anachronism would break the spell of Whimbrel House. At least on the first floor, all was exactly as it would have appeared in Isobel's day. '

"So, what do you think of this forecast?" asked the father, stamping sand from his feet as he mounted the porch. "Do you think this one will hit?"

"Oh, it's so hard to know," said Magda. "They were all excited about that one last week, and now they're fired up about this new one." Like any resident, Magda knew to ignore the national coverage, which was prone to hysteria, and focus only on the local stations, which had no incentive to catastrophize.

"Our flight out is this afternoon. Think we'll be alright?"

"You'll be fine. It's not supposed to start until tomorrow anyway," called Starla.

"I want to see the monkeys," said the girl, who was kicking rocks down the drive.

"Lemurs," said the older boy. "They're not monkeys, they're lemurs." He wiped his shiny nose with the cuff of his shirt, cheeks flush with what might be fever. Magda discretely stepped back.

"We can see the lemurs after we walk through the house," said the mom, clearly anticipating this argument. "This nice lady is going to tell us all about it."

Magda stood up. "Welcome to the Isobel Reyes Estate and Museum!" she said. "My name is Magda Trudell, and I'm the caretaker of Whimbrel House. Have you had heard of Isobel Reyes?"

The older boy nodded dully.

"Who can tell me something about her?"

"She was a *witch*!" yelled the little girl.

Magda sighed internally. Ten years she had been leading tours, and that was still the most common answer. "That's certainly something people say about her. What else?"

The boy thought. "She wrote poems."

"That's right, she was a famous poet. Have you read any of her poems?"

"One. We had to for class."

"Which one did you read?" Magda could guess.

The boy had long bangs that seemed to hang into his eyes. "It was called 'Showman's Rest.'"

"That's one of my very favorite poems!" said Magda. Not true: her favorite was "Antigone," but "Showman's Rest" was included on the sixth-grade curriculum, and this was called "building rapport."

"Well, this is the house that Isobel lived in," she continued, "and we've tried to restore it to look exactly the way it did during her time."

"It's . . . nice," said the boy flatly, glancing around.

"Thank you! Isobel's grandfather, Howard Reyes, gained his wealth as a salvage wrecker. He built this house sometime in the 1850s, and it was among the earliest mansions in the southern Keys and the most elegant at the time. Isobel was born here in 1895 and died here in 1918 at the age of twenty-three. And today people come from all over the world to enjoy her poetry and learn a little more about her life."

"I hear she killed herself," said the older boy.

"I hear she's a *ghost*," said the girl.

"There are lots of stories about Isobel," said Magda, who was used to handling complicated questions. "Why don't we all go see if we can find any here in the house."

She led them through the double doors, through the hallway, and into the main seating area.

The house had been built in the Spanish colonial style, with floor-to-ceiling rounded windows that doubled as doors to the two balconies. Charles Reyes had been a man of simple but eclectic taste, and Magda had tried to select all the furnishings in keeping with his preferences, as described in letters of the time. Therefore most of the decorations reflected either the adventures of his younger years of travel—curios and relics from the far corners of the globe—or the Caribbean influence of the location. Bright walls with heavy, dark furniture; bare wood floors covered with woven sisal rugs. Sunlight and fresh air everywhere.

"Do you think there's a new forecast yet?" asked the mother. "How often do they send updates?"

"There's always a new update," said Magda. If she knew anything about hurricanes, it was that nobody really knew what they would do.

"Seems like the predictions are all over the place. One day it's a category two, the next day a four."

"Those are eyewall replacement cycles," said Magda mildly.

"Is the house really haunted?" asked the girl, who was keeping close to Magda's legs.

"Well, some people say it is," said Magda, which was true. "But I've been working here for a long time, and I've never seen anything suspicious, even when I'm here all alone late at night."

"I think there could be ghosts," said the boy.

"Now, here on the left wall is a painting that Isobel herself painted as a birthday gift for her father," said Magda, waving to the heavy oil painting hanging over the side table. It was a stormy sea, with moody clouds low on the horizon, but there was a crack of light in the center and what might have been a seagull or an osprey suggested by a shadow of wingspan. "Isobel loved the ocean, which you'll see in most of her poetry. In fact, out of the three hundred collected poems that are considered finished today, almost two hundred and fifty of them are about the landscape right here on Key West: the beach, the animals, and the weather. This painting looks a little bit like the forecast for today, don't you think?"

"It looks like it's going to rain," observed the girl solemnly, studying the painting. "It looks sad."

"The amazing thing about this painting is that, as far as we know, Isobel never had any formal training in art. She created this piece after reading a book in her father's library about the Hudson River School of painting. In fact, Isobel never went to school, like you do. Do you know why?"

"Because she went to a magical school instead?" suggested the little girl.

"What? No, dummy," said the brother.

"Matthew Curtis that is not how you talk to your sister and you know it," said their mother, not looking up from her phone.

"Ah, well, Isobel certainly was different from other children, and that's part of the reason she didn't go to school," said Magda, redirecting their attention as best she could. "Do you know what distinguished her from other kids?"

"She didn't talk," said Mathew.

Magda nodded her head. "That's right. In adulthood Isobel was never heard to speak out loud. Also, she apparently dragged one of her feet when she walked. But she still managed to express herself pretty well, don't you think?"

The boy nodded, bless his heart, although Magda was sure he only wanted to hear more about ghosts and witches.

"They're saying it might get stalled out over Cuba," said the mother. "Sometimes they do that, I guess. We thought about changing our flights last night. We probably should have changed our flights. I heard the airlines aren't charging."

Magda nodded soothingly and kept going. "If you look here in the corner of the painting, you can see Isobel's signature. This is one of only a few copies of her signature that exist, because she rarely signed her poems. We have one other copy from the contract she signed with the publisher who distributed her first book, *Wake-Robin*, but the only other copies come from the leaves of the books that were hers in the library."

The painting had been covered in plexiglass specifically, at Magda's insistence, so that the kids could press their faces close to see the blocky, childlike printing. They probably both still wrote the same way.

"As far as we know, Isobel Reyes was born and died right here in Whimbrel House" (*well, out behind it, actually, but no need to get into that*), "and as far as we know, she never left the Estate in all her life. So this place was very, very special to Isobel. She knew every single inch of it. And I like to think that when we come here and enjoy it, it's like we're sharing it with her, and like she's still here in some ways."

"Why did people say she was a witch?" asked Matthew. "Was she really a witch?"

"Well, Isobel was misunderstood in her own time," said Magda carefully. "Her father, Charles, practiced no religion and was an early advocate of agnosticism. In fact he was very outspoken on the point, especially after the death of his wife, Abigail. So there were people who didn't like the Reyes family very much because of that. If you follow me to the hallway here, I can show you portraits of Isobel's mother and father."

She led them around the corner at the same time the door from the kitchen opened and Hank came in, hauling a load of plywood, tracking sand from outside. In his jeans and Florida Marlins T-shirt, he looked about as authentic to the period as a box of Hot Pockets.

"Oh. Hi," he said, looking startled. "Sorry—didn't realize anyone was going to be in here."

"I'm going to step out and call the airline," said the mother, motioning to her phone. Magda nodded and smiled, all teeth.

"We'll be quick and then we'll be out of your way," she told Hank. "This painting is of Abigail Reyes, Isobel's mother. Abigail was the daughter of a wealthy sugar merchant from Louisiana, and she met Charles when she was seventeen. His father, Howard, had died a wealthy man the year before, and Charles inherited this house and a fleet of shipping vessels, so he married Abigail and brought her back here in 1894."

The portrait featured a small, pale woman with delicate features. She looked wistful, if not exactly sad. Magda believed it was painted after her death, possibly using the funeral portrait that would have been common at the time, although such a photograph had never been recovered.

"Unfortunately, five years after the birth of their first daughter, Isobel, when Abigail was carrying their second child"—(*there had actually been two miscarriages in between, one late enough to be considered a stillbirth*)— "Abigail and Isobel were walking out on the beach in weather not too different from this, and they were struck by lightning."

"Oh yeah? They were *both* struck?" asked Hank, who was leaning the plywood against the wall. "Never heard of that before."

"What, were they holding hands or something?" asked the father.

"Most likely the bolt itself struck the beach nearby and then traveled laterally through the wet sand," said Magda. "In fact this still happens every year; you have to be very careful out on the beach, even when the weather doesn't seem so bad."

In case nobody was listening to the history, Magda figured it didn't hurt to throw in a safety lecture every now and again.

"Well, Abigail was killed instantly, and five-year-old Isobel was badly injured. In fact, many people believe the painting we saw in the great room might even be from Isobel's memory of that day" (Magda thought that made it a bit of an unwise choice for a birthday present, honestly). "Today, we believe the most likely effect of the lightning for young Isobel might have been a ruptured eardrum. She developed an infection that left her partially deaf. And that's probably why Isobel was mute, because sometimes people who can't hear well don't learn to talk correctly.

Of course, Mr. Reyes was distraught at the loss of his wife and his unborn child, and also because of Isobel's serious illness. He felt it was bad for Isobel to be out and about in the community where people might make fun of her, so he kept her here at the Estate for the rest of her life, teaching her to read and write from the books in his extensive library. That's where she developed her unique style of poetry."

"Okay, they're saying they're going to wait until the noon update," the mother announced, walking back with the phone in her hand. "At least we're close to the airport. We'll be able to go straight to Security."

"Alright, honey, sounds good," said the dad.

"Oh yeah, airport's right over there," said Hank, nodding.

"Let's head into the library now," said Magda. "We have some original volumes there, including many that inspired some of Isobel's most famous poems."

"Oh shit, sorry, I left some of my bags in there," said Hank. "Let me just duck on ahead of you now . . ."

"Sorry about this—we weren't necessarily expecting visitors today," said Magda. "But we're very glad you're here! Now, Isobel still found ways to make an impact in the community"—Magda steered them slowly down the hall—"and to communicate with the thinkers and leaders of her time. For one thing, her father was very well connected, and he often brought important people from the area to the house for dinners and parties. Isobel didn't speak, but she enjoyed listening to their conversation and sometimes followed up with them by mail. Her original letters are stored in the Smithsonian archives, but we have some reproductions on display, and some of the books are the original editions she would have read."

Not all of them, but Magda was working on that.

"Alright, got 'em," said Hank, ducking out past her with his box of tools and a bucket organizer. "Bye now. You folks enjoy yourself. Safe travels."

"Isobel became well known for her letters," Magda continued, blocking out the distraction. "Sometimes she wrote to disagree with what someone had said or to ask more questions. She also wrote a letter for the local newspaper that started a series of editorials she and her father wrote together about the sharking industry in the Keys. Isobel worried that they were slaughtering too many sharks and that the chum from the processing was causing a hazard for swimmers. Did anybody read Isobel's poem about sharks, 'Bone Slinger'?"

Both the mom and older boy nodded; it was a relatively simple poem (*the Hollow shadow of the wave,*" etc.) and was often included in the textbooks.

"Because of those letters, she began to get local acclaim and was engaged in a few written correspondences with important thinkers of the day, including e. e. cummings and T. S. Eliot, and even a young high school student named Ernest Hemingway."

In fact, some of Magda's most cited research was her argument that Hemingway's sparse prose had been inspired by Isobel's poetry, which had been described by her contemporaries as "the atoll of an undersea volcano." Hemingway had later opined that good writing was "like the tip of an iceberg." Unfortunately it probably wasn't the right crowd for a lecture on comparative lit.

"Isobel's first book of poems, *Wake-Robin*, was published anonymously within her lifetime. It was an open secret that she was the author, and it brought her a lot of acclaim, if not much money."

Isobel's publisher, Robert Margery, had been unscrupulous. The advance from her second book was delayed by over two years after her death and never provided the Estate as much as it should have.

"Her second book, *The Edge of the Water*, was published posthumously, meaning after she died. Today both books are usually published as a single volume just called *The Collected Works*."

Magda pointed to the museum's heavy leather-bound copy of the *Works*. It was actually a reprint from 1965, but even she had to admit it looked impressive in the spot.

"Even in her own lifetime, most people didn't believe such a young girl could be the source of the letters, and they began to travel to the Reyes house to meet Isobel and see if she was really writing them herself. Because of that and also because of her disabilities, she was known as a local oddity, and the rumors started then that she was a witch, which was just a way of saying there was something different about her. Also Isobel was very shy, and her father was protective of her and usually didn't let visitors talk to her directly."

"Was he embarrassed of her?" asked the youngest girl. Magda glanced down; it was an unusual question for a child her age.

"It's not entirely clear, but it's certainly true that Mr. Reyes wasn't always comfortable with his daughter's increasing fame. Many people invited Isobel to travel and visit other places in Florida, and all over America, but he always responded on her behalf that her health wouldn't have allowed it."

"Wait—did I leave an extension cord in here?" Hank popped his head back in.

Magda cleared her throat. "I don't see one. Now, this is the only photograph we have on record of Isobel." She handed around the enlarged reproduction printed on card-stock, which had been resting on the credenza. The original one was somewhere in the Smithsonian annex.

In the photo, Isobel was standing stiff and straight between her mustached father, who was wearing a waist-coat that strained vainly over his rounded belly. She was standing in what Magda suspected was a carefully arranged pose to disguise her dragging leg. It was unclear from the angle if it properly supported her weight at all.

Magda had stared at this photo for hours, trying to understand the young woman who had produced such beloved, timeless words. But Isobel's expression was unre-vealing. She had a clever, pointed face, and something of her mother's small features. Her dark hair was carefully styled but modest, parted low and precisely divided to curl back behind her head. Her body was thin and short limbed like a child. She was wearing a demure dress that looked black in the photo, although it could have just as easily been dark blue or burgundy. Even at the time she would have appeared old-fashioned, her hair still long, her floor-length dress belonging to a previous decade. Her expression met the camera dead on.

"She's not very pretty, is she," said the little boy thoughtfully.

"Oh, I don't know," said Hank, looking over his shoulder. "There's something kind of special about her, don't you think?"

"Yes, I've always thought so," said Magda warmly.

She paused at the base of the staircase, which was roped off. "Now, the second floor of the house is unfinished. We're not really sure what the rooms would have looked like in Isobel's day, but we're working with experts from Florida State to reconstruct all rooms to their original style." And had been working, for as long as Magda had been at Whimbrel House, which was more than ten years. She remembered giving the same line as an intern. Most recently, an engineer had been out to look at the staircase and suggested it not be, technically speaking, quite structurally sound. It was recommended that the public be prevented even from standing around the base of it.

"But if you'll follow me out through the kitchen, I can show you the gardens that inspired Isobel's most famous poems."

"Well, I wanted to check the weather anyway," said the mom to her husband. "Do you think she's almost done?"

Magda led them out through the side door and down the drive. There was a good view back toward the building from here, unencumbered by trees. She paused to let them look.

The house was white, made of limestone that had been excavated from the foundation—fossilized coral—and carved into blocks by Howard Reyes's crew of slaves. The blocks had then been covered with plaster.

The low roof and the balconies were metal, painted dove gray, designed to resist the frequent fires of the time. According to local legend, they were made from the decking of salvaged ships. Magda hadn't been able to verify that, but certainly many of the original interior features, including the marble fireplace, had been rescued by wreckers from ships bound for New Orleans.

Out of all of busy, crowded Key West—jam-packed with bars and tourist attractions—only Whimbrel House had such a large lot: a full acre and a half, each square foot precious to Magda. Howard had purchased the plot drawn into the original survey of the island. The house stood amid its sprawling garden on a rocky rise that overlooked the coast.

"It doesn't look that bad, really," said the father, staring up at the sky: cloudy and sullen. "I guess we'll listen to the update to decide."

"Let's head over this way," said Magda, steering the kids to the right.

The garden was lined with tamarind trees and heavy-headed walking palms whose broad leaves were bigger than a man's shoulders.

It had been Magda's patient labor of the past five years to clear out the gaudy tropical plants that had crowded the garden—the rubber tree, the coconuts—all of which had been planted sometime in the seventies. Oh, the outcry when she had taken out the crepe myrtles! But they weren't even native trees (and such flimsy, fragile branches, at that). The Keys were semiarid, receiving far less rainfall than mainland Florida, and in Isobel's time the house had no running water, so the gardens would never have been lush and green. Somewhere on the property there was supposed to be a cistern to catch rain (there was also one on the roof that had allowed for indoor plumbing before there was municipal water), but that had been covered over long ago. At least the trees dampened the constant roar of jets coming into the airport, which could be glass-rattlingly loud at times, undercutting the illusion of a bygone era that Magda worked so hard to cultivate.

"It's so pretty!" yelled the little girl, bounding over the back steps. A light mist was just starting, not enough to make anything damp yet. Atmospheric, maybe.

Magda had planted native shrubs, according to accounts of the time—joewood, blackbead, fiddlewood, pearlberry, pigeon plum, wild indigo berry. Around the house she encouraged the sea grapes, their leaves like dinner plates, and lucky nut and flaming glorybower. For trees, cinnecord; silver buttonwood, its leaves soft as lamb's ear; and down at the water's edge she let the mangroves come back—black right at the lip of the water, red a few feet behind. It had taken years to convince the Board to let her grow them ("ugly brush," they'd called them) as shoreline protection, since the beach would erode away if they left it bare, and nobody had funds to pay for constant replenishment. Finally a generous grant from the State for habitat restoration had convinced them.

The overall effect was wild, plants asserting themselves every which way, battling with determination for this one acre of paradise that hadn't been mowed under for condominiums or hotels. Magda loved it—it reminded her of Isobel. Savage and indomitable. Even the Board had finally agreed it was unique, in contrast to the other tourist estates on the island, and they were proud of their claim to authenticity.

"We know from her letters that this was Isobel's favorite place," said Magda, turning in a slow circle to wave down to the open water.

The father cleared his throat. "So that's the famous dock?"

Magda sighed. "Yes, it is. Unfortunately, we can't go down to the shore at the moment as it's"—*still an active crime scene*—"undergoing repairs."

The piers of the dock itself were built of good Dade County pine and had remained sturdy since the house had been built, as far as anyone knew. "The beach looks much the same way it would have looked in Isobel's day, based on photographs from the next owner."

At the moment there was a wooden canoe—authentic to the era, although unconnected with the house, since Magda had purchased it up in Manatee Bay—and a modern aluminum skiff overturned and mostly hidden from sight in the tall grass.

"It's strange to be staring at such a famous place," said the mother, finally looking up from her phone, her eyes on the dock. This spot still had a pull, even after so many years. Isobel still had power here.

"So what's the current theory for why she did it?" asked the father.

Magda glanced over at the kids roaming around the garden with a ready eye out for any flower pickers or branch hangers—but the light rain seemed to be keeping them down.

Isobel's death was a matter of public record, but it wasn't something Magda typically lingered over on a family tour. A dry, matter-of-fact sentence, then jumping to the modern history of the house and its ongoing restoration.

"Well, what we know comes from her publisher's account. He printed an excerpt of the letter he received from her father after it happened. Charles Reyes never spoke about the incident on the record."

That short, brokenhearted paragraph had been poured over by generation after generation of scholars looking for some evidence that had been lost to time.

"According to the September letter, Isobel had been working on her second book, which she called *Blood-Root*, after the final poem." The title was changed later by the publisher to capitalize on the sensationalism of her death. The original title was in parallel to that of her first book, *Wake-Robin*. Both plants were found in Isobel's herbarium, which her father ordered for her all the way from the University of Missouri.

Even at the time there were claims that *Wake-Robin* had required extensive revision by her publisher (who had indeed insisted they remove her idiosyncratic capitalization. Isobel's thoughts on the correction were unrecorded—there were letters missing from that period—but it was notable that her second collection featured even more of them).

"We know from her letters that Isobel was struggling with the attention the first book had brought her and dreaded its renewal after her second. She had even considered not publishing it at all, but her publisher, Robert Margery, traveled all the way out to Whimbrel House to convince her. Charles reported that Isobel finished the last poem, "Blood-Root," the next morning."

"Blood-Root" was a dark and troubling poem, the imagery seemingly based on the Book of Revelation, which was an interesting choice for an agnostic.

"Isobel told her father that 'Blood-Root' was the perfect poem," said Magda, starting the story the way it had traditionally been told. "She said that now it was complete, she could finally get some sleep. Charles thought she meant to nap in the grass, but at eleven o'clock in the afternoon, he watched from the window of the second floor as Isobel walked off the end of the dock. She apparently never resurfaced."

This story of artistic suicide was what drew desperate people to Whimbrel House; it was the main part of Isobel's legacy that everybody knew. Magda always tried to de-emphasize it, tried not to make it sound either romantic or inevitable, and yet she knew what most people took away from the tour despite her efforts.

The father swallowed, his eyes on the dock. "Was it, uh—sharks, do they think?"

"Well, it was an unusually brisk day. She was wearing a long dress. It would have been heavy in the water, and she was probably pulled down by the weight of it."

Most researchers believed Isobel had suffered from depression on and off throughout her life, but their evidence was weak, coming mostly from a few lines in letters to close friends. And the poems themselves, of course, but Magda didn't believe in attributing the art to the personality of the artist.

The truth was, of course, that they would never know. Isobel went to her death without ever speaking a word, which meant there was nobody left to explain her poetry or her final act.

She imagined that Isobel, who had been suffering from recurring pneumonia that seemed to be impacted by her neurological symptoms, must have felt worn and old already, at twenty-three, laboring over her precious book of poems. Was she anticipating a long decline, shut away from the world by her own illness, trapped in a fragile body? Or was it the reception of the book, the increased accusations about her character, that she had dreaded most? Certainly the extraordinary story of her suicide had been a huge factor in her fame. Her final book of poetry, *The Edge of the Water*, had outsold the first ten thousandfold.

Maybe the reason Magda couldn't wrap her head around it was because, in her estimation, "Blood-Root" was still an unfinished draft. Isobel, usually a perfectionist in her spelling and punctuation, had misspelled *firmament*, and the final couplet didn't rhyme, which Magda had found was often accomplished in her final revision. Also, the much technically stronger poem "Antigone" was still unfinished at the time of her death— found in a scribbled-over, crumpled draft among her letters. How could anyone feel their legacy ended with "Blood-Root" and leave an achievement like "Antigone" unfinished?

"Antigone" was revolutionary, a completely new style for the time as well as for Isobel herself. If it had been completed, it was the kind of poem that would have changed the course of literature. "Blood-Root" was mostly famous because of the grisly story attached to it.

Magda stopped to pull a sprig of purslane that was out of place. "Six months after Isobel's death, Charles Reyes married a young widow from neighboring Sawtooth Island, an heiress to a sugar fortune out of Haiti. They moved to her family home the following year, but tragedy visited Charles again three years later, when he and his young wife and son were all killed in a shipwreck during a fishing expedition in Bimini. That certainly contributed to the sense that the family was marked by tragedy . . . or haunted."

All of them killed by this place that they loved, in one way or another. There was a fatal beauty to the Keys, as Isobel herself had written in "Bone Slinger."

"Can we see the monkeys now?" asked the little girl, wandering over. Her brother followed eagerly. He sneezed without covering his mouth, and Magda felt the air gust across her cheek. She sighed.

"We can go see the lemurs! These are very special albino lemurs. *Albino* means they're born without the genes that cause them to have colored fur. In fact, one of the reasons why people believed the house was haunted was because of these little guys living in the trees and making a racket. Late at night, they can almost look like ghosts moving between the branches, and they can make noises that sound like human voices, even like a woman screaming."

Running ahead, the little girl did not seem troubled by this comparison.

"They live right here in the walled garden," she said, walking the family to the stone walls off on the hotel side of the house. "Can you hear them? I think they hear us coming."

The lemurs were indeed putting up a fuss, knowing that kids usually meant treats. On the other side of the main gate they were gathered, bobbing in excitement.

"They're so *cute!*" said the mother, clapping her hands.

They were pretty cute, Magda agreed. They were a pain in the neck—the vet bills alone were astronomical, never mind the fruit, and it was a lot of extra work to clean up after their hijinks—but they were pretty cute.

They backed up as Magda opened the gate and led the group inside. Then they climbed into the near tree, their little furry faces peering through the branches, watching the children with what seemed like reciprocal enthusiasm and intelligence.

"Can we pet them?" asked the smaller girl.

"No, they're not pets. They're not used to being handled. They live wild in this garden. But you can throw them some fruit, and they'll hang around."

Magda handed over the bag of dried figs she used to buy their tolerance, or else they would have probably taken to the far trees. There was a low net over the garden that kept them inside the pen, but it was a spacious enclosure and they were free to roam inside.

"Charles Reyes brought the first two lemurs back to Isobel after a trip to Madagascar in 1898," said Magda, while the kids squabbled over the fruit. "The original pair had only one white lemur named Princess Ann, but Charles purchased another white one in 1911 to keep the color in the gene pool. This white color isn't adaptive in the wild. The museum has a special permit to keep them here at Whimbrel House to celebrate their special history here in the Keys."

Which was more than Charles Reyes had done; he'd let the lemurs roam wild over the whole island, where they'd interfered with local species and made themselves pests to the residents. The last feral lemur had been captured and removed in 1980, and Whimbrel House had gone to great trouble to keep their own semi-feral specimens on the property.

"How many do you have?" asked the father.

"Right now, four: Clyde, Perdita, Sandrine, and Cosimo. That's Cosimo there. He was born at the estate." Cosimo, not actually albino but pale in color, with a black-and-white tail, was by far the friendliest of all the lemurs, having been raised mostly under Magda's tenure, who had a soft spot for the furry little creatures, as mischievous as they were.

He bounded over as she spoke, his berry eyes watching her confidingly. She wished she could reach out and touch the top of his soft little head, but the animals were unpredictable.

"Have these gardens been maintained ever since Isobel's lifetime?" asked the mother, looking around.

"No, after Charles Reyes's death the estate sat vacant for many years. It was briefly used as a bed and breakfast, but it was only when the Foundation began to fundraise back in the eighties that the restoration began. And as you can see, we still have a long way to go."

The lemurs, bored, were wandering off with the figs. The kids were no longer paying attention. "And that brings us to the end of our tour," said Magda, smiling, leading them through the gate and back up the hill toward the entrance.

The one exception to her fixation on native plants was here at the crest of the hill, the small stand of shrubby citrus trees; exactly the breed Charles Reyes had grown. They were true Key limes, an unusual subtype unlike those found anywhere else on the Keys. They loved the mist, their glossy leaves turning up to catch the drops. Magda had cultivated them from saplings, determined to return the garden to the precise state that Isobel would have known. She reached to touch one thorny branch as she passed.

"Everybody say thank you to Mrs. Trudell," said the mother promptly. Magda was not a *Mrs.*, but she smiled graciously and accepted two sticky high-fives as she led the family back toward the door, hoping that Starla had set up the gift shop before the closure.

"I want to take that afternoon flight," said the mother. "I don't like the looks of this forecast. It's starting to turn."

"If you think it's best," said the father. "Come on, kids."

Tours of the Estate were donation-only, per decree of the board of directors. Every year Magda upped the "suggested donation" amount on the sign by the door and moved it to a slightly more central location.

The family milled past it without stopping.

*    *    *

Starla wandered out of the gift shop, popping her gum, to watch them pull away.

"Did you hear if they changed the forecast again?" asked Magda. "That woman just said Myra is turning."

"Didn't get a text alert," said Starla, reaching for her phone. "Wish we had a TV here."

Hank approached, wiping his hands on a rag. "You ready for the latest? It's about that time."

"This is the big one. I bet they're going to call it." Starla pulled out the big weather radio from under the break room counter, which Magda thought was a little overly dramatic.

*"This is the afternoon update on the status of Hurricane Myra, which is currently battering into the coast of Cuba,"* said the news reporter's gravelly voice, crackling from the imperfect connection. *"The National Weather Service has issued a weather emergency for all of coastal Florida, particularly Monroe, Miami-Dade, Collier, and Broward counties, and Palm Beach County south of Lake Okeechobee."*

"Now I get the text," said Starla, rolling her eyes as her phone started to buzz.

*The governor of Florida has declared a state of emergency in advance of the storm, which is now expected to make landfall tomorrow afternoon as a category four. Predictions are changing rapidly, with the entire state of Florida within the potential zone. Evacuations are recommended for all counties at this time.*

"Well, shit," said Hank.

"The entire state of Florida?" asked Starla. "They're crazy. No way the entire state is going to pick up and move all at once."

*Alabama, Georgia, and South Carolina are expected to see impacts, as well as states as far away as Missouri and Tennessee and Kentucky. Right now the areas at highest risk are the low lying areas, the barrier islands, and space east of the Federal Highway. In order to give people time to prepare, schools across Florida are closing early and the National Guard is heading down with supplies to set up receiving shelters. Evacuations are effective immediately. Our next forecast will be on the top of the hour. Thank you.*

They paused to digest this.

"Go on home," said Magda, without overthinking it. Starla had school-aged kids. "Go on, get out of here—do what you need to do."

Starla was already turning to grab her coat. "I'll put out the sign to say the museum is closing early," she said over her shoulder.

"I'm out too. I've got a boat to move and a little girl waiting for me," said Hank. "I knew I shouldn't come down here, but it's such good money before these big storms. I hope this place will be okay."

"Whimbrel House has been standing for a hundred and seventy years, through all sorts of storms, and never taken damage," said Magda. "We're on a nice rise here, and these walls are solid limestone."

"It does seem pretty sturdy," said Hank.

"There's no better place to be. And unlike modern buildings, it was designed to run without piped water or electricity."

Starla cleared her throat. "Magda, are you good to lock up before you go?"

Magda was looking out at her Key limes. "Oh, I'm not leaving yet," she said.

Starla paused. "Don't you need to get home and pack?"

"I'm not the one who has to drive across the bridge to get home. I've got time. Go on—go now and try to beat the traffic."

She didn't ask again, although Magda could see her throwing a few worried glances at Hank, who shrugged in reply.

They had bigger things to worry about.

CHAPTER

2

Monday, October 7<sup>th</sup>
1:00 PM

IT WASN'T AS if Magda needed to head home to board up
the windows: she lived in a rented condominium. She
didn't have a cat or a dog to worry about, or children at
school. She had the lemurs at the Estate, the antiques in
the house, and the plants in the garden. She was happy to
stay.

Luckily, Whimbrel House was fairly well prepared.
There was even a sand pile and bags if necessary, and
plenty of supplies stored up—no need to run out and buy
anything. There was a lot to do, but it wouldn't really help
to have anyone underfoot, anxious and twitchy. She walked
around the interior of the house slowly, examining doors
and windows.

Prepping for hurricanes always reminded Magda of
winters in Ishpeming, the elaborate measures people took
to make their lake houses and hunting cabins part of the
frozen landscape without damage. All pipes had to be
stopped off and drained, window covered, slanted roofs

brought to air temperature so the snow didn't melt and ice. Then the weather could just . . . pass over.

Twenty minutes later there was an email from Ernesto Domingo, the current president of the board. He had cc-d all the members, she noted, sighing. He wanted an update on the preparedness plan.

The plan had been tabled last year in a contentious board meeting where Magda had made the case for scanning the original books in Isobel's library to share them with the Smithsonian archive. They hadn't wanted to spend Foundation funds on academic scholarship. And as for earmarking funds for additional supplies—well, it was not compatible with the current budget.

Magda decided her response could wait until tomorrow.

She still had a lot of work to do.

* * *

She was trying to decide the best place to store the extra cans of fuel for the cookstove. The root cellar would be the coolest place in the house, certainly, but was it dry enough? It seemed to get pretty damp down there, based on the frogs and lizards that came up from time to time.

She took the box and went to check. The heavy wooden door was as thick as a cinderblock, swinging on rusty hinges. The stairs down to the cellar were hand carved; the marks of the tools used to hew them out of the surrounding rock were still visible one hundred and seventy years later.

The door swung shut behind her, but Magda made it down the stairs and reached for the pull cord of the single lightbulb with the ease of experience. It cast only a brooding glow. Few parts of the house were properly electrified—much of the old knob-and-tube wiring had been deemed unsafe and disconnected without being replaced.

The cellar had an aura of suppressed anticipation. It was the stillness of the air, like someone holding their breath. There were walls of probably five hundred feet of stone in every direction.

For most of its life, this space had been used to store wine or—back in Isobel's day—probably barrels of rum strong enough to blind a man. Magda theorized it may have originally been built out of a natural crevasse in the rock, which the builders had expanded on and walled in.

As she'd feared, the walls and the floor were clammy, and that might be lichen blooming on the big carved stone in the corners. That was not going to make for great storage. But it was definitely cool and safe from wind or rain. Perhaps if the box was up off the floor?

There were rickety shelves against the back wall, and Magda went over to test them. They were the right height, but when she put the box on the middle plank, there was a groan of metal before the whole thing came out of the wall at the back, leaving her to catch and hold the shelves before they collapsed. "Damn!" A few screws fell out, clattering at her feet. There was a brick wall behind, which had no doubt been added later than the original construction, probably to better facilitate anchoring the shelves, and it seemed to be crumbling.

Studying the exposed wall now, it was obvious that many of the bricks were just resting in their places, the original mortar eroded away. No wonder the anchors had broken loose. When she leaned the shelves back in place, more than one brick fell out of place. Through the holes that were left she could just make out the uneven rock face a few inches back. She supposed if the original cavern was natural, it wasn't surprising there was a hollow space behind the bricks.

Curious if it was also hand cut, she used the flashlight app on her phone to peer behind the wall. No, there were no cut marks. She stood on tiptoes to look down toward the floor.

There was something glinting dully, low to the ground. Something vaguely rounded and low, and for an instant, for some reason, she believed she was looking at the burnished skin of a snake.

A wave of irrational terror overwhelmed her as she imagined great jaws lunging toward her, fangs extended, and jerked back, dropping the phone, hearing it crack and skitter across the stone floor.

Shit! In the gloom of the cellar, Magda could hear her own heart pounding in her ears, her own breath like a bellows in her chest, her eyes dazzled by the outline of the last light of the flashlight before it had gone out.

Perfect silence, which included no slithering, no snapping jaws, no snake behind the wall. She was being ridiculous. There was no reason a reptile would choose to curl up behind those bricks in a closed-in cellar in a closed-in basement in the middle of a house. *Calm down, idiot. Deep breath.*

The lone lightbulb was of next to no use. Owl-like, she navigated by sound, remembering the approximate location of her phone as indicated by the crack of it striking the floor. Finally her fingers found the hard plastic shape of it, completely unlike every other damp, worn surface in the cellar. The screen was cracked but the phone itself still seemed to be working.

Better to come back down with that big flashlight, she decided.

A few moments later, composed again and shaking her head at her own foolishness, she came back down the stone steps with the light. The wall was gaping at her, the missing bricks like the gap teeth of a jack-o'-lantern.

Gathering her courage, Magda stepped back into place, peering down through the gap to see what was glinting, expecting that it might be some kind of old pipe system. This time, with the flashlight, it was easier to see the shape, smooth and columnar, that had attracted her attention. It was the long metal barrel of a rifle.

She felt a frisson of excitement: amazing how, after all this time, the house still held its secrets. Thousands of people had streamed in and out over the years, and she herself had spent a decade here without ever knowing what was sleeping in the cellar, slowly rusting away.

It took Magda the better part of the next hour to laboriously widen the space enough that she could reach down, her whole body pressed against the bricks, and grab hold of the snout of the long gun. Getting it out was even more difficult, but finally she had it free.

It was old, that was for certain. Pre-1900, based on the make of the metal parts, which seemed to be forged instead of cast. Magda wasn't an expert on firearms, but she knew a lot about furniture, and she could tell it had once been a quality piece. Who knew how it had ended up damp and cracked, abandoned behind the wall.

She wondered if it was loaded and if the mechanism was too rusted over, or if it could ever fire again. She would like to see that. She hadn't grown up with guns, but her ex-boyfriend Bryce had taken her to a firing range a few times. He'd spent his youth duck hunting in the everglades and still kept a shotgun behind the bar.

As always, any stray thought that lead back to Bryce made her stomach churn, so she blocked it out and focused on the matter at hand. The rifle should be taken upstairs and documented, put somewhere safe from further exposure to the elements. Who knew? It could even be authentic to Charles's era! She wished she could spend the whole evening researching the provenance, but there were a million other things she needed to do first. She'd have to save it for herself as a treat.

She hurried back upstairs, forgetting the box of fuel cans on the floor; the cardboard would be damp through by the time she remembered.

Upstairs, she wrapped the rifle in a towel and settled it in a place of honor across the hall table.

This was why she could never leave Whimbrel House; even after so many years, the story was still revealing itself. There were so many things left to learn.

* * *

Having spent several hours moving furniture away from the windows and packing fragile items, Magda kept her eyes on the weather updates coming in on her phone. They were still calling for widespread evacuations. The news had descriptions of the backed-up roads, gas stations completely out of gas, and cars stranded in the middle of the highway. It was a relief not to be caught up in any of that.

She answered a few phone calls from people canceling upcoming tours. They all asked if she'd heard about the evacuations but always agreed that there was no way to know if they were necessary yet. Most of them laughed at the idea of evacuating the entire state. It wasn't possible.

All of them asked about the lemurs.

"Oh, they'll do better than any of us," said Magda, laughing. "They have so much space there, and they're used to worse. They're tropical animals, after all—they don't mind the rain!"

After a few more hours on the Landmark draft, Magda headed home at the usual time, driving across the island on a route calculated to avoid evacuation traffic. It wasn't even raining anymore, and even the clouds had seemingly burned off.

Whimbrel House, on the Atlantic side, was blessed with sunrises, but it was the Gulf side that had the best sunsets. In more than ten years on the island, Magda might have become somewhat jaded to sundown in Key West—strolling out to Mallory Square or sitting in Bryce's bar night after night until he rang the brass bell, accompanied by the whoops and hollers of the crowd. But at one point on that drive home, Magda had to pull over to appreciate what must have been the most vivid, spectacular sunset she had even seen. Flaming streaks like the points of a crown that almost seemed to throb and move, like the Northern Lights. That perfect Florida pink that never showed up right in photographs. She could almost hear her father's voice in her ear: *Don't look away from that one, Maggie; there's only a few of these in a lifetime.*

Eventually she had to start the car and finish the drive home.

The apartment building was dark when she pulled in. Most of the neighbors had probably cleared out already. Her landlord had a truck filled with plywood out front.

Her third-floor unit looked the same way it always did: sterile. It was made up of a plain sitting room with scuffed white walls and a small attached bedroom. It had come furnished, and she didn't like any of the furniture. The full bed took up most of the space. Magda usually kept the heavy blackout curtains closed; the view from both rooms was of the parking lot.

She had never really lived here. Whimbrel House was her home.

She had cleared out most of her possessions in preparation to move in with Bryce, and much of it had never been replaced. Only the day-to-day necessities had ever been unpacked. On the afternoon they had had their final blowout, she had thrown a box of his shoes off the balcony and it had exploded on the asphalt next to his car. The closet had been half empty ever since.

Bryce owned a sleek, modern condo down by the pier, and they had agreed it would be easiest for her to move in with him. But she had gotten caught up in the board meeting that week—it was the meeting where they would have approved the disaster plan—and hadn't gotten around to most of the packing, or ordering the van. He had accused her of putting it off deliberately; she had called him unsupportive; he had asked her if she even wanted to get married. The words she meant to say—*Of course!*—had gotten stuck in her throat. Language had always failed her when it really mattered.

He had stormed out, and she had called him, first out loud and then, when he didn't answer, repeatedly on the phone. She had stood on the patio and watched him ignore the ringing. What she remembered now was that the allamanda on the balcony was blooming, and the scent filled the street and the apartment. That and the weight of the box of shoes in her hands.

Later, he had finally texted her back: *I'm sorry. I can't.*

It was fitting that it was Isobel's own poems that captured her feelings at the time. Isobel, who had never known love (as far as anybody knew) and whom Bryce had never cared for.

*Spells break / sleepers Awake / rise blinking, saying*
*I had a strange dream, stay with me now.*

The spell had broken, that was all. In some ways, maybe Magda had always been waiting for something to come along and knock her off kilter. Something usually did.

Now she made herself a plate of scrambled eggs for dinner, eating them straight out of the pan. It had been her go-to dinner as a college student—why not now?

She had started out as a freshman in Ann Arbor studying comparative literature. She'd already been obsessed with Isobel, even then. A lot of her fellow students were double majors in fine arts, wanting to be writers themselves; they considered the lit degree to be hedging their bets (even Isobel had the advantage of being born to a wealthy family). Magda's second major was in botany. She found the creative writing courses to be more difficult than anything else. The other students, whether they were good at writing or not, at least had something they wanted to express. Sometimes their message was stupid—mostly it was self-indulgent—but at least it was meaningful to them. Magda, the daughter of a songwriter, found she had nothing meaningful to say—unless she was talking about Isobel.

She remembered listening to the other students discussing their childhoods: TV shows and Top Forty songs. Magda had grown up on the crosstown bus with a book of poetry on her lap. She usually said she was homeschooled, which was more or less true. ("Do you know what I would have given to be able to skip school?" her father had asked, shaking his head. Magda did know exactly what he would give, in fact. It was something that she didn't particularly want to take from him.)

How could she try to talk now about setting up the amplifiers on the crumbling steps of Cahokia mounds, or driving ahead of the rangeland fires out West, or the sight of the Northern Lights spread out below a single-engine plane? Those were her teenage memories, but they didn't belong to her; they were all borrowed from places she was only passing through. She was a nothing person, from nowhere. Isobel's past was more real to her than her own.

Her best friend at the time (and probably still, although they lived far apart and it was harder than ever to connect) had been her sophomore-year roommate, an art major. Vicki had said if she could make art that made someone see the world the way she saw it, even just for a second—it would be like she'd live forever.

Magda still thought about that when she read Isobel's poetry. There was a line in "Wake-Robin"—*"snow like a secret I've been hiding / it Weighs as much as safety"*—that had changed the way she looked at snow for the rest of her life. Before that poem, she'd seen snow in whatever way was natural to Magda, but after that, she saw it the way Isobel did.

Somewhere crumpled in one of Magda's notebooks was a draft of a poem she'd called "Karma and the Hobo." Magda had been trying to compare the Ishpeming winter that first year she'd moved in with her grandmother to her childhood traveling with her father. She had labored over the poem for years but never felt it was much better than middling. One of her teachers had challenged her: What was she trying to say about winter? About her own child-hood? Beyond the fact they were . . . cold?

Magda still had the poem, but it had never had an ending.

None of her creative writing professors had tried to dissuade her when she'd applied for a master's in museum studies. Now her life's work was preserving Isobel's words, her story, and the magical place that had created them both. Surely that was better than writing an ending to a childish effort like her poem.

The eight PM news reported that the evacuations for all of southern Florida were mandatory. The governor came on, urging people to leave. Magda had met the governor once, at an event in Whimbrel House, and he had spoken of how the Reyes legacy was essential for the people of Florida—a priceless treasure—so she was pretty confident he didn't mean her. Which reminded her: she needed his updated letter of recommendation for the Landmark application.

A few friends sent messages:

*Are you on the road?*

*Stay safe! Be careful!*

*Let me know if you need a place to crash!*

Starla texted that she was taking her kids to her mother's place in Tallahassee. Magda told her to drive carefully and didn't answer the text after that: *Are you leaving yet?*

Her cell phone rang at eight PM. She'd actually been expecting a call from Merrick sooner.

Merrick Bower was the visionary who had first suggested that Whimbrel House should become a museum. It had been in his family through the line of Charles's second wife, Amelia Whitehead, whose daughter by previous marriage had inherited what little was left of the Reyes fortune after the wreck.

She had refused to set foot on the estate, renting it out for use as hotel, but it had suffered neglect along with most of Key West in the depression. By the time of her grandson's inheritance it had long been sitting vacant and was in disrepair. The family, although wealthy by modern standards, was no longer as flush as it had formerly been, and it was expected they would finally sell the lot for development.

But Merrick was one of those people who had been touched by the power of Isobel's poetry. She had always had that ability: to attract a few people passionately. The readers who loved her words understood each other. Merrick had set up a foundation for the house and recruited talent to restore it. He started a scholarship program for graduate students who would agree to work at the Estate—and encountered young Magda, fresh off two years of interning at the Smithsonian, in her first year of a doctoral degree.

The Library of Congress had a collection of Reyes works, and there had been the potential for a position there, but Magda had instead written a grant for the design of the restored Reyes garden and taken an unpaid position as the gardener. Two years later she'd left her PhD program without completing her dissertation—and the rest was history, as she'd clawed her way up to paid staff and then finally to her current full-time role. There had never been another executive director since Merrick had retired, although she'd requested the title twice. The board had determined that "caretaker" was more appropriate.

Almost a decade years later, Magda was still the caretaker of the estate and the author of its every hard-won success. Isobel's poetry was included in the Florida curriculum, the number of visitors was ticking up every year, and as soon the property was designated as a national cultural landmark, Isobel's legacy would be permanently secured.

"Now, Magda, what is this I hear about a hurricane?"

Merrick had lived in Hawaii for the past decade, although as a founding member he was permanently considered a Board of Director emeritus.

"Yes, looks like we're gearing up for another one. Second in two weeks!"

"I'm getting a lot of questions about the lemurs. Are people calling you? We can't move them, right?"

"I don't know if we could even catch them, but it would likely be too stressful for them to try." (It would also be unimaginably stressful for Magda herself.) "They'll be fine. I'm telling everybody they're all set to ride out the storm even if it does hit."

"They don't even know the final trajectory yet. I hear it's still hung up over Cuba."

"Well we're ready for it, whatever comes."

"You know we're very close, Magda. Another year or so and the Estate could really be first rate. If we can get the Landmark designation . . ."

"I know, Merrick." Of all the people who loved Whimbrel House, there was nobody other than Merrick who loved it the way she did.

"Think of the looting after Wilma."

"It's fine. We've got a good security gate this time, and we've got the new generator. I'll make sure to keep the lights and the cameras on all night."

"So you're not evacuating?"

Magda blew out a breath. "No, of course not. I'm going to stay on-site, to keep an eye on everything."

She had always thought of the estate as a living thing. It needed its living heart to beat; if she left, it would die.

"Hmm. Are there still supplies there?"

"There's a whole stash in the cellar, and I'll pack up some more from my house. It'll be fine."

Merrick exhaled, the breath crackling down the phone line. "Alright. I'll tell Ernesto, and he'll put out some kind of statement so people stop worrying about the lemurs. Is it alright if I give your contact information if there's press?"

"Of course."

"I will expect to hear updates whenever you can. Obviously, if it really hits you can expect to lose power and cell service, but use whatever means you can to get in touch as you go."

"Of course," said Magda again.

"Do you have your emergency contacts up to date?"

Honestly she couldn't think of a single person who would need to be notified if she was wiped off the face of the earth. In the will she had printed off some website, any assets remaining were to go to the Foundation. Still, there was no need to drag out that dirty laundry. "Yes, that's all sufficient."

"Do take care of yourself too," he said.

"Of course," said Magda again. "And please don't worry too much. The house has been through so many storms; we'll be fine."

"Right. Well. This has put my mind at ease. Thank you. I have complete confidence in you. And—good luck and all that."

"You as well. Goodbye."

Magda disconnected first.

*　*　*

She dragged a bank box full of papers out of its place on the top shelf of the closet. She tucked a few files into a plastic bag. There was a medical power of attorney, designating her old roommate, Vicki, whom she hadn't talked to in over a year. At least she'd probably pull the plug quickly.

She reminded herself to post an update on her little-used Facebook page, saying she was fine, so people wouldn't worry. There was no need to mention that she was staying in place.

As she packed, she felt a mad burst of her own freedom. If she had been married, if she had had children, it would have been impossible to take such risks. Well, not impossible, perhaps, but shameful and irresponsible. Even if she had had any living family at all, it would have been cruel to scare them. And everyone else's anxiety would have only added onto her own, putting the weight of their fears on her shoulders. With nobody else to consult, she was clear to focus on her duty.

This was the reward of having such a streamlined life.

Some fit of whimsy had Magda rummage through the bottom drawer of her dresser to pull out what her father had called the "go bag." Up until the age of sixteen, she had carried it everywhere. There was nothing terribly valuable in it now: a penknife that was mostly blunt, a plastic butane lighter, a deck of cards. A child's idea of survival. She slipped the lighter and the penknife into the pocket of her raincoat. For luck.

Looking around her half-empty apartment reminded Magda of how little was left after her father had died. All his earthly possessions, which had washed up as a few crates in the back of a pickup—his guitars and equipment had all gone to his fellow musicians, just like he would have wanted. And now here was her own collected material life, barely amounting to anything more.

The Trudells were seven generations deep from Michigan's Upper Peninsula. Sometimes even Magda wondered if her eagerness to relocate to Key West was based on the memory of that snow, which had started in September and continued clear through the beginning of June. The family line included two victims of the Barnes-Hecker Mine disaster, in which a lake overhead had been inadvertently drained into a mineshaft full of men. Fifty-one men drowned, including two of her great-uncles. One man had climbed the ladder as the water came up behind him: eight hundred feet in fourteen minutes. "That's about how hard you gotta work to get out of Ishpeming," her father had cracked.

Magda worked until her eyes started to blur. Time for bed.

She slept soundly that night, having first turned her phone off to keep the emergency alerts from waking her up.

She had missed forty-eight alerts by morning.

# CHAPTER

# 3

Tuesday, October 8th
6:00 AM

*Day Two*

MAGDA LINGERED AFTER her morning coffee, straightening up around the apartment. It was possible the police or fire department might end up coming through. Anyway, people took evacuations as an opportunity to loot, although there wasn't much of value there: the whole place could go up in flames and she wouldn't miss much.

Her fridge was mostly empty anyway—nothing but a year-old six-pack of Bryce's favorite porter, which she didn't like, and a bottle of ketchup. She tossed the latter. The pantry had more, including a whole box of cereal bars. She took everything that made sense: canned food, off-brand peanut butter. Cheap stuff that was filling, that could last. Magda was familiar. She grabbed two bananas off the counter and what was left in a bag of oranges she'd bought the week before.

Besides a few books and her laptop, she added her sleeping bag and a duffel with a week's worth of clothes and toiletries, in case the roads were blocked. Of course she could walk across the island in about an hour, but still, it seemed wise to be prepared for anything. There was a camping cot in one of the closets at Whimbrel House, left over from the days when the estate hosted all night lock-ins for the high school kids—a practice their new insurance plan had put an end to. There was a camping stove in one of the kitchen cupboards and the fuel in the cellar, as well as bottled water.

The bag was light enough to carry one-handed out to the car.

Magda kept a Tupperware container in her trunk, usually containing her dirty gardening equipment. Now she sorted through the few things she needed—important papers, family photos, a spare phone charger—each individually stowed in a plastic bag. This wasn't her first time at the rodeo. She and her father had crisscrossed the Plains states during tornado season, she knew what was essential in a crisis.

The morning news reported that Myra had made its way around Cuba in the night, killing seventeen, with many more missing. There were already relief efforts underway, and she reminded herself to make a donation tonight.

The hurricane was over open water, about to make its final turn, its course still uncertain. The images showed the malevolent swirl of clouds, still large, like a thumbprint over the blue sky. High winds, heavy rain, storm surge expected, but no certainty. Three people had died in automobile accidents while trying to evacuate South Florida—hundreds were stranded on the road.

There was an email from the current board president, who had clearly spoken to Merrick.

*He was concerned about the insurance implications of staff members physically staying on-site. The Foundation could not be liable for injuries.*

Magda replied that of course she was willing to sign a waiver, and logged off.

This was it, thought Magda, frowning back at the white stucco building where she'd lived for the past four years. There was almost nothing she valued that wasn't either in her car or in the Reyes house.

Unbidden, a line from "Showman's Rest" came into her mind:

*Empty we came / to the railroad crossing*
*and each of us empty-Handed / were rolled into our grave.*

Magda shuddered. Even she could acknowledge when there were times that maybe it didn't do to linger over poetry.

She pulled away from the building as her landlord began drilling into plywood to cover the windows; the sound was echoed all throughout the block.

\* \* \*

Magda had been eleven when her father brought home a copy of *The Edge of the Water*. Her life until then had been dominated by his dreams—traveling by bus and by beat-up Chevelle, chasing folk hero status. She had grown up surrounded by his beloved inspirations, Dylan and Ginsberg and Kerouac; sensitive men who lived for the road, their heads full of novelty, leaving a string of brokenhearted women and children behind them. People who were willing to follow their talents all the way to the bitter end.

She hadn't even known until then that it was possible for a woman to be a genius; weren't they too busy being left behind, brokenhearted, by brilliant men? With their unwanted children? The one that leaves is the genius; the one that stays behind is just a sucker. But Isobel never wrote about men, or people at all, actually. She wrote about birds and plants and the water and the sky, and those were things that Magda also loved.

Magda read those poems on nights when she dragged the motel dresser in front of the door to keep out the man screaming in the hallway; she read them on the bus when her father went through his experimental drug phase and was half out of his mind; she read them backstage during the endless sound checks and rehearsals.

It just figured that Isobel's genius had killed her. Of course it had. There wasn't a place for women like that, certainly not in the past—barely in the present—to be strange and moody and brilliant. Of course it ended in tragedy. But at least Isobel had left these poems behind. Magda even worked with her father to set one, "Carrying the Stones," to music, and he had sung it at the festival in San Antonio that year, under a bruised purple sky shot full of stars.

No doubt he thought poetry was an odd thing for a teenage girl to fixate on, even though he himself liked the poems. But he had no interest in biographies of Isobel's life or her family. He didn't think things like that were important for appreciating art, although three-quarters of his own songs contained veiled references to Ishpeming in some form or another (or mining imagery, or themes of claustrophobia and suffocation—sometimes all three). Even though everything that happened to them, no matter how crappy, appeared later, filtered through his songs; not the experiences themselves, but his own feelings and emotions about them, which came trickling through in unrelated premises. That was why Magda knew exactly how tricky, how impossible it would be to

ever untangle fact from fiction, and with Isobel's poems
she never tried.

Now as she coasted down the backroads it was his
scratchy, low voice she could hear, singing, *"You've gotta
pack light, gotta be ready to go; You're never gonna know
until you know."*

\* \* \*

Hers was the only car on the turnoff to the northeast shore
of the key, down to the spit of land called *hueso*, from the
old Spanish name *Cayo Hueso*. American settlers had bas-
tardized it into the current name of Key West, but *hueso*
actually meant "bone." The land that housed the Reyes
estate was still called by the old name.

She was followed on the drive by heavy and sullen
clouds, but not anything that seemed particularly dangerous. It started to drizzle before she parked.

She was sure to drive all the way up to the top of the
hill, not close to any of the spindly trees that might come
down in high winds. Off to the side of the house was a
sheltered spot protected by the adjacent wall.

She made sure all her windows were rolled up and the
trunk was tightly sealed. Now that she was here, she knew
she wouldn't be able to drive out; the radio had reminded
her that Route 1 was set to close. She didn't turn over the
"Open" sign on the mansion, but she did turn on the porch
light.

The rain began to hammer. She ran into the house
with her hood up. It was a relief to close the door behind
her. The heavy, solid walls immediately blocked out the
weather. Inside it was cool and serene, as ever.

For a moment she indulged herself, dreaming what it
would have been like for Isobel when the storms came

through. In some ways it must have saved her a lot of grief, not to have to deal with the forecast being debated for a week and a half. The weather would let you know when it was actually coming, and by then there was only time to brace. They might have had a few hours' warning, when the winds shifted, when the barometer dropped.

According to contemporary accounts, there had been several good storms during Isobel's lifetime—real hurricanes, not just the summer thunderstorms that had killed Abigail Reyes—but neither she nor her father had written about them. Presumably, they'd gotten through the way people had for thousands of years: by keeping low to the ground and waiting for it to blow over. The infamous Labor Day hurricane of 1935, which had killed hundreds, had been nearly 20 years after her death, and there had been no damage reported at Whimbrel House.

Magda turned on the coffee pot she kept hidden in the kitchen, and started to unpack. When there was a break in the weather—it seemed to be coming down in fitful starts and stops—she finished and went outside to walk the perimeter of the house again. The beach was scattered with bits of broken whelks, like alligator scales. Pelicans surfed low over the choppy waves, their wing tips nearly dragging in the foam.

The ocean seemed to be full of churning debris. Leftover from Lawrence, perhaps. Magda turned over what was left of a hand-painted plywood sign that was written in Spanish: *"Mercado."*

She could only fret over the Key limes, which were barely establishing themselves. She wished they had grown up faster, set stronger roots before the storm season. It wouldn't take much to tear them out entirely now.

Back in the house, Magda brought out the camping cot and fetched the little camp stove out of its cabinet. They had used to it heat cider at the Fall Reception, which seemed like a lifetime ago, but at least there was plenty of fuel.

She began filling the clawfoot tub in the downstairs bathroom. The plumbing was terrible, and it would take an hour to fill. The drain plug wasn't a perfect fit, so she laid a plastic bag over it, then packed it down with the rubber stopper. The water was rusty from the old pipes, but she only needed it to flush the toilet anyway. Fortunately, Magda was used to doing her own home repairs because of her childhood—an endless stream of rental rooms, each one falling apart and neglected.

While she worked, she remembered another one of her dad's songs: "All Hands on Deck." He loved witty turns in his own lyrics—meanings that could be folded over on each other and taken another way. It was something he had in common with Isobel, with her cramped, clever epigrams. Magda and he had read them together on long car trips, reciting them from memory.

She spent the next few hours packing up the stock in the gift shop, which she stacked in cardboard boxes on top of the tables. The gift shop was the least sturdy part of the house, she judged, being wood framed and a later addition. She wondered if she should move the boxes into the storage closet, but it would take her several trips with the dolly, and she wasn't sure she had the energy. She did leave out a new copy of *The Edge of the Water* for herself.

It was strange to feel like she must be running out of time, and yet not have that much to do right now. *Stalked by a turtle.* The sky was turning ominous and black. Magda thought of the seventeen dead in Cuba. What had they forgotten to do? They'd known it was coming, just as surely as she did.

Since nothing came to mind, she unwrapped the rifle from the cellar and began to document it, first with a simple pencil sketch and then with archival photos. If memory served, there had been a rifle over the fireplace in Robert Engel's letter describing his tour of the estate after Isobel's first book was published. She wondered if it would ever be possible to verify that this was the same gun.

The last few pages of her favorite book for authenticating antique furniture—*The Glossary of Southern Design, 1900–1940*—had a few pages on rifles, if she recalled correctly. And there was a dealer on Raccoon Key she could probably call, based on the big glass display cases under his counter. What was his name? Earl something.

The next weather alert stated that Myra was making a turn and seemed to be aimed like an arrow straight at Key West. Coming up from the south, it would likely make landfall that night, and "should be considered devastating." The main highway was already closed. Anyone remaining should plan to shelter in place.

Outside, it started to rain again.

Magda made another pot of coffee.

*        *        *

What might have been a few hours later, her concentration was broken by the unmistakable sound of tires rolling down the gravel drive. Who on earth would want to visit the museum today? The news had reported that police were going door to door, urging people to evacuate—but surely they wouldn't be wasting their time at Whimbrel House.

Still holding the rifle—more out of preoccupation than anything else—she went to stand in the doorframe and watched through a knot in the plywood as a familiar black pickup coasted to the porch.

She should have guessed. Like most of the old stalwarts, Bryce never evacuated. In years past, they had spent storms like this holed up at the bar he owned down on the harbor, at his legendary hurricane parties. The top floor of a Mexican restaurant, Bar Pilar was refurbished with Christmas lights and a corrugated aluminum roof, portions of which could be pulled open or closed over the breeze blocks with a system of ropes and pulleys.

"Mags? Are you in there?" Of course, he couldn't see her through the wood and the heavy glass.

"In here, hold on," she called anyway, leaning the gun against the wall, then wiping her hands on her jeans and walking through the kitchen to the side door that wasn't barricaded.

The sky outside was heavy, although the rain seemed to have slackened for now, and there was what might be thunder rolling in the distance—or it might be jets at the airport. Hard to say.

He'd left the truck running. "Starla called me." He looked handsome, Magda thought, and they hadn't been broken up long enough to feel it without pain. She would have once felt a flush of pride at the sight of him, her beautiful boyfriend, and now she had to merely observe dispassionately that he was looking well.

They had been together nearly seven years. It was the longest continuous relationship, of any type, in Magda's life. (Up until age six, barely remembered, she'd lived with her mother until the cancer; after that she'd bounced back and forth between her grandmother and her father until she'd left for college).

"My God, Magda," said Bryce, stepping into the shelter of the porch. "You look . . ."

It was true she had probably lost a little of her glow recently. She was turning forty, and the past year had not been easy. Her body felt hollow and sharp, like the bones of a bird. Her hair was coming in brittle, and although so far it hadn't started to turn gray, she suspected that was right around the corner.

The days when she would lounge in bed with Bryce in his rooms above the bar, drinking rum spirits and eating pastelitos from the bakery on Margaret Street, seemed like a different life. The long weekends they'd spent sailing between the islands, snorkeling—Magda, who had feared the open water since childhood!—or splashing in the clear shallows, were like a dream.

"At least I don't have a box of your shoes this time," she said, and he chuckled.

"There is that."

They had met when Magda was bartending, needing to finance her stint as a volunteer gardener. With Bryce it had been *so easy*—at least until it wasn't. Every other brief and stunted romance had felt like so much work, half talking herself into it, half talking herself out. It had felt impossible to be giving enough, open-hearted enough, available enough.

With Bryce, suddenly all that division was muted, as if he had finally found the remote and pressed the right button. When they had been together, she had felt like a different person—someone who found it easy to love and be loved in return. He had even accepted her passion for history, even though he, a local, was bored by Isobel's opaque poetry and didn't care about the mystery or romance of her story.

She'd told herself a few indiscretions were to be expected. Bar Pilar was packed with pretty waitresses, students on spring break, tourists looking for a distraction . . . Magda, even back then, was no college co-ed. She had always felt herself to be mostly a brain in a jar; how could she blame him for thinking no differently? They had made it work. It had almost worked.

He cleared his throat, and she looked up, startled. "Maggie, Starla says you're staying here? Haven't you seen the satellite?"

"Yes, it looks like it's gonna be a good one." If she had heard a recording of her own voice, she would have said it was completely neutral—but it was as if somebody else was speaking. Sometimes she didn't know who it was.

Bryce was still looking at her like he didn't quite recognize her. "Listen, my friend Cole is sailing up to Fort Myers. He's got his boat ready to go. I'm going to be on it, and I think you should come."

"But—but you never leave."

"This is a Cat four, honey, hitting dead on. You don't want to mess with this one."

"The forecasts can be wrong," said Magda. "Storms turn at the last second. You remember Lawrence?"

"This doesn't look anything like Lawrence."

"Bryce, you know I need to be here to take care of the property, to take care of the lemurs. If I left, it could be weeks before I could get back. What do you think will happen to this place if it sits empty for weeks? . . . I can't believe you're leaving the Pilar."

He shut off his truck, clearly anticipating that this was not going to be a quick conversation. "Maggie, I love the bar—you know I do—but it's a building. It has to stand on its own. What good do you really think you can do if we get the kind of storm they're talking about? All you're going to do is go down with this place."

*Like a captain,* thought Magda. *Like the captain of a doomed ship.* But that didn't seem wrong (it sounded better than "caretaker"). The story was that Charles Reyes had refused to abandon the *Undine* in Bimini after it was taking on water.

"How could I leave, knowing if anything happens, I'll always wonder if there was something I could have done?"

According to the stories, Charles had stayed to wrestle with the controls, perhaps hoping to guide the ship into calmer waters. Instead, they'd foundered on the rocks, and the whole family had drowned. Of course it was all only speculation: no one who was there had lived to report out.

"Anyway, we're the third highest point on the island. These walls are eighteen inches thick. I don't think there's any place safer than this."

"So you're going to squat here, in a haunted house, with no power?"

"If there's any place on the island equipped to be without power, it's here—the house was built before electricity or running water. And I'm hardly afraid of the ghosts."

She had never been able to explain how desperately she wished the house was haunted by Isobel. How she'd been patiently restoring the estate all these years in the hopes of seeing just one flickering smile on that sharply pointed face.

"Maggie . . ." She hated that he still called her by one of her father's nicknames, hated that he could still say it that way, as if he loved her. He didn't, although he had once.

*I'm sorry, I can't.*

For all Magda's years of reading poetry—words so clear and perfect they could make you weep, each one the perfect distillation of language—the words she would hear echo in the darkest times were *I'm sorry, I can't.*

"Magda, this place is right on the water. You're going to be wiped off the map. I don't care how great a poet that witch was—nothing is worth your life."

"I'll be okay. Really."

"Magda, listen, I can't just *leave* you here. How can I? If you're staying, then I should stay too, and then we'll both die here for no reason."

"Don't be ridiculous," said Magda. She wondered if he'd really do it or if he just recognized what the script called for. Either way, it was grotesque. He didn't even care about Isobel.

Of course he could probably *make* her go, if he chose to; he was certainly strong enough to drag her to the car. She didn't think he'd try it, but she did back up half a step.

"Maggie . . ."

"Bryce, I'm a grown woman. I can make my own choices. I'm choosing to stay. If you've chosen to go, then I support you, and I wish you well. But I've already made my decision."

"Because of Isobel?" said Bryce, incredulous. "Because of this nutcase from a hundred years ago?"

"Because her poems changed my life," said Magda quietly. "They can change the world. And I want to do whatever I can to help that legacy reach people. This is my life's work, Bryce. I can't leave it now. Isobel's poetry was only written because of this place, because of her home. It doesn't make half as much sense if you read it without standing here, in the house where she grew up, in the gardens she wrote about."

"'Showman's Rest' is set in Chicago, for God's sake," said Bryce. "'Wake-Robin' is about snow."

She forgot sometimes that he really did have them memorized from his school days, however resentfully. "But there are books here in the library that show where she got those ideas, books with her name written in them by her own hand. Paintings she made herself, with her own signature painted at the bottom. She lives here, Bryce. This is where she belongs. And I won't leave it."

"Then you'll die here, just like she did. Look where all that poetry got her, Maggie. She drowned herself. And you're going to be doing the same thing if you choose to stay here knowing this storm is about to hit."

She thought about it for a second—agreeing to go with him, climbing into his boat and sailing away. Leaving the house behind, the storm, the whole island.

"This is my choice, Bryce. I don't need you to make it yours."

Bryce threw his hands up. "That's the heart of it, isn't it? You never needed me."

And suddenly they weren't talking about evacuation plans anymore. "Is that what you wanted?" asked Magda, feeling sick. "To be needed?" *Of course I don't need you,* she thought but didn't say. She had raised herself in the back of an Oldsmobile, she had rebuilt Whimbrel House from shambles: no, she didn't need him, but she had *wanted* him—surely that was better?

"I didn't mean that," he said, wiping his face. Frustrated.

It wasn't fair. He hadn't needed her either, and she had never minded. Perhaps he needed those other women from the bar, or perhaps they needed him—or, more likely, allowed him to pretend they did. Maybe that was Magda's failure, that she hadn't pretended.

What she really needed was that Cultural Landmark designation. She *needed* that, desperately, for Isobel. Was that really so preposterous?

"I'm sorry, Bryce. But let me give you something before you go," she said. She ducked inside to grab supplies off the side table.

When she came back, he trailed after her around to the garden, as the clouds continued to pile up against the shore. "This way," she said, leading the way to her beloved grove.

Key limes had been a productive crop for the locals in the early 1900s, but now most the limes grown in Florida were the thornless Persian variety; the juice for key lime pie came from Mexico. The plants needed full sun and sandy, well-drained soil (Magda had planted them in carefully mulched mounds), and they could not withstand frost. Nowhere else in the United States was warm enough to grow them, but Key West's coldest reported temperature was forty-one degrees.

Bryce watched as she took the trusty pocket knife out of her pocket and cut a sprig of one of the lime branches. It was too aggressive a cut, and the wrong time to take cuttings, and with the tree so small the parent would probably die now. But grimly she continued anyway, taking three more from other plants. The lime grove was planted relatively close to sea level, and fruit trees had little tolerance for salt. The loss of the individual plants was worth something if she could at least save the garden.

She trimmed off the thin, straight thorns, then wrapped the switches in damp paper towels before sliding them into a bread bag. A few rubber bands held it all together.

"Take these with you," she said, handing him the tied-up bundle. "They're an old heirloom breed, and there's barely any left. If we need to replant someday, we can use these cuttings."

He took them. "Magda . . ."

His phone chirped. Bryce glanced at his smartwatch.

"Is that Cole? Are you holding them up?"

"Don't worry about that," he said, his jaw tense.

"Bryce, you shouldn't make anybody wait. If you're going to get out ahead of this thing, every second counts."

In "Blood-Root," Isobel had written, *There are Worse deaths / than the final pang.* Magda always wondered if she had been remembering Abigail, who had reportedly dropped without a word, struck dead in an instant. It was Isobel who had lived, burned and deafened, mute.

Where Magda got the courage, she would never know. But she leaned forward to kiss his rough cheek, and when he automatically reached for her, sliding his arm around her waist, she let him draw her in. The safest place in the world, she'd thought once, little knowing how the memory of those words would haunt her later.

"Be careful," she told him. "I can't leave. But be careful. I'll check in on the bar after the storm, okay?"

He kissed her hair, the way he used to do when she was half asleep. Magda had never known before those days what it was like, to feel that somebody else's body was only an extension of your own. Tearing herself away from him had been like losing a limb. Almost a full year later, she still felt the phantom pain.

"Just—be safe, okay? Promise me. Promise you'll do whatever it takes to take care of yourself. Even if it means letting this whole wreck sink into the sea."

"You too," she whispered, not promising. "Take care of yourself."

He shook his head.

"Safe travels."

They hugged again, and then he gripped the sapling in his fist—*Careful,* she thought, but didn't say—and he was gone.

CHAPTER

4

Tuesday, October 8<sup>th</sup>
4:00 PM

IT STARTED TO rain with intent just as the afternoon
turned to evening. Magda had resolved to benefit from
the internet for as long as she had it, and was drafting
emails to the Board about the likely funds necessary for
repairs. She had revised the opening of the Landmark
application, deciding that "preeminent voice in literature"
sounded better than "unsurpassed poet of the era." Now
she had nearly finished going through the monthly
accounts—as usual, several grant-related expenses had
been miscoded.

Somehow the media seemed to have caught hold of the
story of the caretaker refusing to leave the estate, and there
were a few requests for quotes or interviews. A lot of the
questions, of course, were about the lemurs. A few school-
children had written to ask if they would be okay. Magda
replied that they were used to tropical storms and didn't
mind a little rain.

She hoped she wasn't asking for trouble by publicly
admitting she was staying, since technically the evacuation

was mandatory. Magda emphasized that Whimbrel House was of immense historic value and had stood through many prior hurricanes, including Andrew and Wilma. And then yes, she went on to talk about how the lemurs were basically wild animals and it wouldn't be possible to corral them, so it was kinder to let them ride it out in place.

She could already tell which part would be heavily featured in the coverage.

When she was finished, Magda pulled on her heavy raincoat and tucked the hood over her head to walk down to the dock. In her heavy rubber boots, it was difficult to make her way through the wet grass. There wouldn't have been a spectacular sunset from Mallory Square tonight, she was sure: just a burning glow behind the clouds, like fire on the horizon.

As usual, it felt like there were eyes on her as she moved through the garden.

It had always seemed like human hubris to think that only people would come back after death, to hang around the places they had loved. Surely if there were ghosts at Whimbrel House, it would be the ghosts of plants and animals, not people. Perhaps the ghosts of the old lime trees, or the ospreys that had formerly, when the house was vacant, raised generations of chicks in the sprawling nest that for years had been tucked into the eaves.

The water had receded out from the bottom of the dock. She couldn't resist walking out there while the rain was relatively light. There was no moon or stars. The clouds were invisible but she had the sense of them overhead, heavy with more rain. It was fairly warm out. The wind wasn't cool and didn't seem all that strong yet.

Magda looked at the dark, unrevealing water. This ground might have once been Isobel's resting place.

Although years of storms would have long since sent any remains many miles from the dock (there had been divers out once, in the sixties, who had found nothing), there could be a fragment of her left here, transformed into reef. Strands of hair made into an eel's nest, maybe. Fish that were still made of her proteins and cells, eaten by osprey that had hatched from the nest under the eaves under her bedroom.

That was why she was here. This place *was* Isobel. Everything that was left of her.

For tonight, there was nothing to see but wet dark brown sand, turned gray in the low light. From what Magda could see, it had recessed probably about twenty feet out—which probably meant all that water was going to come rushing back in sooner or later.

She checked on the lemurs next. They were fine, huddled in the cement house at the back, eating the bananas and ignoring her. They had tipped over one of the water barrels, so she flipped it back. One of the females walked quite close to her, chattering, and Magda held a hand out for her to sniff. But she moved back to her family without complying.

Magda walked slowly back to the house, where she hung up her raincoat and left her boots next to the door. As strange as it seemed, she was glad to be here. If she were anywhere else, she'd be frantic about the estate, about the lemurs, imagining death and destruction. In "Carrying the Stones," Isobel had called it a "relief" for the Captain to go down with the ship: *No longer straining at the Horizon, searching for the guide star / beneath the water Stars are endless.*

That was how Magda felt now, having made the decision to send the crew off in the lifeboats and stay on her ship. One way or another, at least she'd know what happened.

Most people remembered that poem because of the death of Isobel's father—it was just another spooky part of her legacy, as much as scholars had their doubts about the necessity of Charles's decision to stay aboard the *Undine*. But that was with the benefit of hindsight Isobel certainly didn't have at the time the poem was written. She was speaking more of her own mortality, Magda was certain (and it was no stretch since that was the subtext of most of her poems). Maybe those were the lines she had been thinking about when she walked down the dock that last time.

In another hour Magda was listening to classical guitar on the radio, thinking of her father, and maybe remembering the day she and Bryce had driven up to Little Havana to walk around taking black and white photographs on his ancient Canon. He'd wanted something authentic for the walls of his new bar. He'd been completely confident that between the two of them they had the requisite artistic skills, although Magda had warned him that her real talent lay in grant applications.

The rain picked up suddenly, from zero to one hundred. One minute it had been gently keeping time with the strumming of the strings, and in the next it was louder than the *sforzando*, and faster, vicious. Magda held her breath and stopped the laptop to listen. It died down with the wind, returning to the backdrop of ordinary rain, but with the next gust it escalated again. After that it came in waves, slowly building in intensity the way she'd imagined labor must do. Once it reached a new level of strength, it never went backward, but continued to climb, like someone slowly turning up the dial.

By six PM the weather forecast was getting repetitive—
*get out, get out, we're all going to die*—and Myra was still
offshore and closing in. It was too late for it to turn now,
said the weatherman. Even if it did, it would still strike the
Keys with full power because it was more than three hundred miles across. Magda tried to imagine a storm that
wide, but her imagination failed her.

There were also several pieces about Whimbrel House,
Magda noticed, notified by her Google alert. She was
amused that the story seemed to be gaining traction. She
supposed it was good local human interest.

It was certainly possible she had bet on the wrong
horse this time. Every other forecast had come to nothing,
the no doubt excellent models thwarted by the shallow
unpredictable waters of the coast. The Keys had their own
patron saint and she kept the storm from the door. But it
seemed that in this case, she was asleep at the wheel, or had
abandoned them. It didn't change the decision Magda
would have made, but she could admit she had been hoping for a different outcome.

She had the big battery-powered lantern at the ready,
expecting to lose power. They usually did, even in ordinary storms. The wind was still picking up outside.
When she finally lost cell signal, she turned off her beat-
up old phone and took out the battery. She had an external one charged in one of her ziplocks, but it was better
to save whatever power she had for a time she might
really need it later. She tucked it all into her duffel of
clothes.

The weather reported that sea level had dropped
around the Keys. Residents were advised to shelter in place.
The bridge was closed. Rescue workers would not be able
to get the island until the storm had passed.

She put her hand on the heavy marble of the entry way. "Well, I guess it's just you and me now," she said aloud. The stone was cool under her hands, but she could almost imagine it throbbed like a living thing. "I'll take care of you, and you take care of me, okay? Just like you did for Isobel." For twenty-three years, at least.

She took the spare cot and her sleeping bag into the kitchen, which felt like being safe underground, the walls were so thick and strong. It was always the room that felt the most natural to her, as a member of the staff. The main rooms were for the family.

She got into the makeshift bed. The wind was still exultant outside. It had developed the distinctive hum of the big storms. In Magda's experience the wind could shriek, moan, or scream like a woman. The sound now was lower than that, and building, like someone was running a vacuum under the wind.

Magda opened *The Edge of the Water* at random, pulling the lantern closer to read. By chance, the poem selected happened to be "Antigone."

Hmm. There were hundreds of poems in the book; maybe she didn't need to read the creepy ones by lamplight. She still had a long night ahead of her.

She was several lines into "The Great White Bird," which seemed innocuous enough, although as she kept reading she was reminded that the bird was intended as a metaphor for the spirit after death.

She bet this never happened to the Whitman people.

\* \* \*

Magda awoke what might have been minutes or hours later. It was still dark, although the interior was always fairly dim once the windows were boarded. The walls seemed to be pulsing with the energy of the wind and rain outside. Her instinct told her it was not yet morning. She was surprised she'd been able to sleep at all, but she felt certain that she'd been soundly dreaming and that something specific had woken her.

She sat up and reached for the lantern. She had heard something, surely.

The ambient weather sounded just the same, dampened by the solid building, but she was hearing something soft and whispering. Then a loud *crack*.

She wormed out of the sleeping bag and hurried to the door, shivering in the night air. She had fallen asleep fully dressed, but she paused to put her rubber boots back on to protect her feet from the cold floor. Whatever the sound was, it was coming from the gift shop. Now she was closer, she could smell—*smoke*, and hear crackling and popping. What she had taken for darkness ahead was also smoke, thick enough now to make her cough as she ran.

The rear wall of the gift shop was already alight, sheltered from the rain by the overhanging roof. There was something heavy and gray shoved through the wall. Sparks were still popping and flashing around it.

Magda realized she was looking at the front of the skiff. It must have been picked up by the wind and thrown straight through the wall like a projectile.

She ran to grab the fire extinguisher. She had to keep the fire out of the main house, which—despite stone walls—also had wooden floors and ceilings and several heavy hanging tapestries. If the art, or any of the antiques were soiled by the soot . . .

She yanked out the pin and started spraying from the adjoining wall outward, starting at the floor and sweeping up. The smoke was thick, and Magda pulled her shirt up over her nose and mouth to cover her face so she wouldn't breathe in the burning fumes. She couldn't even remember if fire extinguishers worked on electric fires, but the flames seemed willing to be subdued by the heavy white foam.

The extinguisher ran out before the last of the fire did, but she'd beaten it back to the area directly around the nose of the skiff, and she beat that back with her jacket. There was still some sparking around the edges. The damn faulty electric.

She had to turn off the power. Whatever wiring had gone wrong in the walls, it would soon be burning again. *Think, think.* The electrical box was around the side of the house, in the maintenance shed—she'd have to go outside.

She hurried now out the side door, which now fit badly in its hinges, possibly swelled up from the heat and the rain.

It was like walking into a wall of wind and rain. The storm itself felt charged, a pounding like a heartbeat that seemed to fill all the space. Magda was soaked immediately. Shaking her head, she pushed on to the rear of the building.

A small shed had been constructed to protect the meter and the main electric panel from the effects of the ocean, so at least there was some cover ahead as she waded through the gathering stream. Unfortunately it looked like something had slammed into the door, ripping it off its hinges, and causing the whole thing to tilt drunkenly. Inside, the rain hammered ominously on the plywood roof. It felt like standing inside a drum solo.

She splashed to the electrical panel at the back, which was a nest of wires and switches. Every year Magda fought to keep a reasonable budget so that, under ordinary circumstances, she could hire a professional to address any issues with the wiring, but there was no one to call now.

She shivered, her skin clammy and damp under her plastic raincoat. The fuse box looked foreboding in the gloom, dented gray metal. She wiped her hands on her pants—both were damp—and cracked it open. The frayed wires around the panel made her nervous, and the plastic casing was already cracked. When had that happened? It hadn't looked like that the last time she'd been in here.

Her father's voice reminded her that standing in a puddle in the middle of a storm wasn't the best time to play with the electric system. But what else could she do? The sparks in the gift shop had probably already set the walls back alight. She didn't have time to delay. Turn off the power now, or the house would burn.

Maybe there was something rubber or wood she could use to knock the main shutoff switch. There was a box of tools in the corner. She kicked it over and found a claw hammer. That was better than nothing, right?

She gripped the plastic handle and reached the head up toward the main circuit. It was all or nothing.

She hooked the handle and pulled it down with a dull *thunk*.

For what felt like half a beat there was silence, just long enough for her to exhale in relief.

Then she felt humming in her fingertips, her toes—she tried to jerk her hand away from the hammer, but it was too late, her fingers weren't responding—and the room lit up like a kaleidoscope, like being in the center of a firework, like turning into a shower of sparks, flying in all directions. She heard—she swore she heard—an angry buzz like the timer on the washing machine in her apartment, as though she had taken a nap with clothes tumbling merrily away.

There was a smell of burning feathers, very strong and close by, and she almost grasped, faintly, that it was probably her own eyelashes, her own eyebrows, the hair on her arms—

A great hand reached up out of the ground and closed around her, tight in a fist, and everything went black.

# 5

Tuesday, October 8th
10:00 PM

THE SUMMER MAGDA turned fourteen, she had been driving with her father to a folk festival in Goshen. They had been on the road for two months at that point, bouncing from gig to gig. They were down to one set of reliable speakers and one amplifier they kept alive by dint of alternate coaxing, jiggling, and judicious application of electrical tape. He had promised to teach her how to solder when they next got to town.

The weather had been unsettled all week, with thunderstorms, but now, as they hit the open vista of US-20, the sky had turned greenish and churning. She remembered the hair on her arms standing up, twitching like a divining rod.

The radio had cut out into a weather alert, and they'd had five minutes' warning, no good place to pull over. In her memory she hadn't really been scared. Maybe a little excited, even. "Are we going to stop?"

She could see her father's bare forearm, the cuffs of his shirt rolled up. "Can't stop out here. I guess we can outrun it if we have to. Look at the map again. Is there anything coming up?"

Magda was good at navigation. Besides wiring repair, that was her contribution to the team. It was grounding to have a job.

The laminated county roadmap showed an empty stretch for at least another three inches. She knew without checking the scale that anything more than a thumb span was out of reach.

Her father stepped on the gas when she said as much. He was watching the sky in his rear view. "How about other roads—will we cross anything bigger?"

"There's a little turnoff for a lake up ahead, but it doesn't look like much. Then there's I-69 after that."

Her father's eyes were on the clouds. "How long?"

"Maybe ten miles?"

"Okay, we can make that. Don't worry, Mags. A tornado is a real specific kinda thing. We probably won't even see it."

The clouds were roiling as they crested the hill five minutes in. Neither of them mentioned it, but the tires turned faster. "There," said Magda, pointing to the bridge on the horizon. "See it?"

His voice was calm and steady. "Well, if that's the best we can do, I guess it's gonna have to work, eh Maggie?"

Later Magda had learned that an overpass was a crappy place to wait out a tornado. According to the statistics they would have been better off lying down in a roadside ditch than doing what they did, which was gun it to make for the bridge.

Her father pulled carefully off to one side, and they both watched while the storm that had been following them finally swallowed them up.

"Well, we might get a real show," said her father.

Black clouds, stirred up like a hornet's nest sending out whips of smoke. It seemed like something that shouldn't exist in the real world. "Do you think it will come close?" she'd said.

Her father put his arm around her shoulders. "I just think it might. But we'll be just fine. Just hold on to me, okay? I've got you."

The next few minutes were a blur. The day turned to dusk, and then came the hail and lightning. The sound of the wind was like one of the trains they had raced outside of Chicago. The temperature dropped like being plunged into ice water.

"It's not that close," yelled her father. "We're good here."

Magda didn't remember being frightened—although she must have been. What she remembered was the feeling of his flannel shirt under her cheek, and the strength of his arms around her back. His voice in her ear. "Wow, ain't it something, Magpie? Look quickly now—it'll be gone in a flash. You don't want to miss this."

"It's beautiful," she said. But the rain turned sideways, an unnatural angle, and Magda closed her eyes.

"Don't look away!" he shouted. "There, Maggie, look, there!"

It wasn't like on TV, where you watched that needle coming closer and closer. It must have been shrouded in the storm. Between one minute and the next it appeared, almost on top of them. How close was it? In her memory, it was right there in the overpass with them—but perhaps it had never been that close. Perhaps it was still a mile or more away, tossing cows and overturning a grain barn, killing three farmers and a storm chaser.

Except for the grit from the road blowing up into their faces, they had been unhurt as it blew past with a blare like a semi overtaking them on the highway, cussing them out and throwing up rocks. By the time she realized it was over, it was already long gone, with nothing but her ears popping to tell her it was real.

"Well, hot damn," said her father, looking down at himself. "Hot damn. That's good fodder for a song, baby girl. 'High Winds from Goshen,' maybe. How does that sound?"

He wrote it, too: *Hold your ground, we're grounded by the road now / Watch the sky, She's taking what she's owed now.*

In her memory of that year, her father had known everything. There was nothing he couldn't fix, not the car when it broke down—and it always broke down—or the motel AC, or a tricky E chord she couldn't quite get her fingers around.

But he had been younger than she was now, that summer. He hadn't known what to do either.

Sometimes now she thought about the sheer insanity of raising a teenager on the road, stringing together a mishmash of schools, leaving her to sleep in vans or motel rooms while he played bars and small stages across the country.

A tornado was the least of their problems, really.

\* \* \*

Magda opened her eyes in the dark. Her cheek was pressed against damp soil, and she was breathing earth.

She sat up, very slowly, every joint aching like she was getting over the flu. She was soaked through. She wasn't sure how she'd gotten on the ground. Her head hurt badly, her neck—it was hard to swallow. Her eyes were dazzled. She looked down at herself, blankly, feeling like she didn't recognize the vague shape of her own body.

Her palms were stinging. She looked at them for a long time and then finally succeeded, after a delay, in curling the fingers into a fist. Alive. She was alive. As long as she could make a fist, she was alive.

She clambered to her feet. Her knees refused to lock until she concentrated. Ugh, how much time had passed? *The fire—the breaker.*

Based on the position of the main switch, the power was off. At least that had been a success.

The battered shelter around the power box hadn't been enough to keep her lower half dry. Fortunately the fury of rain seemed to have slackened for now, although a sudden gust of wind caught her as soon as she was standing. Her feet, clumsy, disoriented, found their way to taking a step, although they wanted to slide out from under her. She wondered if the plastic of her shoes had melted.

She fought to gain control of her shallow, panting breaths, trying to find a rhythm. *Two in, long exhale.* Like they did for pregnant women—what was that called? Lamaze. Just keep breathing and everything would be fine.

Coordination returned as she crossed back over the rain-soaked grass and under the overhanging porch of the dark and silent Whimbrel House.

It was a relief to slam the heavy door behind her and brace it with a plywood board. The house inside seemed wonderfully still and silent. The outraged howling of the wind was muffled, distant. It could rage, but it couldn't get in.

*See? I needed to be here,* thought Magda. The fire would have spread if nobody had been there to put it out; the art, the antiques, everything could have been ruined.

It had been worth something. It was worth anything if it saved Isobel's house.

*    *    *

Stripping off her sodden and clinging clothes Magda staggered back to the doorway of the gift shop to at least check that it was not actively burning: if it was, she wasn't sure she'd have the strength to put it out again. But the seeping rain and her previous efforts seemed to have quenched it.

She stumbled to the fold-up cot in the kitchen, unzipped the sleeping bag, and managed to pull herself into it, shivering. She still felt icy cold inside. Rather than passing out immediately, she had to warm up and let her muscles, particularly the long muscles in her thighs, stop twitching and clenching before she would be able to find sleep.

After a good show—and it didn't take much: solid amps and a backup band that could keep pace, no drunks in the audience yelling for "Freebird"—her father would come back to the motel giddy. "This was one for the record books, Magpie," he'd say. "If you figure heaven is the Greatest Hits album, this was a show that's gonna make the replay."

That had been all he needed, the easy weight of his guitar, or his mandolin, or his banjo, and a list of all his favorite songs. How could Magda blame him for leaving an oversensitive teenager out of the montage? Years later, after the accident, that was how she pictured him: endlessly reliving those nights, the floodlights and the crowd. Forgetting her.

Lying in the dark she pinched the fleshy padding at the point of her chin with nerveless fingers. Behind it she could feel the shape of her own skull. Sometimes it seemed so close to the surface—at the orbits of her eyes, the eruption of her teeth—that she could picture exactly how it must sit behind the skin. As if she could hold it in her own hand.

Isobel had written once that she thought people were reincarnated as birds. She had been pretty mad on birds—well, she'd been raised in a house named for a seabird, after all—and knew every species that passed through the Keys on their way north or south. It would probably be difficult to pick a few highlights for Isobel, for whom each must have been pretty similar to the one before, except for the slow turn of the seasons, which were barely appreciable here on the southern tip of the US. A bird made as much sense as anything.

And Magda herself—she remembered thinking, even back when her father had first said it, that only the dying would be able to pinpoint their best days. Everyone else could still dream the greatest moments were right around the corner.

But now, slowly warming in her sleeping bag on the metal cot—she reached to turn on the lantern despite knowing she should preserve the battery life, keeping it within arm's reach but safely out of flailing distance—Magda was grimly suspicious that it was those days on the beach with Bryce she'd relive in paradise.

There were days when the ocean was so mild and mirror clear, she could look down through the water to her own feet on the white sand, swirling in a cloud of tiny bright-colored fish. And then Bryce would come back from examining whatever conch or crab he had found and sweep her up, and she would be weightless. Almost without a body at all.

Magda rolled herself onto her side, to stare at the low lantern light. She closed her eyes.

CHAPTER

6

Wednesday, October 9th
8:00 AM

*Day Three*

THE ELECTRIC CRACK of a shutter being torn from its hinges jolted Magda awake. She had been dreaming of her grandmother's house in Ishpeming falling into a mine shaft, Magda reaching uselessly from sturdy ground.

She sat up and started coughing. She felt like she'd swallowed a bale of wire. Her head pounded like the night after a boozy celebration at Bar Pilar. She sat up slowly, grunting, wishing she'd thought to leave herself a bottle of water by the bed. Ah well, if she had, she'd only have used it on the fire last night.

She took stock of herself. Other than her throbbing hands there was no other sign of injury she could find. She just felt heavy and tired, run-down like the morning after any other night without enough sleep.

And the house was still standing—nothing else had broken through the walls in the night. The wind was still wailing outside, but it was evident by what little light there was that it must be morning. All that and the world didn't end. The Keys were obviously still standing.

She checked the weather radio first. The weatherman must be somewhere far away from Florida, because he sounded calm and even bored as he reported that Hurricane Myra, now a category five, was stalled just to the south of Key West, where it was delivering sustained winds of over one hundred miles an hour with gusts of up to one hundred twenty. It was still moving very slowly north.

Power was out over the entire lower half of the state. Any residents stupid enough to be caught in the storm (he didn't say that, but Magda felt it was implied) should shelter in place. The severe winds were expected to continue for at least another twelve hours, but there was no guarantee how long the storm itself would stick around.

She switched it off to conserve the battery as long as possible, knowing it might be weeks before power was restored.

Her palms were scorched. She reached for the medical kit and slathered them with cream, then laid a square of gauze over each one, and wrapped both in a roll of fabric. They stung like the next morning after a bad sunburn.

She loaded up on clothing from her duffel—careless of her to have slept naked last night, but she'd been far too tired to locate, unzip, and root through her bag in the dark—and, when fully dressed from head to toe, including heavy socks, checked first on the gift shop.

The wind was knocking on the door, *thud thud thud*, but she wasn't about to let it in.

The skiff was still wedged firmly halfway through the wall. It looked as if it had poked its head inside to say,"*Hey guys,*" unconsciously singeing the wood all around.

She couldn't leave it where it was. Covering herself in her coat and stepping into her boots, she ducked through the side door, into the rain, and hurried around the side of the building, staying well back under the eaves.

Outside, the other end of the skiff, slightly crumpled, emerged from the wall. She gave it a solid pull, groaning, and after a brief battle it shifted with a metallic squeal of protest. Another good tug had it starting to move. Fortunately it was made of fairly light aluminum, or she wouldn't have had the strength. When it came out the front half was dented but it was still whole.

The hole that remained in the *wall*, however, would let in the rain if she didn't fix it.

Magda was careful not to let the skiff catch the wind again as she dragged it back to the side door, which she'd left swinging open. Although it had been securely staked— she'd thought—there must have been a solid gust that had caught it and torn it straight out of the ground. Fortunately another didn't come up as she maneuvered it inside.

When she finally slid the boat up against the inner wall, she breathed a sigh of relief. Now to repair the charred gap that was taunting her, deeply blasted in all directions.

She moved the radio into the gift shop so she could keep track of the storm. Then slowly, taking shallow breaths and pausing to rest after every move, she got to work.

It took two heavy plywood boards to cover the hole, drilled straight through the wooden walls, and braced with a tall display stand, which Magda could only push by leaning all her weight behind it. She wasn't sure it was entirely solid, but she wasn't seeing a lot of other options.

The walls of the addition were rattling ominously. There might be some busted beams somewhere. It wasn't surprising, the way the wind was whirling around, looking for weak spots. When she put her hand on the plywood, she could feel the storm battering against it.

Water leaked around the edges of her patch job and onto the floor. She wasn't sure it was worth it trying to sop it up. She sealed up the edges with plastic tape and caulk from the tool box. Her hands were clumsy and the gauze soaked through quickly. She had to rewrap them twice. She got splinters in her fingertips. At one point she dragged the duffel over to rummage for another layer of shirts.

The forecast was getting repetitive—the storm was barely moving—and finally she turned it off. Nothing they said was going to make any difference to her.

When the wall was as good as it was going to get, she made her way to the kitchen and heated water on the camping stove for coffee. Breakfast was a cereal bar and a few slices of bread with peanut butter, and then she forced herself to eat half a banana, which wouldn't keep long. She wasn't hungry at all, or even thirsty, really, although she made herself drink. She felt like she was coming down with something. The lack of sleep and being out in the storm probably hadn't helped her immune system. Suddenly she remembered the flushed cheeks of the boy on the last tour. Great. That was just her luck: survive an electric shock but then come down with some random bug.

*"Clear liquids when you're sick,"* said her grandmother, *"as much as you can handle, and then some. Flush the fever right out of you."*

When she finished, she made a slow circuit of the house to look for other damage, avoiding the eyes of Abigail Reyes as she walked past the portraits. This was no time for gentleness or timidity, she reminded herself. These were times for Charlie's swarthy, confident face and ambitious mustache. *"Carry on, Carry on,"* he told her, waving his hand with impatience. *"For heaven's sakes, girl, keep it moving."* He was a sailor, after all, a merchant and a traveler; he had no doubt seen many storms. The thought cheered her only until she remembered that the last one had killed him. She avoided his eyes, too, after that.

She stacked up a few more sandbags all around the interior doors—just in case any water started to leak in. The original extant of the house was still water tight. The walls seemed to have a lot of strength left in them.

She could hear one of her father's tunes bouncing around in her head as she worked. She had never minded being alone, but it was strange now to feel almost crowded out by voices.

Finally satisfied, she wrapped herself in her unzipped sleeping bag (she had always run cold, and being sick made it worse) and sat on the bottom step of the grand staircase, with the leftover wine from the Fall fundraiser. It was a cabernet, not especially good, but the lid was a twist-off. *Thank the Lord for strong coffee and red wine.* That didn't seem like a line of Isobel's poetry—maybe from one of her father's songs.

She definitely felt worse. She kept coughing into her sleeve—it didn't sound good, but nothing came up—and wasn't sure if it was the smoke from last night or another symptom of whatever cold the kid from the tour had. No doubt her nighttime misadventures had multiplied any crap that was building up in her lungs.

At one point she blew her nose on a few squares of toilet paper and found that the product came out sooty and black. She had heard somewhere you weren't that sick if you could still touch your chin to your chest. She did it a few times, just to be sure.

The bottle of wine went down easy. It was only early afternoon, but Magda had time to savor it. Or would have, if it didn't taste like ash.

True to the forecast, the storm seemed to swell with every hour that passed. At some point Magda risked climbing the stairs to the second floor, where the slats in the old hurricane shutters still permitted a view of the outdoors. She sat by the window in what had been Isobel's bedroom, looking out at the coastline.

The rain was nearly horizontal, and formed such an opaque mist that it was as if the house was an airplane ascending through clouds. Although her watch told her it was almost noon, it looked like dusk outside, the sun blotted out by the heavy clouds.

At first everything was gray—gray sky, milky gray air, gray water on the horizon. Her eyes learned to find the new contrast settings, like switching to black and white photography. Even after she adjusted, it took her several seconds to make sense of what she was seeing in the gloom.

She could barely make out the garden at all, but the wind was not quite continuous, and when it slackened, the familiar shapes of the dock and the water came into focus.

From here she could see the gusts whipping down the beach, bending down the palm trees at the hotel. The surf, all the way out to the horizon, was truly awful; nothing but endless choppy, churning waves, each one hurling itself at the shore to erupt with a shower of sparks. It was fortunate that the shape of the inlet itself kept it somewhat protected from the biggest of the waves, but she could see down the shore how they were eating away at the cement seawall, curling over it like a clutching hand, pulling it out into the water. It looked like stretches of it had already started eroding away. The big public dock at the other end of the beach was totally in ruins, pylons standing stalwart but unbraced, a few brave crosspieces still hanging on.

She spent the next several hours drinking the wine and squinting through the heavy rain to watch the dock down the beach be demolished to nothing, beam by beam. The wind and the waves were vicious, attacking it from all directions, never giving it a rest.

She was also watching the surf as it came up the end of the lawn. Their own dock had a low profile, and the water had already overtopped it, which was fine—that might actually be preferable than having it exposed to the wave action, from what Magda could tell. But now the waves were curling over the grass, irregularly at first, then more often, and finally even as they retreated, the water level was still up over dry land. Magda estimated the ocean must have risen six feet at least.

There was still a good stretch to the lemur's garden. They were fine. Magda was keeping her eye on the distance. She could see the edge of the stone wall from this window, and all seemed to be well.

She knew even a few inches of running water could knock a person off their feet; six inches could transport a car downstream. And it seemed to be moving over the lawn at quite a clip. Would the ground be eroded away? If so, where was the money going to come from to restore it? The beach might be completely gone, or then again maybe the outgoing storm would deposit more sand there. They had never had a seawall, just the old oyster beds, and Magda hadn't pushed to add one more inch of hardened shoreline to the Key. She'd wanted it to be the way it had been in Isobel's day, of course, before cement and rebar had come in to reinforce what had formerly been a free-wheeling, drifting island.

Now it was possible that decision would cost her the Key limes. The water must already be on top of them, and they couldn't survive any saltwater intrusion in their soil. She had never had the chance to taste their pale yellow fruit; they didn't bear for at least four years.

She thought of the cuttings she had sent away with Bryce. She wished the phones weren't down, as it would have been comforting to at least know he had made it to safety. She tried not to imagine them—Bryce, Cole, and the lime switches—all drowning like Charles Reyes and his new family in Bimini.

It was funny, parts of her family had drowned too in that Michigan mine. Really, there was nowhere safe. She wondered if that water looked like this—foamy and frantic, hungry—as it had come rushing down the shaft.

Was her fever better or worse? She knew wine was probably not the clear liquid her grandmother would have recommended. She hadn't liked it at first, but she was kind of warming up to it. If she could have offered some to the victims of the mine disaster as that swamp water poured in on them, they probably would have taken her up on it.

Still a reasonable span to the lemurs. Ten feet at least.

It was obvious from her viewpoint that the winds were constantly changing directions—they'd attacked the dock like a pack of wolves, surrounding it on all sides, testing for weak spots, then coming in from all angles. What would they do to the garden walls? The water was gaining ground up over the lawn.

Just as she looked down for her glass, she happened to catch sight of what must have been the biggest wave yet, making straight for the edge of the yard. Where the others had started running out of steam once they reached land, this one almost seemed to grow and spread.

There were more waves behind the first, as if encouraged by its success—eager now, sensing the weakness, storming the gate. Each one of them seemed to cheer on its neighbor, until finally Magda could see that the water level itself was rising, right over the grass, right to the edge of the wall—and still coming.

Oh God, it would sweep the walled garden. The lemurs had no way to get out.

The next wave swept right up into the pen, followed by another one. The ocean had gained so many feet in just the last hour. She wasn't sure how much longer the storm would last, but if she was going to get down to the pen, she needed to do it now.

Before the whole thing starting coming down.

Wednesday, October 9th
3:00 PM

MAGDA THREW HER storm gear back on and ran down the stairs to the side door of the gift shop.

The door was hard to open—then it was ripped out of her hand and slammed against the wall, making the whole structure rattle ominously. Magda couldn't pull it shut so she left it gaping, hoping that when the winds shifted she'd be able to do it then. Going outside was like stepping into a wall of water. She had to lean forward to even walk, with the winds buffeting her back, catching her raincoat like a sail, threatening to pick her up off her feet.

She wondered if she'd end up crawling, in the end.

She scrambled across the grass to the near garden wall, a distance of maybe two hundred feet. The gate was on the other side, closer to the water, but she took the long way around the outside rather than cross in front of the ocean.

A sudden gust blasted by her with a howl. She could hear the rattling of the gift shop roof from here, and an ominous groaning creak. *Oh God*—the supplies. The med kit, the duffel of clothes, her phone, the weather radio—she'd left them in the gift shop where she'd been working. Even the sleeping bag. She almost turned back to move them, but another huge wave was already sweeping toward the garden.

It hit the shore at full force and sent the spray flying into the air, heavier and colder than the whipping rain.

No, she had to get to the lemurs first. She was a *caretaker*—she couldn't just let them drown.

She held an arm over her face and pressed on toward the gate. Her foot kicked up something—ice? Was that possible?—in the grass. The Key limes were long gone, she noted, barely stopping. Either the wind or the water had swept them away.

The wall around the gate of the garden was already starting to erode from the bottom and wasn't going to last much longer. Magda kicked her way around it trying not to lean on the loose stones.

Finally she slipped and slid through the opening and into enclosed space, where all four lemurs were packed against the back wall watching the water coming with wide eyes. "It's alright, it's alright, I'm here," she murmured, her hands shaking as she tried to pull the gate closed behind her. The lemurs shrank back, terrified. She wasn't cutting a very reassuring figure just now, windblown and bedraggled, her heart pounding, her eyes streaming from the saltwater.

A sudden gust drove the eroding wall, and Magda bit her own tongue hard to hold back a cry as the bricks started to fall in. God, the whole thing would come down soon. But the animals wouldn't walk downhill, toward the sea— they were crouching on the highest ground at the back. Although the cement structure was solid, it was clear to Magda that the storm surge, if not the winds, would soon overtake it. The lemurs would drown if she didn't let them out.

It was wrong, she was sure, to try and let them go free—they weren't tame, and for all she knew they might never be recaptured, if they lived through the storm at all. God knew what trouble they would get into. Maybe the calculus might have been different if she'd been on some unspoiled paradise full of rare species. But Key West was built over on top of old buildings, crumbling skeletons over skeletons, more cement now than sand. The spit of land that housed Whimbrel House—and maybe the golf course, and the empty fields around the airport—were basically the last places on the island that even felt like a natural space, with most of the rest of it being built up on top of Navy yard fill.

She didn't know if the lemurs could even survive the storm on their own, but she knew they would rather try than die trapped in their pen.

She didn't have any tools but the penknife in her pocket. Fortunately she knew how the netting was attached to the back of the wall and where it would be easiest to take up. She hurried to the far corner, where the bolts holding it down had recently been replaced. She tuned out the surf and the wind and focused on the careful work of unscrewing the fasteners, then sliding the metal attachments out of place.

The biggest lemur, Clyde, came over toward her as she used her hands and the knife to pull the netting out of the frame. Magda wasn't sure how he would react, but his attention was absorbed by the sea, which was even now coming up to his front door.

The mesh came lose. She cut and tore the rest of it, making a hole plenty big enough for a small animal to

climb out. "Go that way, Clyde," she said stupidly, pointing up the slope of the garden. She wondered if he understood her, having lived with humans his whole life.

He sent her a look of distain and did not come any
closer. Cursing, Magda backed away, staggering in the
water that was now up to her ankles. The lemurs
scattered.

"Go on you stupid monkeys!" Although they were
primates.

She sloshed back all the way to the wall, hoping if they
avoided both her and the sea they would be more likely to
end up at the exit. She braced against a standing portion of
rock, afraid to turn her back fully to the ocean.

The grout began to shift underneath her and she
cursed. Everything was falling apart. What the hell did
you do when even a stone wall wasn't safe anymore?

She looked up as Clyde started to move. Finally he was
making his way to the opening in the netting. Magda held
her breath.

"Go on, go on," she whispered. "You can do it."

He looked dubious, examining the hole.

"Go, you little bastard, go!" She really thought he was
going to change his mind just to spite her, but obedient for
once in his life, he climbed out at last and started loping up
the grass. Now he was determinedly making his way
toward a low mass of standing trees that marked the edge
of the drive. She didn't know if it would be any safer in the
winds, but it would certainly be drier—much more of this
and the pen would be engulfed completely.

Clyde's mate, Perdita, was next, following him without
so much as a glance at Magda. Leave it to a prosimian to
make you feel inadequate after you've risked your life in a
hurricane to save them.

The last two were huddled back against the wooden frame of their sleeping bunk. They were watching the water, and Magda wondered if they could understand the situation or not. She debated whether she was doing her part by merely enabling their escape if they chose to take it, or if she had to actively carry them away from the floodwaters to do her moral duty.

Since her moral duty was probably to comfort them while they drowned rather than release them, she guessed the time for debate was over.

"Come on, Sandrine," she whispered, getting down on her hands and knees to crawl closer. "Come on, babycakes, time to go."

She reached one heavily cloaked arm toward the little lemur, still trying to talk soothingly over the howl of the gale and the water outside. Sandrine shifted anxiously, chattering, finally distracted from the view through the door to turn her attention to the caretaker. "Come on, baby, this is no place for a nice little girl like you."

Sandrine surprised Magda by letting her get close without a murmur, seemingly frozen by the storm and the sight of the water coming to carry her away.

Magda took off her coat—soaking yet another T-shirt, but what could you do?—and was prepared to try and catch her and swaddle her up in the fabric, but Sandrine skittered ahead of her when she bent forward, making for the wrong side of the pen.

"Damn it!"

Magda forced herself to hold still and take two steadying breaths. She could do this. There was still time.

Abandoning the other lemur, Cosimo, for now, she herded Sandrine in a slow circle, waving her arms and splashing her feet until finally, *finally* the lemur made it all the way to the opening in the mesh where her fellows had gone.

Looking up the rise, she couldn't see the other two, but Sandrine was chattering with interest, staring into the bushes. Magda hoped she wasn't seeing a crocodile or a boa constrictor. But the lemurs were going to have to be left to their own fates now—Magda had done what she could for them.

Apparently trusting the instincts of her elders, the lemur reached to pull herself through the netting and into the branches on the other side.

"Stay low, Sandrine," Magda advised. "And get to higher ground. I'm going back after your buddy."

She forced herself to head back down the hill one last time to find the final lemur. If she was hoping he'd used the opportunity of her absence to crawl out by himself, she was in for a disappointment. He was huddled down into the furthest corner of the pen.

Cosimo was the tamest of the lemurs, having been born on the estate. Magda thought her odds were pretty good of being able to catch him if she had to, but the odds of him biting her face off didn't seem terrible either. Quite a fate, to survive the storm but be mauled to death by an animal you were trying to rescue.

She was ready with her jacket, but when she got close, he reached carefully and deliberately to climb up her arm to her shoulder, and sat perched there, his fingers buried in her hair.

"Well, okay then."

Cosimo's black and white tail curled confidingly around her forearm.

Outside, there was a terrible creak and groan, and the loudest sound yet, like an avalanche. Magda was fairly positive they'd just lost the gift shop. *The supplies,* she thought uselessly. But it was too late.

The walls of the pen rattled with the force of one of those sudden gusts, and Magda crouched with her head in her hands, as Cosimo peed spectacularly down the front of her shirt.

The winds lasted for what might have been a sustained thirty seconds, but which felt to Magda, about to be crushed to death in a lemur pen, like it might have been a thousand years. She was an idiot to have come out here, she concluded. She might as well have left the lemurs to their fates. She could have been snug and safe inside with her bottle of wine right now.

Then the gust broke off with a snarl and Magda figured this was as close to a chance as she was going to get. She stumbled out the front of the gate, holding Cosimo bundled under her chin so the wind didn't blow him clear away. He seemed to understand the situation because he huddled down lower in her neck, his little human-seeming hands gripping hold of one of her ears.

She almost tripped over the fallen stones of the wall, half buried under murky water. She needed to get back inside—this was nuts. But she slogged up the hill, still clutching Cosimo, who was also clutching her.

Sandrine was still in the branches on the other side of the pen. She ran ahead when Magda made for her, Cosimo beginning to chirp when they got close. When they made it to the low trees, Magda was thankful to be able to reach a branch that seemed relatively stable—Cosimo reached obligingly, pulling himself into the trees.

Her last sight was of the two of them huddled together. Then the thinner branches were whipping in the wind, and Magda had to hold her face away.

"Good luck," she whispered as she spun around, her eyes full of tears. Who knew if she would ever find any of them again.

From further up the hill there was an audible yowl. She guessed Clyde was calling the rest of his band together. Hopefully they had the instinct to head for shelter.

The water seemed certain now to reach the mansion itself before long, and who knew how the foundation would hold up once it was inundated. Magda was already picturing the grant application she'd need to write as she struggled back toward the house.

Another gust came up while she was walking—rising to gale force, enough that she had to drop down to the grass and let herself fall forward, grabbing a handful of earth, suddenly terrified of being swept straight down the hill and off the edge, into the ocean. If she'd been standing upright it would have no doubt knocked her straight off her feet. She could imagine now how easily it must have tossed the skiff.

Then she staggered back toward the house, pushed up the hill by the wind like a kite.

The gift shop had collapsed entirely on one side, the broken wood frame scraping along the limestone side of the house in a pile of rubble. It was sagging like a drunk against the still standing section that connected to the side of the house, the roof now a steep slope down to the ground. She had to make a wide circuit around the wreck just to reach the back door of the kitchen, now the only way in.

It was strange to see a formerly habitable place, one where she had spent many hours working, transformed into a towering wreck. It reminded Magda now of the shantytowns on the sailing trip she had taken with Bryce.

She shuddered to think what Myra must have done to the tropical islands, where this kind of structure was considered well built.

The wooden door of the gift shop still hung from its hinges. Magda turned the knob and pushed it doubtfully, in the vague hope that her duffel bag and the med kit would be somewhere visible inside. It swung open about a foot with an ominous groan.

The rain was coming in through cracks in the roof and streaming over what had been the laminate floor. The debris had mostly piled up in the back. It would be suicide to go in and try to pick through it. So much for her supplies.

All that was left was a sheltered, cave-like space close to the original wall of the house, the sagging crossbeam still supported by a limestone wall. One good gust would bring it down too.

Although what didn't make much sense, as she squinted out into the unrevealing gloom, was the shape the water was describing with its flow, just beyond what had been the entrance from the house. It should have been simply an empty open space, but now the water was drawing an elegant spiral in the middle, smooth on the edges in and out. Like Charybdis, rising out of what had been a laminate floor. She couldn't understand it until the sloshing water drained another inch. Then she realized that the center of the floor itself had caved in like a giant sink hole and was sucking the water down in a spiral.

Through the newly opened floor Magda could make out what looked like a circular structure, perhaps six feet by six feet across, with smooth ceramic walls, earth toned like terra cotta.

*The old cistern,* she recollected—contemporary letters had referenced it as the way Charles managed to keep the tropical plants growing in what should have been a dry and unforgiving habitat. It was gone before the house was sold the first time, and she had never known its exact location or what had become of it. She had assumed it had been taken out.

Squinting now into the newly revealed feature, huddled under a folded cover of the roof, Magda amazed herself by still feeling a bolt of delighted curiosity. Forget the headache pounding at her temples, her soiled shirt, the wind and the rain; this was an object Isobel must have been familiar with, one that had been buried from sight for a hundred years.

It was half filled in now with rubble and silt. Although—

It was only from this angle that it was visible—from anywhere else it would have been obscured by the wreckage—but Magda could distinctly see what looked like a black corner of what might have been a square solid shape. Right in the center of the cistern. Was it a rock? No, there was something about the weight of it, the perfectly straight sides, that looked humanly made. There was nothing that had been in the shop that looked anything like it. Was it an old crate or something? Trash caught up in the whirlpool? But it was clearly mostly buried in silt, only that one visible corner exposed.

It bothered her. She knew perfectly well there were many more important things to worry about, but—well, she was still a historian, first and foremost. If it was some kind of water control structure, she had never seen such a thing. If it was a box, which it resembled most, then why? What was in it?

She wondered if it would be possible to get in there and see it for herself, although right at that moment the storm seemed to be building back up—and the roof and walls around it were evidently unstable . . . it was obviously not the best idea—but that clearly *was* something dark and square she was seeing.

Another sudden gust had her shaking herself as well as the walls. How stupid she was, standing outside in the storm. Hadn't she already pushed her luck far enough for one day? She needed to be inside, making sure there was no damage in the house.

"Alright, come on, Magda, for heaven's sake, focus—*oh!*"

The white heron was standing only a foot away when she turned, maybe the same one she'd seen only a few days before. The bird's bright eyes were fixed on the open doorway, its sides heaving. Magda looked back at it. Something made her push the door open a little wider and step aside.

Daintily, deliberately, its neck extended in a graceful bobbing curve, the big bird walked inside the cavern created by the wrecked addition.

*I'm not going to name it,* Magda decided, letting the door swing closed in its broken frame—because at this rate, she might end up having to eat it.

*       *       *

Back inside she changed quickly and examined her face in the bathroom mirror. Even in the light of the lantern, her skin looked sallow, her cheeks fever bright, although she felt cold. Her forearms also itched badly, and in the gloom she could make out what looked like raised red welts on the skin. It didn't look like any insect bite Magda had seen;

it might have been stress. She didn't have even basic medical supplies anymore, not even Advil or Tylenol. No more antibiotic cream either. And without the radio, no way to know the predicted path of the storm.

The only thing to do was assume the worst. Assume this flooding was only the beginning, and that as the center of the storm moved north, conditions were only going to devolve. Stronger wind, more rain. And there was nobody coming to help; it was all down to her.

Her head was pounding sluggishly now, whatever cold she'd picked up only compounded by the exertion, not to mention by being soaked, freezing, and tired. *Don't think about it,* she told herself. *Don't think about it now.*

At the kitchen window, she peered out the crack between the plywood boards, to watch the ocean water streaming up over the lawn. The next wave brought it up into the lemur's garden, quickly inundating the entire enclosure. The corner posts slanted precipitously. There wasn't that much elevation left before the ocean would come up to the steps of the house.

Numb, she walked around, rearranging the sandbags she had left out, even though she was pretty sure it wouldn't do much good. She lined the insides of the doors, then each entry way to each room, in case any of them could be spared by another twelve inches of breakwater. Her mind was still, blank. Her hands were steady. She needed to make a plan. She felt certain she was running out of time.

The art was first. The painting Isobel had made was priceless—that was the first thing to go. She lifted it down off the wall carefully, aware that even the stain of finger prints could be spoiling the original frame. But she didn't have time to go find her gloves. Her cheek was pressed to Isobel's blocky signature like an imprint as she carried it up to the landing of the stairwell, the bottom of which was ringed in sandbags, and leaned it against the wall. Then she went back for the books in the library. Forget the cheaper editions she had picked up at book sales and giveaway piles, and the text books she had selected mostly for their appropriately worn and illustrious covers. They could molder away in the supply closet for all she cared. But there were still many rare and original volumes. The ones with Isobel's signature went first, into Tupperware containers that had once contained leftover food from some long-ago event—then wrapped in plastic bags, then stacked into wooden apple crates. The humidity would be terrible for them, Magda fretted, but what else could be done? The other boxes were all cardboard, which wouldn't be any better. At least these kept the loads to what she could lift.

*Idiot,* Magda blamed herself. Why hadn't she sent them to the Smithsonian when they'd requested them? She had to have known on some level that the entire chain of the Keys was only biding its time until sea-level rise literally wiped it off the map. What had she been thinking, storing priceless pieces of history here? She wished she had made better-quality copies of everything, stocked the house with reproductions. What was the point of trying to summon Isobel's departed spirit back to a place that was also doomed?

Back and forth, she systematically packed and transported the crates from the library, serving as every link of a human ladder. By now she imagined she could hear the waves knocking on the front door. Somewhere in the back rooms, rattled by the window, a mirror fell over and broke, shattering from the sound of it. *Bad luck,* thought Magda, and in the next breath she thought, *Not authentic—don't worry about it.*

The antique rugs in the dining room, the wall hangings, the more valuable works of art. One by one Magda packed them up as best she could, watertight when she could achieve it, and carried them to the second-floor landing. These stairs that the engineer had questioned the integrity of, now their best hope. The kitchen was low; it would be the first to flood, and then what was left of the gift shop would be cut off.

The rain was picking up again outside. She could hear the churn of the ocean, and it sounded unusually close, but she didn't let herself check. She just began to move faster, snatching whatever she could that seemed worth saving, filling crates and bags.

One of the long windows in the sitting room was leaking. Even an inch of water coming in would destroy the original hardwood floors. The first money she had ever raised was to refinish and stain them . . . but no, she needed to stay focused on practicalities.

Magda could only save what she could carry, and her strength was flagging.

The painting of Abigail was still hanging, and Magda decided it was worth more than the less valuable of the two antique rugs, and though she couldn't move it—it was far too heavy and anchored securely to the wall—she debated cutting it out of the frame, but it was so fragile it was sure to crack. Finally she wrapped the entire thing in tarp and tape, hoping it might offer some protection. Abigail's melancholy eyes followed her until the features disappeared beneath a swaddling of plastic. Magda examined the final product critically—if it wasn't watertight, it would just be trapping moisture in against the paint—but it would have to do.

The furniture was hopeless. Most of it was too heavy to push more than a few feet. There was a curio cabinet full of fossils that she left behind. The floor lamps, which were antique—forget it. The gilt of the fireplace she could do nothing for, but it might have been fished out of the ocean originally anyway; perhaps it would be fine. She went for two oil lamps and the ceramic ewer from the kitchen, which was original to the house, and then forced herself to go back for a wall clock that had been authenticated.

Then she had to stop and lean against the wall of the landing, panting. She probably needed to take the most important things—the painting and the books at least—even higher. All the way up to the attic, if that's what it took. That painting was ungodly large—why the hell hadn't Isobel thought to paint something small and portable? A nice cameo, maybe—maybe something waterproof?

She was afraid to linger on the creaky landing too long. Who knew if it would even support her weight with the added bulk of the antiques.

Just the painting. If she could just get that to the second floor, she'd rest. And maybe one box of books . . .

The last trips up the second flight of stairs were nightmarish. Magda was sweating, swearing, trying not to lose her grip on anything priceless. The walls were definitely rattling now, and what sounded like important pieces of the exterior were coming loose. She worried the still-standing timbers of the gift shop might take out the walls of the mansion if they collapsed and hit at the wrong angle.

Finally she stood for a minute in the window of Isobel's room, staring out at the unrecognizable landscape revealed to her. The house was like an island in the middle of a lake. There was no more division between the edge of the land and the ocean—just one endless stretch of open water, churning madly. And incredibly it was still raining, the wind still howling on.

Who know where the lemurs were. She hoped they had moved quickly and that there was land left for them to go to. Maybe they would have some instinct for survival that she apparently lacked.

There would be nothing left of the gardens. Even the shape of the coast itself might be different. She had reconciled herself to the loss of the lime trees, but it was possible that every palm, every shrub she had watered during the hot summer months and sheltered during the brief chills of winter, every flower she had tracked in her log for the past ten years was gone.

She should probably have moved her own cot first, the sleeping bag, her few remaining supplies, she realized stupidly. Her remaining stores of food, the fuel cans in the cellar. It was all still waiting to be dealt with.

But Whimbrel House belonged to the ghosts, not the living.

Now that the immediate work was done, her temples felt tight, as if they were trapped in a vise. She leaned her forehead against the glass.

There was no light at all down the whole stretch of the coast. No flashlights in the windows of the hotel, which must have been fully evacuated. Not a buoy in the water or any structure to give her any sense there was *somebody* alive out there, somewhere. That she wasn't truly the only one left. Maybe she was.

In a burst of fancy, she took up one of the hurricane lamps and set it in the deep wooden window frame. It was stocked with oil; they all were. She still had her dad's lighter in the pocket of her raincoat. She flicked it over the wick and let it catch. There were no curtains to worry about setting alight, and it was safe enough under glass.

Then she set the lamp in the window as a rejoinder. *I'm still here.* She hadn't abandoned the house entirely to the ghosts yet.

She forced herself to get back on her feet and go down the stairs to retrieve whatever she could.

There was still work left to do.

# CHAPTER

# 8

Wednesday, October 9th
4:00 PM

DOWNSTAIRS, ALL THAT was left of what she had brought to the house was right where she had left it. Despite her fears and the still steady wind and rain, the water level so far seemed to be about the same. She wished badly for the weather radio so she would know more about what to expect.

The doorway into the ruined gift shop taunted her. It was impassable now, with beams and plywood blocking the way—she'd have to go out the kitchen side door to get in through what had been the exit, if she wanted to get back in. No doubt she should board it up to keep water out.

She peered out hopelessly into the space. The inside was a mess of water and wood and chaos. She could barely make out the shape of the old foundation. No sign of her supplies. No sign of the heron either. Just the cistern and that mysterious shape.

Doing nothing wasn't going to make her feel any better, she reasoned. If she took it easy, the mystery could serve as a distraction. That was logical, right?

It was kind of amazing to think that without the hurricane, and her mad decision to stay through it, this cistern might never have been found. At least that was one positive outcome of the whole storm—she had discovered something nobody had even known to look for.

But what *was* stuck in the middle?

She couldn't take it any longer. With the interior door blocked, she slipped out onto the porch and back around to the external door, keeping both ears tuned for any kind of creaking or shifting overhead.

Standing at the edge of the cistern, she wished she had her phone or a camera to document what she was seeing. The mud would probably cover it up again eventually. She knelt in the sandy earth and dug out the space around the box with a broken-off piece of the floor tile.

She was able to clear off the four corners and then the dark square of the top. It looked like the lid of an old steamer trunk made of heavily lacquered black canvas with rusted metal rivets around each corners. What the heck it was doing in the old cistern she couldn't say.

It was packed into a load of cobble and soft soil, all saturated now with rain and sea water. It wasn't terribly hard to push that aside, excavating the trunk slowly, one side before another, but she would never get the whole thing out that way.

There was still water trickling in from the holes in the roof, and the more she dug around the sides of the trunk, the more the water seemed to backfill the space. It was stuck deep in the mud, like quicksand. If she didn't move fast enough, she was afraid it was going to sink further down. She wasn't sure how deep the cistern went or how thick the silt inside of it was.

It was wedged quite tightly, and she couldn't get a grip on any point to pull it out. It made no sense that as the task got more difficult, she only became more determined to retrieve the box. She should have been giving up on the idea, deciding it was better to go back inside, where it was warm and safe, instead of staying out here splashing around in the mud like a pig under a roof that might collapse at any minute.

But she felt like a woman possessed. It was illogical, but this whole adventure was somewhat illogical, and damn it, she wanted to know what was in this box. It couldn't have been left here on accident, surely, as tightly as it was wedged. Someone had put it there deliberately. The cistern had been active as late as the 1920s, so it wasn't as if pirates were burying gold doubloons by then. Maybe it was a time capsule? It might have been hidden from human eyes for a hundred years and might only appear for this instant. What else was a historian for?

She took up a broken-off strip of plywood and jammed it down underneath the edge with all her weight, sinking it as deep down as it would reach. Then, with all her remaining strength, she tried to pry out the trunk, using the wood as a lever. Was it Archimedes who had said something like *"Give me a fulcrum and I can move the world"*?

She must have pulled too hard—the plywood bowed and then snapped, leaving her holding the broken end. The box was still stuck tight, but the lid had come unjammed from the impact, and it burst open in a shower of dark sludge.

Magda knelt in the knee-deep mud, panting.

Inside the box was the skeleton of a woman.

* * * `

There must have been some movement of air and water through the sodden box, because the skeleton was picked clean, with no flesh remaining at all. Within the folds of some kind of material—something that had resisted decay—the bones were childlike, curled up and sleeping in the dank coffin under the cistern. And yet it was clearly a woman, even to Magda's half-trained eye, not the least because of what was left of a pair of small high-heeled boots that were rolling around the bottom of the box.

Was this some kind of unusual burial? An old woman perhaps, or some servant's child who had met an untimely death and been interred at the estate?

The boots dated the body, to Magda's experienced eye, to the early 1900s. It was an era with which she was intimately familiar, after all.

She had to move the bones. The water was still trickling in, filling the cistern with muddy brown sludge. If it continued to rise, it would start filling up the box itself—and Magda was struck with the need to keep the skeleton safe.

But the box was heavy and still wedged too tightly to the cement. She couldn't work her hands down around the crumpled corners, and although she could fit them into the straight sides, scraping her knuckles, the box weighed too much to budge with just her fingertips.

And the sea itself was still rising, and the whole gift shop could come down any second. She couldn't get it out, and she could leave it there. She needed something she could fasten around it so she could hoist it out. Was there a rope anywhere in the house, or a chain?

Magda was still debating when she heard the unmistakable drone of an outboard motor. It was the first evidence of living human beings she'd seen the storm had descended, and it was momentarily disorienting, like waking after a long dream. Her next thought was, *Who the hell would be insane enough to be out on a boat in the middle of a hurricane?* The open water must be roiling, and the inland was studded with shoals and debris.

She pulled the lid of the trunk back down, determined that if she couldn't get it out, she could at least keep try to keep the bones preserved. There was a bent brass fastener in the front of the trunk, half buried and filled up with silt. She dug it out with her fingernails and cupped palmfuls of the rain. Then she patted the lid of the box as she snapped it shut tight.

"I'll come back for you soon," she whispered.

She ducked her head out to look for a boat, but she couldn't see anything in the gloom of the rain. She could still hear the whine of an engine, distinct over the crashing waves.

She hurried into the kitchen to grab the big lantern off the counter, shaking off a sudden wave of dizziness—then back out the side door to stand on the big front porch, where she was at least somewhat protected from the weather.

There: coming from off to the right, where the old road ran alongside the airport. She could see a blinking light, and she flashed her own lamp in response. At first she thought it hadn't been seen, but then the sound of the engine shifted, as though turning.

She was expecting it to be a Coast Guard boat coming through the trees, but instead a battered white runabout rolled into sight, listing badly. It could float most of the way up the driveway, but no further; the water over the gravel around the house was too shallow.

"Hey there!" hollered a man's voice. "Help us!"

Magda waded out to them, more and more amazed; the boat, she saw on closer inspection, was dented on one side. She made her way over to it as the driver cut the engine, and she reached to grab and stabilize the closest edge.

*"Hank?"*

No doubt about it, it was Hank, the handyman who did odd jobs around the Estate. He was barefoot, wearing a dark green weather-beaten raincoat over what looked like a cotton shirt and jeans.

"I can't believe we found you," he was saying, taking off a black ballcap and wiping his brow. His hair stuck out in wet, tufted curls. "We saw the light—I just kept trying to aim for it."

"The light?" Magda turned to follow his eyesight; he was staring reverently at the window to Isobel's room, where the oil lamp was still burning, lower now, almost out. "I—I forgot I put that there," she admitted.

"My daughter Emily, she's hurt." He motioned to the back seat, where a small, forlorn form was huddled under a raincoat. "We need to get out of this storm."

"My goodness," said Magda. "Honey, are you alright?"

The shape stirred, and a pale face emerged, squinting at Magda; Emily looked no more than fifteen or sixteen years old. She looked away immediately, shy.

"Well I'm not sure what's really *safe*, but—the house is dry," said Magda, pointing back to the building.

"Sounds good enough to me," he said, climbing laboriously out. "When we got caught out, I remembered what you said about the walls and the high ground. Seemed as good a chance as any. It felt like a sign when I saw the lamp. But Christ, I wasn't sure we'd make it."

They each took one side of the boat and hauled it in as Magda cast a longing last look back in the direction of the cistern and its mysterious contents.

"When the water came up like that, I really thought we were done for. We should have evacuated sooner, but I've been looking for Emily—and when I finally found her, I couldn't load us up fast enough to get out."

Magda peered back at the girl, who was still huddled in her raincoat.

"Did you call for help?" While she had personally resolved not to call emergency services no matter what, nobody else could be held to her promises.

"There's no one to call. The bridges are closed. Phones are down. Everything's underwater. We barely made it out."

*Jesus Christ.* Together they dragged the boat all the way up to the low end of the side porch, where the water was already tapping at the edge of the concrete step.

"There's a lot of debris in the air down there. You're lucky here—there's not as much flying around. I'm surprised you've got so many trees holding up."

"They're mostly native, so they're used to this," said Magda. "Although if the ground gets eaten out from under them by the water, they'll come down alright."

"More worried about the water coming up again." He looked up at the house, skeptical.

"Plenty of dry ground left," she said, encouragingly. "And there's a whole second story."

He shook his head. "It'll have to do. I just don't know if anything will stand. I think—I think the whole island is going to go under. Just be swept off the map entirely."

He was probably chilled and in shock, Magda reminded herself. They had made it this far.

"We were holed up on the third floor of a hotel at first, down by the harbor. I thought it would be okay. The windows blew out, everything's shot to hell, and I'm still thinking we'll hold on, until the water—the water came right up the stairs. It was coming in under the door. The whole place was going down, we barely got to the boat in time, and it was just getting worse behind us. It's not even the wind. Jesus, it's the surge."

"How do you want to tie off?" she asked, focusing on the practical. "I've got some supplies inside—not much, but it's better than nothing. You must have been desperate, to leave without shoes."

"I have boots, but they're soaked. I took them off, they weren't helping much. They're in the boat. I can throw some real solid knots that will keep this thing in place, I think."

So between the two of them, they fastened the dock lines to the corner cement pillars, along with plentiful foam fenders, and Magda tried to hold the bow steady while Hank climbed back inside to fetch Emily from the back seat.

"Here we go, sweetheart," he said, his voice muffled. Magda heard low groaning, and soft-spoken reassurance. "Look, we made it. She's soaked to the skin," he added to Magda, lifting the limp bundle of limbs up into his arms. "We need to get her inside."

He carried her slowly through the ankle-deep water and carefully up the damp, slippery steps. He wasn't a tall man himself, although barrel-chested, and the weight of the girl, small as she was, wasn't nothing.

Magda hurried after him to hold the door. Emily's face was hidden in the hood of her raincoat, turned into her father's chest, but a few pale strands of hair and a flash of blue-white skin were visible. She must be half-drowned.

"Hold on, baby girl, hold on now," said Hank, navigating the hall with difficulty and following Magda into the sitting room, where the biggest settee was arranged against the back wall. "We'll getcha warmed up in no time, okay?"

He laid her down, bracing his back and grunting as he stood. Magda moved to unfold her legs on the couch—she was short enough that she just about fit.

"Here we go." Hank was kneeling down to unzip the rain jacket, which appeared to be a man's, far too big for the girl inside. He lifted her upper arms enough to get her out of it and tossed it over onto the wood floor.

Without thinking about it, Magda pushed it with her foot onto the rug before the water could soak in.

Unwrapped, the girl was slight and pale. She had sun-streaked blonde hair that fell into her eyes, and her face was wrinkled up in pain.

She was wearing a sweatshirt from Disney World, also dark with water, despite the jacket. Her father took it by the waistband and dragged it up over her head, tugging hard when it trapped around her forehead like a crown. He handed it to Magda, who added it to the pile on the rug.

Down to a last T-shirt, the shape of the girl was distorted at the waist.

"How's the little boy?" Hank asked her. "Still kicking?"

Emily put her hand on her stomach and nodded.

Magda felt suddenly ill. "She's . . . pregnant?"

"Seven months," said Hank grimly. "My grandson. Do you have blankets?"

Numb, Magda did the best she could in a pinch, which was to offer up the calfskin rug that had been arranged over the back of one of the heavy wooden benches.

Hank shrugged and covered the girl as best he could, tucking it in tight around her neck. "Is that better, honey? At least a little?"

Emily barely responded, seeming only partly conscious now. Magda hoped it was nothing more than shock and the relief of being finally out of the elements, because they didn't have much to offer if it was something worse.

Hank was watching his daughter with anxious eyes. This close she could see he looked battered, a bruise blooming on his temple.

"Are you alright?" she asked, motioning to his face.

"We got tossed around pretty bad in the boat," said Hank. "Plus climbing out of the window in the storm, trying to get down to the boats. God, this storm. I've never seen anything like it. It was right behind us most of the way here, like a shark following a hooked fish. Another hour or so at most, it'll be on top of us again. This is only the outer bands of it now."

*Like being stalked by a turtle,* Magda reminded herself. No surprises, just some wind and rain. "Whimbrel House has seen worse," she said. "It's stood in this spot for almost two hundred years."

Hank shook his head and said nothing.

"Her hair is wet," said Magda. "Do you have a hat or anything?"

"Everything we've got is soaked," said Hank.

Magda went to the search through the drawers of the side table to see if there was anything they could use. There was a folded stack of sheer curtains that hadn't been used for months. She shook one out and no visible spiders dropped out. Good enough.

"Here," she said, bringing them back. Between the two of them, they got one of them wrapped like a turban around the girl's head, with all the wet hair tucked inside. She was almost entirely nonresponsive now, her eyes closed.

"Is she hurt anywhere?" asked Magda. "Did you see if she hit her head?"

"She's just a little banged up, I think," he said.

Magda looked away as Hank moved on to strip off the girl's sodden jeans, socks, and shoes. Then Hank wrapped the other curtain carefully around her lower half, piling the sweatshirt and raincoat on top of her feet, visible as slight protrusions under the material.

It put Magda in mind of a shrouded corpse, and she tried to push the thought away. She watched him taking her pulse, first at the neck, then the wrist, then the ankle.

"How's she holding up?" she asked, afraid to even raise the question in case the answer was dire. The girl hadn't even moved during the exam and, as far as Magda could tell, wasn't showing much signs of life. The stillness seemed unnatural, and Magda's heart clenched.

Although she had seen her share of bodies in the water, Magda had only been present at one death in her life. What she remembered most was the silence, the stillness of that room once the tiny sounds of another living body— the rustle of the sheets with every exhale, the faint rattle of dry lungs, perhaps on some level even the whoosh of blood in blue veins—were noticeable for the first time only in their absence.

In that moment it had been clear to Magda that there was no living thing in the room but herself, as if her father's body had been converted into merely another part of the mattress and the heart monitors (which had been silenced by a compassionate nurse). Even the low-intensity hum of the electric lights, the sounds of footsteps outside in the hall, the soft tones of women talking—all of it had been drowned out by the unimaginable silence.

The last of her family.

"I think she's dehydrated," said Hank as Magda blinked back to attention. He took his daughter's face in one hand, turning it, brushing the hair out of the way. There was an egg-sized lump hidden in her hairline, she saw now. The girl stirred, her face wrinkling, but didn't wake. He turned back to Magda. "Do you have water?"

"Yes, of course," said Magda, turning to the kitchen. "Wait here. Are you hungry? I don't have as much as I'd like, but we've got cereal bars."

"I'll take one. We can try with Em, but she hasn't wanted to eat much; I'm worried about the baby. I'm just not sure what we can do."

Magda went to go get one of the few remaining sealed bottles of water and the box of cereal bars. One would have lasted her an afternoon, but Hank ate all of his first in a few bites and looked like he was hoping for more. "Much obliged," he said when Magda offered him a second.

Magda had estimated she had enough supplies to make it through about a week—she revised that downward to maybe three days.

"I wish we could get her to take something sugary," he said, starting in on the water. "You got any soda, anything sweet?"

Magda started to say no but then remembered the oranges in the kitchen. "Fruit?" she said. "We could—we could mash it maybe?"

"Yeah, that would probably work."

Magda went back to the kitchen to fetch it, using the penknife from her pocket to cut it into sections and stacking them in a cheap reproduction cup and saucer from the cupboard. She used her fingers to crush the fruit as well as she could. The juice was not plentiful, but she could mix it with clean water from one of the remaining bottles. She brought it back to the sitting room to do so, then watched as Hank lifted the girl's head and set the cup to her lips. "Yeah, that'll do." His fingers were almost too big to fit through the delicate handle of the teacup. He gripped around the whole of the silver rim to hold it steady. "Come on, sweetheart," he murmured, peeling back the pale lips and coaxing in a little of the pulpy mash. "Here we go, baby. Just a little now."

It was hard to say how much he got down, but at least some of the liquid went in before the girl spluttered and Hank drew the cup back. She turned her face away with a low moan of pain.

Magda tried not to think of all the things that could go wrong with a pregnant teenager stranded in a storm. She could go into premature labor from the stress—or the baby could be dying inside the girl already, which could lead to septic shock, even if the labor didn't kill her.

"Better than nothing," said Hank, setting the cup aside. "We'll try again once she warms up a little more."

"Let me know if there's anything else she needs. I know hydration is extra important when you're . . . expecting." Somehow *pregnant* seemed crass.

Hank cleared his throat. "Didn't exactly expect to be a grandfather at my age," he said.

"Congratulations," said Magda, hoping it didn't come out lamely.

"It's not good news. Emily's just turned sixteen. There was some boy at a party, I guess." He rubbed his face. "She's been living with her mother, who isn't good for much. We split a while back. But then on Monday, as I'm leaving here, her mom calls saying she's run off—they're always fighting. It took all the time we should have spent getting out for me to track her down. Found her holed up with a friend down at the harbor, and by then it was too late to try and leave. Even after we got to the boat, we had a hell of a time getting out. It was a madhouse down there."

He seemed to be deflating now that there was nothing to do, putting his hands in his pockets and looking down at the wet cuffs of his pants.

Magda wasn't sure what to say.

He cracked his knuckles, looking away. "I thought there was a generator here?"

"Not working—we lost the wiring right off. But the house was built before electric or running water, so we don't need it as much as a modern place. We can hole up here off the grid for as long as we need to."

He nodded, not seeming reassured.

"We can heat water," she added. "There's a cookstove."

That he seemed encouraged by. "You got enough gas?"

"Two tanks."

He shook his head. "I guess we should save it. Boil everything we need all at once, not use it up in drips and drabs."

Magda had actually had the same plan, but somehow it felt wrong to say so. "Do you have medical supplies?" she asked. "Even painkillers, if she—if she can take those, with the baby? I lost my kit, unfortunately, in all this confusion."

"There's an emergency kit in the boat," he said, rubbing his chin, which was coming in with gray-speckled stubble. "I can't remember what's in there—I don't—I don't know what she can take. I can't remember—aspirin? Or wait, not aspirin, I think? Maybe it's Tylenol."

Magda had supportively encouraged many pregnant friends over the years, so she knew the rules were specific and complicated and ever changing, but she did not actually remember too many of the particulars herself. She had an IUD specifically to ensure that she didn't have to memorize which soft cheese carried listeria.

"How about a working radio—does the boat have one?" she asked eagerly. Even just to hear the weather report could be lifesaving, if they knew the storm's location or timing.

Hank shook his head. "Was just a cheap thing," he said, "it fell out of the cradle and cracked on the way down."

"Maybe we can fix it," said Magda. "You're a handyman, and I'm sort of handy." Which was to say she had spent a fair amount of time in her youth fiddling with speakers and amplifiers or watching her dad fix up their various beater cars.

"I'm a *carpenter*, part time, when I'm not taking out charter boats," said Hank. "But I know dead when I see it. And that thing is dead. You're right, though—we need whatever supplies we can get. And I left my duffel under the seat, which at least has a change of clothes. Seems like we're short even of towels and stuff. I need to go get it . . . can you stay with her if I go salvage whatever I can?"

"Of course, but—I feel like I should admit, I don't know much about medicine," said Magda. There were medical books in the library, but they were from 1910. "I was a museum studies major."

Hank patted her arm. "Yeah, and I'm a high school drop-out. Just sit with her. If she wakes up, tell her I'm just outside and I'll be right back. Don't let her get off the settee."

That sounded doable. "When did you say she was due?" asked Magda. "Not too soon?"

"Another couple of months. Don't worry, she's not going to go into labor right in front of you. I doubt she'll even wake up."

"Okay," said Magda. "Go. Be careful."

She shuddered at the heavy creak of the floorboards as Hank swept out down the hall.

He had a big presence; his absence was felt immediately, as if a draft had picked up in the room. Even the girl, Emily, whined and shifted under the bundle of fabric. To Magda her breath seemed shallow, as though it could cease at any second. The rain hammered outside.

Somehow, although she'd been alone since the storm struck, Magda had never really felt it until now.

\* \* \*

Not sure what else to do, she took up *At the Edge of the Water* and let it fall open to one of Isobel's poems. She flipped past a few of the apocalyptic ones first, before settling on "Bone Slinger."

Emily shuddered, tossing her head on the pillow. Magda sat down next to her, patting her hand. She cleared her throat and then read aloud:

> *Dream of birds rising like recollection*
> *black gulls screaming Wait, wait*
> *but the ocean turns my own voice back.*

Emily raised a hand to the wound on her forehead and moaned.

"Emily? Can you hear me?" There was no response. After a moment of interminable silence, Magda searched out the place she'd stopped on the page.

*I am calling Want, I want,*
*but the ocean turns my lone voice back*

There was a sudden slam from outside; Magda was relieved for an excuse to get up and go to the window to watch Hank wrestling a duffel bag out of the badly listing boat. The prow was ramming up against the wooden decking of the porch. As she watched, some of the wood splintered off. She wanted to yell out to be more careful, but held herself back; what did it matter, really?

Just then a big gust knocked the boat sideways, and Hank, who had been climbing down the side, disappeared with a muffled shout. He didn't come back up. Magda dropped the book and ran out the kitchen door, down into the knee-deep water. She didn't have her wellies on, but waded out in what she was wearing.

Hank was crouched on the other side of the boat, cussing over his hand or forearm. He had dropped the duffel. Magda reached for the bobbing nylon straps—it was heavy, water laden, and dragged her almost off her feet, slamming her into the side of the boat. But her fist was still clenched tight around the strap and didn't let it go. "Hank!"

"Hold on," he yelled back through gritted teeth, wading around to reach her. "Hold on, honey, I'm coming. You got it?"

"Take the bag," she said. "Quick, before I drop it."

"There's nothing in that bag worth our lives," said Hank, but he did reach out and take hold of the strap, awkwardly, with the wrong hand. The right one he offered out to Magda to grab. "Take my elbow, now, I busted the hand just then. Hurts like a bitch."

"Is it broken?" Magda reached out and took hold of his ropy forearm, still bracing herself against the boat, which was liable to roll again at any minute. Hank was as steady in the waves as an island, even as the mud squelched under her socked feet.

"Ain't you even wearing shoes?" he asked, looking down through the murky water.

"I thought you might be hurt—I mean, hurt worse." It took the two of them working together to get back up to the porch steps without losing the duffel or their footing.

"Damn, I wish I hadn't dropped it," said Hank, sinking to his knees when they made it up onto the dry wood. He held his right hand up in front of him—Magda could see it was mottled blotchy red across the skin, which already looked tight and swollen. "Caught this on one of the cleats when she rolled. Could've been worse, though—I could have been trapped underneath." He shook his hand out. "It'll be alright. It'll have to be. Can you open the bag?"

It was held closed by a zipper, which might start to rust after the sudden saltwater bath. Magda pulled the leader down through the teeth and held the sides open.

"Not much to write home about," said Hank glumly. "Mostly my own change of clothes, not good for so much now that it's wet too. Might still be a dry pair of socks in the middle."

"I'm sure most of it's fine," said Magda, although she was disappointed too. Was it too much to ask for at least a few more bottles of water? She wondered if there was any more still in the boat. It might be worth going after, if so, but since they had only just escaped their last effort, it seemed impolitic to bring it up now. "It might be different if you had a fancy camera or a book or something. Where's the med kit?"

"Stuffed down the side, should be."

She dug it out, a square plastic box with the familiar red "plus" sign on the lid. It didn't look like it was stocked with much—two of the little pill samples were for motion sickness.

"What about the radio?"

Hank shook his head. "I guess this is the best we can do," he said, clearing his throat.

He dropped his jacket on the floor to puddle on the rug, this time fortunately missing the hardwood. It had kept his shoulders and upper arms dry, but he hadn't fastened up the front, so the chest and stomach of his long-sleeved cotton shirt ("Roll Tide") were dark with water. He bent forward, the motion ungainly, to pull it forward over his head, and suddenly Magda was standing with a half-naked man.

His chest was sparsely haired with fine gold hairs that might have been close in color to Emily's in his youth. The skin was pale and pebbled with cold, but he was powerfully built, barrel-chested with narrow hips. His gut was soft, revealing his age, probably from many beers drunk out on the open water. His neck and shoulders were deeply tan, which only made his soft, vulnerable belly paler by contrast.

Magda had known her share of men over the years and had always thought Bryce was about as close to the masculine ideal as she was likely to see—swarthy and tall, long of limb and corded with muscle. Hank was built on a different model. He must be Irish or Scottish, with skin like that.

"S'cuse me," he murmured, opening the placket of his jeans.

"Oh! Sorry." Magda handed him the calfskin without letting her eyes stray and turned away. "I'll just go into the other room, so you can change."

"Don't need to apologize to me," said Hank. When Magda looked up, he met her eyes calmly. "It kinda gets under your skin, being alone in a place like this, huh?"

"Yes," said Magda honestly. "It does."

"There's something about this house. I can't imagine staying here by myself. And time goes funny in a big storm. It's the not knowing—what's coming next, how it's all going to play out. You have to—you have to be in the moment, you know? No past, no future. Just what's right in front of you."

"I know just what you mean."

Hank wrapped the rug around his shoulders. "I didn't tell you how grateful I am, you taking us in like this," he said. "I don't know what would've happened to Em and me if we'd had to keep going. There's nothing out there. I realize we're probably a burden on you—my girl being sick too—but it's a real act of kindness, you helping us out."

"Oh, don't—don't even mention it," she said. "Times like these, we have to take care of each other."

She stepped back, leaving him to change. "I'll go sit with Emily while you get dried off," she said.

"I hope she's feeling better soon. She was confused the whole ride over, kept saying crazy things. Didn't know where we were, didn't know who I was most of the time. Maybe the pills from the kit are helping some."

Emily was still seemingly insensate on the couch. A few minutes later Hank came to join them, dressed in a damp pair of sweatpants. It was unfortunate the air was full of moisture; nothing was ever going to really dry out.

"Her color's good," said Magda, trying to be encouraging.

Hank checked her forehead. "No fever." Emily stirred, and he brushed her hair back. "That's it—you try to rest up," he murmured. "Give that little baby the best chance you can. And wake up feeling better—I wish could do the same." He looked up at Magda. "Do you have a proper bed here, or anything?"

"Just a camping cot set up in the kitchen, but it's pretty comfortable. Do you want to lie down?"

"Maybe we can bring it out, set it up in here?"

"Of course. I can do it. You stay with her."

The hallway creaked as Magda headed back to the other side of the house. The wind was picking up again. Somewhere nearby, something wooden was hitting something metal. Was it coming from the gift shop?

Although she recognized they had bigger problems, Magda's mind kept returning to the skeleton in the cistern. Someone had put it there deliberately, she was sure. It hadn't just washed in there, not wedged as tightly as it had been.

The cot was heavy and awkward. Magda caught her fingers on a screw that was sticking out from one of the joints and cursed. She regretted offering to do it herself—some things were just easier for a man to handle. And hadn't she resolved to take it easy? That had gone by the wayside. But in all the excitement, there wasn't time to notice being sick. Deliberately she turned her mind to the matter of the cistern and kept walking.

Before she'd started restoring the gardens, Magda had reviewed all the plots, plans, and aerial photographs of the grounds that had existed over the years. She had, in fact, been reviewing them again just recently for the Landmark application. There was certainly no cistern visible after 1920. There had been a small garden off on that side of the house, and then a greenhouse before the giftshop.

So the body had been put in some time before that. And she had at least one other piece of the mystery to work with: the trunk itself. It was of the kind that was commonly referred to as a "steamer trunk," but technically speaking those were relatively shallow (less than fourteen inches deep), so this would be more accurately called a wardrobe trunk. It was old, but not as old as some that Magda had seen. She was experienced with furniture and estate sales, and the oldest trunks were hide or leather, not coated canvas like this one. If she could get a better look at it, there might be more clues about its owner or origin.

Whatever else was going on, she needed to get back to the box.

# CHAPTER

# 9

Wednesday, October 9th
5:00 PM

FINALLY MAGDA GOT the cot all the way into the sitting room.

"Oh, that's a sight for sore eyes," said Hank. He was still crouched next to his daughter, wiping what might have been tears out of her eyes.

"This is the best we can offer, unfortunately," said Magda. He had finished the second bottle of water, or Emily had stopped pretending to be asleep while she was gone. Magda reminded herself to bring another, grimly noting how quickly three people would go through them all. They'd be drinking rainwater in a day or two. Still, there was nothing to be done about it. At least the water came down clear; it was contact with the land that polluted it. There was almost something poetic about that.

"Look, my daughter and I are exhausted, and we might only have so long before the weather hits again. I think it'd be best to sleep in shifts, if that's okay with you."

Magda nodded. "I don't mind staying up first. You get some rest." While she didn't exactly feel one hundred percent herself, it was safe to assume she'd had a less hellish past few days than the two of them.

"I appreciate that. Come on, darlin', brought you something that might be a little more comfortable, hey?" With her father's assistance, Emily managed to get herself laboriously out of the chair and to shift over onto the edge of the cot, then sank down with a heavy. *oof* of exertion. Without a word, she lay back and curled onto her side, and Magda handed Hank the curtains and the calfskin rug. He arranged it over her and patted Emily's shoulder. She didn't respond or move.

She was a sweet-faced girl, Magda couldn't help but notice, with a small, upturned nose and chin, which made her entire face into a crescent moon. Her hair was very pale, like rose gold. At the moment her pretty features were marred by a slow trickle of blood that had trailed down from her hairline. It had been wiped away but was still visible in the creases around her eyes and the corner of her lips.

Magda hoped she would stay asleep: Who would want to wake up like this, trapped in this storm with a stranger?

Hank nodded and got himself settled on the settee, his feet dangling off the end. It was kind of endearing. Also, now they were out of beds as well as supplies, noted Magda—she'd end up sleeping on the floor. How had it come to this so quickly? She shook her head.

Magda moved the book of poetry to the windowsill (it fell open, as it usually did, to "Antigone," and Magda shuddered).

"I guess it's just us and the poetry here now," said Hank, watching her, his voice low.

"You could say that, yes," said Magda.

"Don't really truck with poetry, myself."

She bet he liked music: loud music with heavy drums and screaming guitar solos. "Maybe you'd like this," she offered lamely.

"Maybe."

Hank sighed and shifted, but eventually seemed to find some sleep. Emily hadn't seemed to even move since her father had bundled her up on the cot. It couldn't possibly be a good sign for her to sleep so deeply.

Magda waited a respectable amount of time to be sure nobody needed anything, then took the lantern and crept back down the hallway to the kitchen.

The water was still coming up, and she was taunted by the knowledge that the bones were still out in the cistern.

There was a kayak paddle leaning by the side door, which Starla must have brought inside from the dock; Magda took it with her into the ruins of the gift shop.

There was six inches of water already, and in the cistern it was rapidly filling up underneath the sealed box. Settling the lantern on a convenient beam, she splashed through the water, reminding herself it made no sense to be worried about snapping turtles or barracudas right now. Realistically, she should probably be more afraid of spilled oil or sewer waste, but it was definitely something living she worried about encountering. Strangely, the skeleton didn't scare her at all. She just needed to get it somewhere safe.

She paused to cough into her shoulder.

*In the contest of the living and the dead,* Isobel had written, *the Shades have the whip hand.*

She had been right about that.

The water actually made the job easier. Kneeling by the cistern, Magda forced the sharp blade of the kayak paddle down into the muck, all the way underneath the base of the box, and when it was as deep as it could go she began to slowly lever it up, one hand on the top. It came slowly, resentfully. The box was degrading, and Magda didn't think it could be carried without falling apart.

Finally, it emerged in a flush of black water.

She rested it, now freed, on the level top of the cistern—the floodwaters were teasing at the lip already—and hurried back into the house to grab the hallway rug (it was imitation anyway—placed there to absorb the impact of a thousand sandy, grubby visitors' shoes) to make a sling for it. Then she carefully transferred the box on top, moving it incrementally until finally it was centered. Then, holding one side in each hand she could gingerly carry it a few steps to the kitchen door. Beyond the awkward size it was also quite heavy, likely more from the weight of the sodden box than from the bones—but she could just about manage it.

That damn heron was back as she struggled to get the box over the step, watching her from the corner of the garden. "I don't suppose you want to help?" she grumbled. She was holding back a cough again. Damn, she was going to run out of steam soon.

The bird, clapping its bill warily, took a low hop through what had been a shattered window frame and disappeared into a gloomy corner.

"No, I didn't think so." Magda wiped the wet hair out of her face and carried on.

Using the rug, flipped facedown to make a sledge, she could drag the box up onto the porch, without having to pick it up by its disintegrating sides, and set it onto a piece of plywood. Now she could pick it up using the wood. She just needed to find a safe spot for it, higher, away from any risk of the water.

Huffing and panting, she carried it up the outdoor metal steps that led to the second-floor balcony. Where the stairs turned, there was a sheltered overhang, and she carefully slid the box all the way up against the side of the house, where it was protected by the roof. Then she carefully wrapped the rug around it. If she didn't want to bring it inside, this was the next best thing.

But it was dark, and she couldn't exactly do much more by lantern light. At least the box was safe until morning.

"Sleep tight," she whispered. Then she slipped back to the sitting room, where Hank and Emily slumbered on.

The night stretched on. They all slept badly, with Hank and Magda taking turns staying up to keep an eye on both Emily and the storm. After a few hours, Hank got her dressed in their driest collective outfit, from the very center of the duffel. By mutual agreement they stayed nearly silent, exchanging shifts with a tap and a few grumbles.

True to Hank's prediction, the water rose throughout the night. By morning it was already threatening to climb up onto the porch.

CHAPTER

10

Thursday, October 10<sup>th</sup>
6:00 AM

*Day Four*

MAGDA DRAGGED HERSELF to the kitchen and ate a breakfast bar, which tasted like ash. She had reached the stage of illness in which everything was phlegm. On the other hand, there wasn't much edible food left anyway. At least she felt a little stronger, a little more steady, with whatever rest she had managed to catch.

When she crept back to the sitting room she found Hank flipping through *The Edge of the Water*. She watched him squint at the pages. "So what do you think?" she asked.

"I don't think I really get it," he said. "It's a lot of birds and waves and clouds."

"Yes, Isobel was famous for using the natural imagery of her surroundings to talk about bigger themes. That's one of the reasons this specific place, which provided so much of her inspiration, is vitally important to preserve."

"But I mean, what does any of this matter nowadays? Don't people have better things to do than still read this old stuff? . . . Or couldn't you at least read something written in this decade, maybe?"

Magda had tried to answer this question a thousand different ways. "The point is that it's a way of seeing the world," she said. "Isobel wrote about self-inquiry and suffering and immortality through metaphors of nature. She was a true genius. And every time you read her words, you're communing directly with the voice, the mind, of this one exceptional person, a hundred years after her death. I think that's incredible."

"I guess," said Hank, unconvinced. "She sounds a little nuts though, huh? I mean, I read this foreword."

"She wasn't nuts. But it's true that not everybody is passionate about poetry. If you're more excited by the chance to wash up, there's a sink in the kitchen and a bucket I filled from the hose before all this started."

Hank raised an eyebrow, but either he realized he wasn't going to get very far with this line of conversation or he really did want to clean up; he zipped up his coat and headed down the hall.

As dawn broke, both of them went out to inspect the damage and shore up whatever they could with the sandbags. Magda paused to brush her teeth on the back porch, spitting white foam into the dirty brown water. She heard Hank splashing somewhere on the other side of the house, probably peeing. Outside, it was raining steadily and didn't look pleasant, but it didn't actually seem to be raging as hard as it had been.

Clearly what little food Magda had brought with her wasn't going to last the three of them very long. The rain was endurable and the water wasn't going to get any lower. While she felt up to it, it seemed like as good a chance as any to try and scavenge what she could.

She and Hank came back in at the same time. He checked on Emily, who was neither better nor worse, and coaxed her into swallowing another quarter of a bottle of water. She hadn't peed the whole time she'd been here that Magda was aware of. It didn't seem like a good sign.

She tugged on her rubber boots. "Will you be okay staying with her if I go out and see what I can find to eat?"

"What, out there?"

"There's a coconut palm at the top of the drive, and there are a fair number of plants in the garden that are edible—sea grapes for sure, and I know there's a patch of those left. I'll see what else I can find." She shrugged back into her heavy raincoat, pulling the hood up. "Luckily I'm a botanist, so the world is my grocery store—and my pharmacy."

Hank shrugged. "Well, she's sleeping easier, so I guess—go for it. Just be careful, huh?"

So Magda went out the side door, casting another longing look at the second-floor balcony. The body in the box would have to wait a little longer—the first priority was finding calories. *Then* maybe a little investigation.

The porch was soggy and seemed unstable under her feet. Magda resisted the urge to tiptoe, and flattened out her weight instead, like creeping over ice. Everything south of the house all the way down to the shore was underwater, but that still left some reasonably dry ground to the north, which had a gentle slope up to the main drive.

She made it to the side stairs, which creaked loudly, splitting paint fragments off the wood. Out into the rain, which was coming down in straight lines on the sodden

grass. It barely felt solid under her feet, like she was crossing a bog. Magda waded out.

What were the chances she'd be wandering around
and lightning would find her like it had once found Abigail
Reyes? Pick her out of all the upright objects on the shore
and strike her down. There wasn't usually lightning in a
hurricane . . . right?

*   *   *

There were still standing trees at the top of the hill. Magda
was glad she had let the lemurs go when she had—although
if she later learned they had starved to death, or been eaten,
or given somebody rabies, she reserved the right to change
her opinion. She hoped all of them had made it through
the night and were off playing in the trees somewhere. Or
maybe the whole rest of the island was gone and the lemurs
had drowned. Maybe *she* was still going to drown and just
didn't know it yet.

She gazed out through the blurry gray-brown of the
storm. *Calories, Maggie.*

The driveway was a low spot, submerged but still passable. Magda splashed across it and then up the muddy hill
to the sheltered space at the top of the road, where she
found a few green coconuts that had been shaken loose by
the wind of the night before. "And to think, I almost had
you taken out," she said, squinting up through the rain.
There were enough loose branches around that she could
throw a few at the nuts still being held under the leaves and
catch a few more.

The sea grapes only had a few fruits left, but she did
pull up a few runty little peach palms to bring in the
shoots, which she'd heard could be eaten raw. Or did they
have to be roasted? She wondered if any of the books in the

library would have told her. Probably not—Charles Reyes paid for good produce to be brought down from the mainland; he hadn't been eating his own garden plants.

There were downed trees in the road, she noted—those ridiculous non-native Christmas palm trees people planted because they thought they looked "tropical." Too bad it wasn't the season for their fruit. No cabbage palms either, the leaves of which were considered a delicacy.

She had enough to carry as it was, juggling the coconuts with the palms clenched in her fist. At least that was some food and water. It was amazing how quickly they'd fallen: from a thermos of coffee and a box of cereal bars, to foraging off the land. But there were worse things to be in such cases, she reflected, than a horticulturalist.

It was hard not to slip as she came back down the slick slope. She had gotten so used to being rained on that it barely even registered anymore. She returned with her arms full to find Hank standing out on the porch where she'd left him, squinting into the gloom.

"We still need more protein," said Magda, putting her bounty down on the porch. "I was thinking maybe we could try to catch some fish or something."

Hank squinted. "I'm not sure how many fish we're going to catch in the middle of a hurricane," he said.

"Well, it's not like we have anything to lose, right? We could give it a try. But I don't have the supplies."

Hank considered. "I think there's tackle in one of the compartments on the boat. Let me go check."

Both of them walked along the porch to the place where the runabout was secured under cover. "Do you think we should pull this up out of the water?" asked Magda.

"Nah, I've got three half hitches here, see? She'll be okay for now." Hank climbed in and rummaged around by the steering wheel. "Aha!" He held up a roll of clear fishing line and a box of hooks.

"Well, that'll work," said Magda. "The pole seems like the easy part."

"Sure is. You got any bamboo here?"

"Uh, no. It's not native. We took it out. But there's some that comes up from the condos down the way."

A sudden chittering on the roof attracted her attention—it was Cosimo, clinging to the gutter of the second-story porch.

"Hey! Oh, buddy, I was hoping you were already in the trees," said Magda. "Did you get separated from the others?"

"Will that thing let you get close enough to catch it?" asked Hank.

"Possibly—he was born here on the Estate."

"There you go—you said we needed protein. See if you can grab it."

"Absolutely not," said Magda. "If we need to eat, we can eat fish or bugs or crabs, not—not *pets*."

"Then we're not feeding it," said Hank shrewdly. "We're not wasting what little food we have on a monkey."

"Cosimo is a *lemur*," said Magda. "And if we need more food for him, I'll find it—he was here first!" At the angry tones, Cosimo backed off, cackling, and disappeared onto the roof.

Hank raised his hands. "Alright, peace, peace. I won't eat your pet," he said. "We'll look for something else."

"If you see a white heron, not that either," said Magda suspiciously. "It's practically tame." She was still straining her eyes in the direction Cosimo had gone. The way the roof was overhung, it was impossible to see him or tell if he was with the others.

"This would be a lot easier if you hadn't made friends with all the creatures we could eat, Snow White," said Hank. He pushed himself up onto his feet and climbed back onto the porch. "You said you know where there's bamboo? We're going to need it to fish—unless you're too close to flounder and tuna, of course."

Magda bit back a smile. "Yes, I know where there is some. I'll go get it."

She judged the shallowest water on the route down the shore, clambered back down off the porch, and waded out. Her headache was back, she noted. She'd have to make this the last trip.

It was hard to move through the water without picturing the possibility of a shark swimming next to her, or a boa constrictor underfoot, or an alligator (hell, maybe an American crocodile, with her luck). There were also plenty of fish that could bite, not to mention jellyfish. Leeches. Any or all of them could be lurking in the muddy brown water, just waiting for something moving to come within range.

There were also plenty of other straight-looking sticks floating about, she couldn't help but notice, and yet here she was looking for the specific one Hank required.

*This is your house, Magda*, she reminded herself. *Yours and Isobel's. Hank came to you for help. You're in charge.*

But she still walked on through the murky water until she found what was left of the patch of bamboo, badly beaten down and broken from the previous night's winds, and collected as many long, straight branches as she could. The poles were light and easy to carry, slung over her shoulder like a hobo's bindle.

She would just set Hank to fishing, and that would keep him out of her way while she checked out the box. She had been alone too long—that was the problem: she was too set in her ways. Bryce used to tease her about it too. Silly things like where the tools were put away, which cups went in the dishwasher, what washer settings to use on different clothes.

What had any of that really mattered, she thought now, compared to the—brief, doomed—joy of being with a partner who loved her? She should have thrown all the dishes out into the street and eaten off paper plates. She should have burned her wardrobe and only worn a swim-suit for the rest of her life.

Hank had been watching her progress on the return. "It's picking back up out here," he said. "Wind's coming back around, I guess."

"I thought it seemed a little better." Magda hoisted herself slowly up onto the porch. He offered her a hand, but she didn't need it.

He shook his head, turning back to the water. "It's building up again. I can feel it just in the time I've been out here. Preparing to hit us again. I don't know how the hell we're going to ride out even another few days."

"You know . . . you don't have to stay here just because I'm staying," said Magda. "If you wanted to make a break for it while it's clear, I'd understand."

"I thought about it," said Hank. "But the idea of get-ting caught out if we push off from here and don't find anything before the next swell hits . . ."

Magda nodded. "Well then, good luck with the fish-ing," she said. "I'm going to take this stuff inside."

"You really wouldn't come?" he asked, looking at her sideways.

"What?"

"If I said we were setting out now, heading for higher ground—you'd still stay here, knowing everything you do about the storm? Look at this place." He waved an arm over the sodden landscape; it looked like it was melting all around them. "I'm no meteorologist, but whatever reprieve you were hoping for, it obviously ain't gonna happen. I know you feel like you've got a duty, but in another day or two there's not going to be any of this place left to save."

Magda shook her head. "It doesn't matter what I'd do," she said. "You just said you didn't think it was safer to leave. You think the best bet is to try and hold out here, where at least we have a roof over our heads."

"Until we don't," said Hank. "I don't know what's the right call. I just can't see loading up that girl into my little boat and sailing out into nothing. Maybe that makes me a coward, I don't know. Maybe I'm damning us both."

"Well, I'm staying no matter what," said Magda. If she was thinking of the bones in the cistern, that was nobody's business but her own.

"Then at least we're in good company." Hank grinned, his teeth shockingly white. Favoring his injured hand, he carefully untied his boots and left them by the door; they were soaked through to his socks. "Guess I'll go set some poles. Hardly seems much use, but maybe I'll try some further out."

Magda left him the bamboo and let him get down to business. She wondered how hard it would be to ferment sea grapes into alcohol. Probably not worth trying. She wasn't sure exactly how she was going to break open the coconuts without spilling the milk. She wished again for the tools that had been lost in the giftshop.

Was there any chance there was anything useful in the boat? Hank didn't necessarily know what they were missing—and she had wanted to take a look at that broken radio, she remembered now. She glanced over to see where he was: clear across the garden. Well, it wouldn't hurt to check.

Magda made her way over to the runabout. It wasn't much to speak of, really—just a fiberglass shell and two bench seats.

There was a glove compartment next to the steering wheel; Magda opened it and rummaged through the laminated maps and registration papers, muffling a cough in her sleeve. No tools, nothing of use. Then she checked under the seats and finally found the marine radio sloshing in six inches of water. As Hank had said it was a cheap handheld model, no GPS. It was clear the runabout wasn't ever intended to be far from port; he'd probably figured he'd be able to use his cell phone if he needed help.

The battery case was indeed cracked from the bottom, and it had been submerged for God knows how long. It seemed dumb to hold out any hope if Hank, who probably knew more about such things, said the thing was dead— but Magda and her father had once resuscitated an amp using parts from a waffle iron. She dropped it into the pocket of her raincoat and then headed back inside.

Emily was lying, corpse-like, under the thin blankets. Magda got close enough to check that she was breathing— she was, shallowly—but didn't disturb her. Well, what could she do quietly, while sitting and regaining her strength?

Setting aside her stash in the kitchen, she made sure Hank was still occupied—he was—and then climbed up the metal stairs to the trunk, which was right where she'd left it, seemingly no worse for wear.

She didn't have rubber gloves and perhaps that would have prevented a true professor of restoration studies from proceeding, but Magda was feeling less and less academic as the storm raged on.

Setting up the lantern—although her eyes were so adjusted to the dim light at this point that she barely noticed it anymore—she started her examination with the metal latch. She knew only a little about steamer or cabin trunks, but she knew enough to check there first for the date the trunk was made. It was covered over with rust, and Magda thought about going for the toothpaste; it was an old trick for cleaning metal. Instead, she used her thumb and her own spit to clear away what she could. *Harold and S-something*, seventeen—no, that made no sense, must be one-nine - 1912. Okay, that was something. Even if the trunk had been brand new when the skeleton was placed inside, the woman couldn't have been buried before that date.

So she was looking at a woman who had died sometime between 1912 and 1920.

Well, there was one she could think of, but that was— that was ridiculous, of course.

Time to continue the investigation. Carefully, Magda opened the top of the chest and rested it on the ledge of the next stair. She forced herself not to turn to the bones yet, still focusing on the box itself. These wardrobe trunks often came with inserted drawers, even upright hanging bars, but this one was missing all the parts. Only the wire framework was still visible.

There was a space on the front in which the name and address of the trunk's owner might have been recorded, but it was heavily degraded by the water. Only because it was tucked into an inner pocket of what she presumed to be celluloid, she could make out the first letter of each word, in flowing script: perhaps an R, and either an N or an M.

She thought furiously but could identify no connection with those initials among the extended Reyes family. Perhaps the trunk had merely been used to transport a delivery or something. But the quality seemed rather good for that. Of course it was possible there was no association to the household at all—just a trunk they had purchased secondhand or something. There could have been a servant of the house who had borrowed it.

Then again, if the trunk was made in 1912, the Reyes's financial situation had been on the decline then. Magda knew for a fact they had employed only one servant, a cook and housekeeper named Sallie, who lived in town. Presumably she would not have brought a borrowed travel trunk to the house.

Satisfied with her examination of the box, Magda took a breath and then had her second look—her first really good look—at the bones inside. There was no flesh left, just a brown staining at the bottom of the trunk, so the remains didn't smell beyond the musty odor of the sea. Magda couldn't see any immediate damage on the bones, but she was no forensics expert; nor was she a doctor (and it wasn't the first time since deciding to stay in the storm that she had regretted it).

The skeleton was no longer perfectly articulated. She suspected the material tucked around it was what was left of a tarred canvas; it had kept the bones more or less in the order they would have been in life. Perhaps there was still some cartilage that kept the big bones together long after the flesh had eroded away. There was an imprint of material pressed into the tarpaulin, presumably from the clothing; maybe linen or muslin, now long since eroded away. Somehow she pictured the folds of a long dress.

Again, her immediate impression was that this person had been slight. Surely that skull was smaller than her own. Morbidly, she measured her own hand against the skeletal bones that were caught in a fold of fabric. Well, perhaps it was not so far off. Perhaps skin and fat took up more space than she realized.

The face was obscured by what was left of a few pieces of hair, which was lank and tangled and resembled nothing so much as seaweed. But it was long and had not been gray in life. So much for the theory of an old woman. No, this was a younger female, of small stature but not an actual child—not with those heels. From a good family, dead at Whimbrel House sometime around 1918.

Magda shut the box and leaned back on her hands. This was insane. It wasn't possible.

Was it?

She needed—she needed to stop being foolish and— and go be productive. If Hank didn't catch fish, they needed protein. That was—that was probably more important than this.

Yes. She needed to stop.

She rewrapped the box and backed away, promising herself she'd come back after clearing her head a little.

She wasn't that sick yet. She could make one more trek out while the weather held. Really, she was feeling better; it was mostly just the headache.

There was a relic in the corner of the sitting room that she'd marked as an Indonesian fish trap, brought back from one of Charles's early travels. It had been described in one of Robert Engel's invaluable letters, when he'd depicted the house as "scattered with flotsam of a life spent traveling the oceans—fish nets and ship's bells and glass witch balls."

The trap was simple in construction: woven vines into a narrowing tube, with a space at the bottom to set bait. The idea was that fish would be drawn in but be unable to turn around to get back out of the narrow opening. Magda didn't have a lot of food to spare, and she wanted something stinky, like a sardine, for bait. Maybe Hank was right and there would be no fish hunting during the storm, but she might as well try. She needed to—it was better if she kept busy.

The wind was already picking up as she slipped back outside. She could hear it rising in pitch, back to that eerie howl. She looked over toward Hank, astonished by how much it had picked up in so short a time. It was good that she hadn't taken her gear off yet. He saw her looking and waved.

A young woman who had died between 1912, when the trunk was made, and 1920, when the cistern was filled. Isobel had died in 1918.

Taking the fish trap Magda made for a birdbath in the side garden that usually had a few snails in it. She was in luck; there was a large one, dead from saltwater intrusion. *Fortune smiles,* she thought, as she would have had to steel herself to kill one. Softhearted, her father had called her.

She crushed the dead snail against a brick, with a rounded rock, and then dropped the smear into the back of the trap. Now, to find a place to set it. After consideration she selected a corner where it wouldn't be easily swept away when the waves were higher again.

Of course, there were many women who had probably died within that range of eight years. It was foolish to jump to conclusions. Magda should know better: she had been in school for too long to just *assume*—

Granted, it seemed ridiculous to hesitate over putting an authentic fish trap into the water. But it *was* an antique. And for all Magda knew, it would have had to be maintained—conditioned with oil, maybe—to hold up underwater. Come to think of it, it was probably used in freshwater, not salt. Her only consolation was that she had done the last appraisal of the furniture, and this item hadn't ranked highly. Determined, she plunged it in. It was probably happy to be used again, she told herself. Tools wanted to be at work, not on display.

Yes, there could be other women, surely. Other women who were also slight and small. A visitor to the house, perhaps.

She anchored the trap against the wall with flagstones from the destroyed path and made sure it was half buried to resist the currents that would take it out to sea. Who knew if she'd ever be able to check it? But just the attempt made her feel more cheerful. The trap had a woven rattan flag that was weighted to bob in the water right above, revealing its location; she'd never noticed how cleverly it had all been constructed.

What could she do next? Tools wanted to be at work.

Thinking of other sources of protein, she knew a few spots close to the house where there were so-called "gypsy chickens" nesting under the bushes. More than once she had found rotten eggs under the broad leaves of her precious plants—well, it was time for payback.

How was it possible? It couldn't be. Isobel's suicide had been *witnessed*, for God's sake! Everybody knew that. Her father had been watching from a window on the second floor of Whimbrel House when she'd gone off the end of the dock. His account of the incident had been included as a prologue to the second book of poems, a fact that had enraged Charles Reyes, who considered it exploitative. The angry letters he had written to the publisher were still in the archives at the Smithsonian.

It was thunderously loud as she made her way to the trees. Magda checked a few places she knew the chickens often roosted—including a hollow tree a few inches off the ground, where she found a clutch of small brown eggs. It was hard to know how old they were exactly, but they didn't smell. Magda doubted there were ever baby chickens inside, but—well, in other parts of the world people ate those eggs too. Beggars couldn't be choosers. She filled her pockets.

Alright, it was true that officially Isobel's body had never been found—but perhaps she had eventually been washed back in to shore, like so many of the suicides of the present day. It seemed odd, but might Charles have wanted a private—though unconventional—burial? A suitcase for a coffin was a strange choice, but he hadn't been a religious man, after all.

R. N. The trunk had belonged to an R. N. No one in the family or the Estate was an "N." She skimmed mentally through the list of visitors. Nothing. Of course, there was one "R" personage associated with the house and the Reyes family: the publisher, Robert Margery. And he was known to visit the house. He'd even come down at least once, shortly before the suicide, to convince Isobel to publish again.

Robert Margery was a disreputable man by all accounts. He had defrauded several famous clients. And he had been eager to get the book that Isobel was resisting sending. There were letters in the archives from him to

Charles, encouraging her father to persuade her to finish. Charles's replies were curt; he would talk to Isobel but could make no promises.

Magda could probably even check the household ledger to confirm the exact date he'd been down.

She found another egg and added it to the collection, dizzy with the possibilities. Ironically, if she'd been one person, just with the eggs and plenty of fresh water, she wouldn't have starved. But with three, there probably wasn't going to be enough to last beyond another day or so.

Her throat was sore again; the rain wasn't helping—she needed to wrap this up and go back inside. Was there anything else she could grab? Purslane, perhaps—it was growing as a weed in one of the side gardens, and it was edible. And it was supposed to be an anti-inflammatory. It was unfortunate that bending over to gather it made her feel worse, but she gathered what she could, chewing a few of the mild and juicy leaves, and filling the front of her sweatshirt, which she held folded in front of her like a bag. She looked pregnant herself as she waddled back down the steep slope toward the house.

A burst of wind caught her and she had to turn away from it, leaning over to protect her stash. Bending over made her realize she was dizzy, maybe a little short of breath. The headache she had been battling on and off for the past few days was more or less subsumed in the blasts of rain, but she could feel the tightening at her temples, the drumbeat of her own pulse there. There wasn't enough purslane in the world.

Enough time outside.

Turning, her eye was caught by what appeared to be a tall, dark shape standing on the porch. It wasn't Hank, who was wearing green, and anyway he had been on the other side of the house the last time she had seen him. This was—it was the shape of a man, dressed in black clothes with a brown bowler hat, and he was watching her.

Between one startled blink and the next, he was gone. Magda rubbed her face, getting grit in her eyes. There was nobody on the porch. She was probably running a fever; she was under a lot of stress. She needed to get the supplies inside. She forced herself to start walking. Her legs were shaky.

Once back in the house Magda headed down the hallway. It had been a good morning's work, but perhaps she had overexerted herself. She had the gritty, heavy feeling of too many days in a row without sleep, so when she reached the sitting room, she first assumed her eyes were just slow to catch up to the challenge of the dimly lit room.

But no. The bed was empty.

"Hank? Emily?" she called, turning in a circle. But he was still outside, there was nobody in the house. The girl was half dead—surely she couldn't have gone far. She must just be crouched in one of the dark corners, no doubt confused at having woken up alone in an unfamiliar room. Even the curtains that had been used as towels were gone.

"Emily? Are you in here?"

The room was empty.

She went to the window, calling for Hank. She heard him answer—something indistinct—as she checked the hall closet, the dining room, the bathroom. Nothing.

Hank came up the front stairs, his heavy footprints echoing through the house. "What's the matter?"

"Emily is gone!"

"What the hell—?" He went back into the room she'd already inspected to see for himself, as if she might have missed a sixteen-year-old girl in there. "Emily? Em, sweetheart?"

"She didn't come past me down the hallway. You would have seen her on the porch. She couldn't have gone upstairs?"

Magda hurried up to check, ignoring the ominous creak of the landing as she passed the stacks of the antiques she had relocated. It seemed incredible that Emily would have been strong enough to climb them.

The second floor had three bedrooms, some storage space, and the remains of what had been a bathroom, which was no longer functional. Magda checked that first since it was at the top of the stairs, but there was nothing, and no place to hide—the walls were bare down to the studs, all the appliances having been taken out. Neither of the storage closets was hiding a teenager.

One room, the smallest, had been for guests—empty except for a few boxes stored there—and the largest room was Charles's—empty.

The last room on the second floor was Isobel's. "Emily, are you in here?"

She threw open the door and found her, standing at the window, staring out through the shutter at the unrevealing gloom. "Emily! For heaven's sake. How did you get in here? Hank, I found her—she's in here!"

Emily didn't turn. The dock and the shore itself should be indistinguishable now, but that seemed to be the direction toward which she was looking. It was fortunate the hurricane shutters were closed, because each room had a set of big double doors onto the second-story porch.

"Hey, hey," said Magda, hurrying to her side and putting her hand on Emily's shoulder. The girl was burning with fever. "Emily, honey, can you hear me? Do you know who I am?"

It was evident that she was both dizzy and weak. She was clutching the edge of the windowsill as if the walls were shaking wildly.

Her eyes were still straining into the darkness in the direction of the dock.

"Take it easy—you're okay. You're safe here." For now, at least.

The girl's feet shifted. Her strangely colorless eyes skated over Magda's face, uncomprehending.

"My name is Magda—I'm the caretaker here," said Magda. "You're in Whimbrel . . . you're in an old house on Key West. There's a hurricane. Do you remember that?"

A slow blink, reminding Magda of a cat.

"Can you tell me your name?"

"Em-Emily."

"That's right. You arrived here with your father. You were trying to escape a storm. Do you remember that?"

"My—father?" Emily's eyes were drawn back to the covered window. Through the cracks between the plywood there was nothing but a thin gray light and the horizontal stripe of blown rain. "I . . . I feel like I know your voice. Like—something from a dream."

"I was reading to you before. I guess you were partly awake."

She heard Hank's heavy clomping on the stairs and then he burst into the room. "Good lord, Em, how the hell—?" He wrapped his arms around her shoulders and pulled her against his chest, one of his broad palms buried in her hair, cradling her head. "Jesus, honey."

"She must have gotten confused, not knowing where she is," said Magda.

Hank hummed and didn't answer, rocking her from side to side.

"Should we take her back downstairs?"

"Maybe we should move her up here," suggested Hank, glancing around. "Then we can keep the doors shut, and this way she won't be bothered by what's going on downstairs." Magda saw his eyes linger on the empty wine bottle still sitting in the corner, and flushed.

The door-length shutters on the second floor were original, the permanent kind that folded shut and bolted from the inside; Magda had never let anyone work on them. He'd probably never seen the second floor before. Most people hadn't.

"I suppose that makes sense," she said. Now that the excitement was over, she felt herself losing steam. "But be careful of the stairs, they're not fully sound. We've been trying to fundraise to fix them and finish the upstairs, but . . ."

"Yeah, well, we'll have to make do, I guess. I get the feeling we're all going to end up moving up here anyway," said Hank. "The higher, the better."

So Magda let him drag the cot up to what had been Charles's bigger bedroom (a fact Magda decided wouldn't be of interest to the current crowd). He got Emily to take a Tylenol, and Magda took one too.

"You've got to rest up for that baby, sweetheart," he murmured, settling his daughter down. "No more wandering off, okay?"

She blinked up at him, uncomprehending, and he sighed. "Just try to get some sleep," he said.

Once she had drifted off, he stood, moving toward the door. "I left the poles out there," he said, looking outside with a frown.

"That's okay. You were right, it was a silly idea."

But he was turning to go. "Nah, it's alright. If you can stay with her, I can still grab them."

Magda slowly followed him out into the hallway, pulling the bedroom door carefully closed behind her. "Are you sure it's a good idea to go out? It seems like it's picking up again." She rubbed her head, which was aching, and trailed him down the stairs to watch him shrug into his raincoat. He left the front open; unlike her, he always seemed to run hot.

"Last chance to check for a bite, then. I'll take a walk around, make sure everything's secure; then we'll hunker down."

"How's the hand?" she asked.

"Better, I guess," he said, clenching it. "It'll have to do." He took up the rifle that had been leaning beside the front door. "This thing doesn't work, right?"

"No. It's an antique. The whole mechanism is rusted over."

"This is an 1862 Springfield," said Hank, looking it over with appreciation. "A Civil War rifle."

"Really, are you sure?" She wondered if he was a Civil War buff, or a gun buff. "I knew it was old, but I wasn't sure how old. I found it in the cellar when I was locking up. It's part of the history of the house."

Nobody in the Reyes family had served in the Civil War, being all the wrong ages, but there had been a lot of activity in Key West related to the naval base, which was in possession of the Federal troops. She supposed it wouldn't have been too difficult for an old soldier's rifle to find its way into the house.

"Look, there's a place for a strap. I bet—" Hank moved to his duffel and unhooked the shoulder strap. The metal ends were clips, which he attached to the hooks on the rifle so he could sling it over his back. "Maybe I'll take this out with me, in case anybody's out there. Better than nothing, I guess," he said.

Magda debated trying to dissuade him—the rifle was an antique, after all—but she was tired herself, still sick with whatever bug had gone to her lungs, and she wanted to be sitting down. She didn't feel like arguing.

It was just like a man to think he needed some kind of weapon. At least the gun was only good to scare strangers, and she hadn't seen signs of anybody else in the past three days.

"You make sure to keep an eye on the door while I'm gone, okay?"

As if anyone else was going to show up. But she nodded (resisted a salute) and he turned on his heel to head out onto the porch, letting in a blast of rain. Resolute, he stepped out onto the storm, barely pulling the door closed behind him.

CHAPTER

# 11

Thursday, October 10<sup>th</sup>
10:00 AM

MAGDA TOOK THE duffel by the shorter straps and *The Edge of the Water* and went back up the stairs to Emily, who was shifting around on the cot, restless.

"Hey there, honey," she said softly. "It's okay. You're fine now. You're safe." She sat heavily on the floor, pawing through the duffel; everything inside was still wet. She wished she could sleep, but she wasn't going to risk leaving Emily unattended again.

An unfamiliar weight in the pocket of her raincoat reminded her of the radio. Well, this seemed like as good a time as any.

"What do you think, Emily?" she asked. "Shall we take a look?" She scrabbled around the battery case with her fingernails. Bryce's friend Cole had once had a better-quality version of this one; it was charged like a phone, with a battery that was powered by the boat's motor when it was running. In this case, it hadn't been plugged in for hours—but when she got the back open, there was also an AAA battery backup.

She peeled the old battery out, dumped out the rusted AAAs and then cleaned out the grit with her fingers. Then she wiped them on her shirt. The smaller flashlight also ran on AAAs, so she sacrificed its light for the power. She dropped them in, then held her breath and turned it on.

Nothing. "Well, it was worth a try," she said, to a still-sleeping Emily.

She tried swapping them around, one at a time, feeling for the positive end with her fingertips, then turned it off and back on again. When that didn't work, she tried switching them the other way. Still nothing.

Magda pulled them out and set the smaller flashlight on its end to see better.

Magda could remember her father, in the early hours of a Super 8, when he wanted his free breakfast, fixing an electric skillet with a nail file. "Cleaning the contacts," he called it. So she took the batteries out again, and examined the crusted place where the wires connected. She fished in her pocket for the penknife and used it and her fingernails—split and full of dirt—to scrape at the places where the wires connected. If necessary, she'd take the whole damn thing apart, try with the wires from the switch. She hadn't actually packed a nail file, but there was probably sandpaper stashed away somewhere.

When she felt like she'd made some progress, she replaced the batteries again, the right way this time, and flipped the power. For a second nothing happened, but then the cracked screen flashed and it crackled to life.

Magda flipped eagerly through the channels, but there was nothing but static—either it wasn't actually working, or the problem was that they were indoors and surrounded by trees. A marine radio wasn't exactly made for interference. What if she could take it out on the balcony—or hell, the roof?

Emily stirred, moaning. Magda clicked the radio off to preserve the life. "Emily? Can you hear me, honey?"

Leaving the back of the radio open to the air so it could dry out, Magda moved to the girl on the cot. She soaked a handkerchief with some of the bottled water and dabbed gently at the wound at Emily's hairline. She could see how the spot had now swollen up, disrupting the smooth roundness of the little face. She wrung out the cloth and draped it gently over the reddened skin. Emily stirred, fussing, but Magda shushed her. "It's alright, sweetheart," she whispered, although it was not alright—they were trapped, the water was still rising, the radio still didn't work, and who knew how much longer the storm would last.

Large pale-colored eyes rolled, light brown eyelashes fluttering. *Awake.* "What—what?"

"Hi there, Emily, do you know where you are?" asked Magda, bending over the younger woman. "Do you remember talking to me before?"

"You're—the woman who's crazy about the creepy house."

Magda huffed out a laugh. "I guess you could say that, yes. You gave us quite a scare getting up out of bed."

Emily coughed. "Are we—are we trapped here?"

Magda took a moment to picture how terrible it would be, to wake up disoriented and alone in the middle of a disaster like this. She could have been dreaming of safety and warmth. Now, instead, she'd woken in the dark and the cold with the knowledge that the situation, which she could barely remember, was dire.

"This is a good place to be trapped," said Magda. "We'll be okay."

"I'm so tired," said Emily, breathing heavily. She touched her forehead again, making a face.

"You should sleep more, if you can. Get some rest—there's nothing else to do right now."

"I'm scared," said Emily. "Can you just . . . talk to me?"

"Sure," said Magda. "What do you want to know?"

Emily lay back again slowly. "Are you married?" she asked, closing her eyes.

"No," said Magda, adjusting the pillow.

Emily reached down to rub at her belly, wincing. "Did you used to be married, and it didn't work out?"

Magda remembered that Hank had split from her mother. "No," she said. "Never married." In retrospect she hadn't really even gotten all that close, really.

Emily's eyes opened. "Do you have any kids?" She was starting to look skeptical now.

"Ah, nope, no kids either."

"So just . . . poems?"

Magda couldn't help it—she laughed. "That's right," she said. "Just poems. But they're really good poems."

Emily's pale lips turned up at the corner. "I guess that's cool," she whispered.

"How are you feeling, really?" said Magda. "You've been terribly out of it. Can you tell me what hurts?"

"I feel awful," said Emily. "Everything hurts. I wish—I wish I was back with my mom." Her eyes filled with tears.

Magda put her hand on Emily's shoulder and squeezed. Hank should be here, she realized. She should call him.

Except that in her excitement over the radio, Magda hadn't noticed Hank had been gone so long.

How much time had passed, anyway? Wasn't he just fetching the poles?

"I know it's scary, but we'll be alright," she lied. "Just . . . think pleasant thoughts. Try to get some more rest, okay?"

She waited for Emily to close her eyes. Then quietly she went to one of the windows to look out through the crack in the shutter. She couldn't see Hank.

Peeking at the sleeping girl, she crossed the hall. Isobel's bedroom had a view of the famous dock and was the spot where her father had *allegedly* been standing, putting away one of her books, when she walked off the end of the dock. Now looking out, Magda had an open view of the coast.

On the southern side of the house there was nothing but open water in all directions. The waves on the beach were startlingly rough. The dock was already overtaken again. Where had Hank set up the poles? It was too dangerous for a lone person to be out there; it would be nothing for a wave like the size of that one—or the next—to sweep a grown man out to sea.

Had he fallen? Been struck by something, perhaps, or slipped?

She hurried to the hall, trying to keep quiet so as not to disturb Emily, who seemed to have managed to get back to sleep. Feeling guilty, she pulled the bedroom door shut tight, wishing for a lock. But she could only deal with one wayward member of the family at a time.

She hurried down the stairs and through the kitchen to the back door.

From the porch it looked as if the house was in the center of a lava flow, although on closer inspection it was a quickly moving sheet of mud. Mud in all directions, streaming off the land and into the ocean. All of the grass seemed to be gone, although it was possible it was simply submerged under water. The opacity of the flood meant Magda at first thought it was deep water, but closer inspection revealed it was probably only a few inches deep.

"Hank? Hank, where are you!"

She circled the porch. If her back wasn't to the house, she would have been disoriented—she could only see a few recognizable features of the landscape to give her an estimate of where she was—most notably the standing corner of the lemur's garden, a pole of which was bent at an angle out of the earth, like a felled flag.

Fruitlessly she scanned the expanse of the lawn, made wrong shaped under the mud. "Hank!"

A whistle. There! Halfway down the garden—Hank, soaked to the skin and shuddering, his teeth shockingly white in his muddy face.

He was trying to wade through the flooded lawn, but the water was streaming down the slope, threatening to knock him off his feet. Between them, what had been the driveway was now a fast-moving channel.

"Good lord." He was going to be swept away in front of her.

"Go back!" she shouted. "Go around the other side!" Instead, he plowed forward to grab hold of the heavy terracotta sundial, which was cemented at the base but likely to be soon eroded out from underneath.

"A little help!" he called out, bracing with both hands.

There was only maybe ten feet—the width of the drive—between them, but how would he ever get across that river? She needed something that could stretch across the distance—a rope or something—but she didn't have anything she could throw to him. She could think of a few things in the house that might float, but given the current that was doing its best to sweep him straight out to sea, that didn't seem especially useful.

The paddle, maybe—wasn't that kayak paddle tucked away somewhere on the other side of the porch? She ran to fetch it—it was extendable, so it could reach at least half-way between them. She made her way carefully down the porch steps. The rain was blinding. Taking off her rain-coat, she wrapped it around her waist, then tied the arms around one of the solid metal railings. Using it to anchor herself, she braced her own feet as best she could in the muddy earth that was washing out from under her. Hank likely outweighed her by more than fifty pounds, but in the water, weight was relative, surely?

Magda reached as far as she could with the paddle, but he'd have to leave his position to grab for it, and risk being swept away. A fraction of an inch one way or another and it was over.

"Hold on!" he shouted, unnecessarily.

Magda bit down on her lip, suddenly convinced she would fail now, when it mattered most.

He made the grab, losing his footing almost imme-diately in the rushing of the water. Like a fish on the line he briefly flailed but managed to keep his hold as Magda automatically squatted lower. She gripped the end of the paddle, the edges of the plastic paddle cut-ting into her hands, the raincoat digging against her hips. His hand had been wrenched by the boat, she remembered suddenly—hers had been recently scorched by electricity. If either of them lost hold, he'd be swept away.

She had a sudden vision of his body, transformed into another pile of bones—Emily, already half-dead, would be right behind him—and then it would just be her, left in a house full of ghosts.

"Back up," sputtered Hank, through a mouthful of water. "Magda, back up!"

But she couldn't move. She didn't know how long she could hold on. She felt frozen, unable to do anything but stare at him, waiting for one of them to lose their grip.

"Damnit, come *on*!"

Hank got his toes under him and pushed; Magda felt the force of it through the paddle, traveling through the bones of her arms into her shoulders. A demand. She gasped, and as suddenly reanimated, she managed to dig in, inching back toward the safety of the porch.

Hank was still on his belly, sinking his feet and knees into the muck as Magda hauled them backward. Once she was closer, she could wrap one leg around the corner column and use its strength to bolster her own, but it wasn't enough to gain traction. Hank was still wiggling forward, straining with effort—almost within reach—

He still had the rifle swung around over his back. Magda grabbed for the barrel end of it. It felt wrong to point the dark, empty muzzle at her own chest, and she was half in fear it would fire, although she knew it was impossible. But it had to be done—the strap around his chest held, and she dragged him in the last few feet. The paddle was tossed down onto the wooden beams of the porch as she untied herself and dragged him up the stairs out of the water, then collapsed onto her knees.

"Lord almighty," coughed Hank. He bent forward at the waist. Incredibly, he laughed. "Well, I'm—much obliged to you, for that timely piece of assistance. Was looking like I was done for there for a minute."

Magda put a hand on her chest, panting. "Are you alright? Injured? You were gone so long!" It seemed like the wrong time to mention that she had lost track of time entirely. What if she hadn't come looking for him? She never even would have known what had happened to him; he would have just disappeared.

"Thought I could get some crabs, got turned around in the trees, that's all," he said, trying to wipe his streaming eyes with his equally soaked sleeve. "God, I'm wet through. Do we have any dry clothes?"

"You were wearing them," said Magda. She had to cover her face with her hands for a minute, trying to breathe.

"How's Emily?"

"She woke up briefly, then went back to sleep. I was just with her." She shook herself. "Hold on—you stay here while I get those rugs, they're better than nothing."

She grabbed the rugs they had used for Emily, which were still the driest option downstairs. Hank was shirtless and shivering when she got back. "Who would have thought I'd come down with hypothermia in Florida," he joked through clattering teeth, managing a smile.

Magda didn't smile back, remembering from some article she'd come across that you really *could* freeze, even in the jungle, if you got wet and couldn't get dry. "Here," she said, handing over the wrappings. "Strip down and try to dry yourself off with these."

If her grip had slipped, if he hadn't pushed when he had, if he'd lost his end of the paddle . . . she could see him, swept out by the water like the stone wall around the lemur pen. Solid one minute, and in the next minute *gone*. That was all it took: a single second.

"Hey, you alright?" said Hank, mopping himself off.

"Oh, fine. Fine."

He stepped closer. "It's okay. You did it. I'm okay."

"I know," said Magda. "I just . . ." she trailed off, shaking her head. "This is all crazy."

Hank took another step closer and hesitated. Slowly he reached to slide a hand through her hair. *It must be disgusting,* she thought briefly; it was sticky with humidity, unwashed for three days, still damp with rainwater.

She debated moving away, didn't.

"Tell me if I'm reading this wrong, won't you?" he said, leaning in.

How was it possible that his body, compared to hers, was still so incredibly warm?

This was a mistake, she thought, a distraction. It wasn't love, or even lust, but it was *something*—it spoke to the same part of her that had sat in the middle of the storm getting drunk on leftover wine. She shouldn't.

"Get undressed," she told him. "Your clothes are soaked."

Grinning, he kicked out of his shoes, which squelched, then his sodden socks to reveal pruny, pale feet. Then holding her eyes, he shucked open his belt and let his jeans drop around his ankles, standing in dark gray boxers. His knees, Magda found, were the only part of him that reminded her of Bryce—knobby and thin. Something about his helplessness, the innocent way he exposed himself, without any shame—tugged at her. Bryce had been the same when they'd swum together naked, off the side of the boat. Magda always thought of her body as a secret. She supposed that was how women were raised.

"Should I keep going?" he asked.

She took the last daring half step in order to fit into the circle of his arms and lifted her head to kiss him. Because he was warm, and she was always cold; because he was so *alive*, unlike everything else in the house, including maybe even herself. Because he wanted something from her, and what Magda wanted was not to think anymore.

He tasted bitter, a hint of tobacco, but then fresh like rainwater and ozone, like the storm. His chin bristled with unshaved hair. It was different from Bryce, who had been careful to maintain himself to a certain standard—she had teased him for his use of moisturizer, for his twice-daily shaves, for oiling his hair. *I have to look good,* he'd say. *Nobody's gonna tip an ugly bartender.*

Hank was ungroomed, sweaty and dirty. But so was she. His hand slid down her back and Magda groaned, softly, stepping in closer to press against his chest.

"You want to lose a few layers, darlin', come down to my level?" he asked, his voice gritty and low.

In reply, Magda shrugged out of her shirt, tossing it over a reproduction captain's chair, accurate to the period, and bent to untie the laces of her sneakers. There was nothing alluring about it except that the storm was still going on, and they were only alive in the current moment.

His injured hand didn't seem to be bothering him as he caught her around the hips when she was done. He pulled her in and Magda let him do it. But when he tried to guide her down onto the (cheap imitation, late forties at best) upholstered settee, she pushed him down first instead. "Like this," she whispered.

Hank didn't resist being positioned the way she wanted him, the way she preferred it. Maybe with Bryce she'd been willing to experiment—but Hank was almost a stranger, and strangers mated carefully.

She kicked out of her cargo pants and her cotton underwear.

"I didn't think I had a chance with you," said Hank, watching avidly.

"Well, you're kind of the last man on earth," said Magda, and he laughed.

There was no protection, but Magda was pushing forty and had taken bigger risks than this. It was appropriate, anyway—it was authentic to the original era of the house. She didn't really have time to locate the intestines of a sheep, in the French style.

She reached down to line them up.

"Ahh," said Hank, a soft noise of contentment of the kind Magda would make sinking into her own clean bed after changing the sheets. He tried to thrust up and found himself stymied by her not-inconsiderable weight. He needed his hands on the bed to hold himself up, which meant that he couldn't reach for her, couldn't hold her to him the way he might have otherwise wanted to— or touch her back, her hair, her face—he had to remain still underneath her, except for the restless movement of his hips.

Magda began to move slowly, the rhythm that the waves might beat against the dock on calm days. Unbidden, a line of Isobel's poetry ran through her mind—*the unfailing Beat of the ocean's blood*—although Isobel had presumably known nothing of sex.

"Ah, darlin'," said Hank, trying to match her as best he could from his position. "Beautiful, ain'tcha?"

Magda didn't need his compliments—she leaned forward to muffle him, and that was sufficient to keep him occupied while she used the strength in her thighs and her core until both of them were gasping, and finally his patience snapped and he came up around her like a trap, his hands on her shoulders, his legs pressing up against her, and Magda reached down to bring herself pleasure before he took his, which was always her personal objective.

This was a different kind of thing from what she'd had in her few real relationships, feeling truly connected; this was merely the scratching of an itch, a drink of cool water after a thirsty job. But it had its own charms. It reminded her of freshman year, when it was a pleasure to be able to do such things without being overly concerned by the experience of her partner. This kind of sex was catch as catch can, and she accepted it.

Fortunately, he fell back, gasping, when it was over, and Magda was once again free to break the embrace. She realized too late that her bleeding hands, cut by the paddle handle, had left streaks of rusty blood over his ribs. Hastily she reached to wipe them away with her fingertips.

"Ahh, darlin'," he slurred, his hands up over his eyes. "That's the stuff. Wish we had a cigarette, eh? Mine are all wet."

"I have a lighter, but no smokes," said Magda, who would never have let him light up in a historic house anyway, and so was glad of a reason to avoid the debate. She wondered if they needed to have the *this-shouldn't-happen-again* talk, decided it was implied.

She went to the washroom to pee and wash herself, then got dressed again in the clothes she had discarded. Everything she wore at this point was pretty ripe, but frequent exposure to the rainwater was the best she could do. Hank was still lying back, possibly thinking about sleep. Magda felt invigorated, and she wished there was something more she could do to help them prepare for the second wave of the storm, which was no doubt coming.

She went to the window and looked through the cracks in the hurricane shutters. The water had already risen again outside. If Hank had been trying to cross the yard now, he'd be up to his waist, and there would be no way an oar would save him.

She had forgotten to tell him about the radio, in all the excitement. But he was going to be useless now, and she still didn't even know if she could get a signal. Perhaps this was the right time to try.

"I'm going to check on Emily," she whispered. "You sleep." He managed a lazy salute.

*   *   *

Magda crept up the stairs and confirmed that Emily was still asleep right where she was supposed to be. She scooped up the radio and took it into Isobel's room, which had the least obstructed view of open air. She squatted in the window well, reassembling the parts by feel.

She had often gone sailing with Bryce and his friends, so she knew the basics of marine radio. She tuned to channel 16 first, the US Coast Guard channel. In a disaster like this, it should have been alight with messages and warnings for ships in the area, locations of various rescue teams, and so on, but instead she heard only heavy static. Damn, that station was probably the strongest signal she was going to get. And that meant no weather report either, at least not on the marine frequency.

Well, it seemed safe to assume there was a small craft advisory.

A little radio like this only had line-of-sight transmission; the signal couldn't be reaching more than a few miles, blocked by trees and buildings. She switched to channel 9, the frequency for ship-to-ship communications, even though any vessel this close to shore in the hurricane was probably in more trouble than she was.

She held down the button without waiting the requisite thirty seconds. "Is there anyone out there? Can anyone hear me?" There was a whole procedure to marine communication, and this wasn't it—but she figured these were exceptional circumstances.

There was no answer except crackling.

"Hello? Anyone out there?"

There was a static crackle that sounded deliberate. Magda leaned against the window and raised the radio higher, hoping every inch would help. "Hello? Say again?"

"-Ixty –Ay. Switch to—Six. Eight," said the voice.

With shaking hands Magda turned the dial to channel 68, which was presumably for conversation. By convention this would keep their chatter from distracting other boaters on the main channel. "Hello?"

The voice on the other end was crackly, but audible as long as she held it high enough. "This is a marine radio frequency, ma'am. Are you on a boat?"

She was straining to hear. "I'm—I got the radio from a boat. Docked. This is Magdalena Trudell at the Isobel Reyes House and Museum. Who is this?"

"Say again? This is Francis McKinley, I'm a radio operator at the Naval Air Station. I've got both marine and CB hookup here. You say you're where? I'm having a hard time reading you. Are you in trouble?"

"I don't—I don't know about that. I'm here at Whimbrel House—just off Smather's Beach, on Atlantic Boulevard."

"Oh yeah, I saw in the news someone was staying there in the storm. You regretting it yet?"

"No, of course not," said Magda. "But we lost radio here, and I've got two stragglers that showed up, one a pregnant teenager."

"Ay?" There was an ominous crackle. "Say again?"

"Look, I don't even have the forecast here. Is the storm still coming on?"

The reply was indistinguishable static. Frantically, Magda tried standing up, holding the phone out into the open air.

"Hello? Hello, can you hear me?"

"I'm trying to—adjust—rig so I can get a better signal for you, but . . . Copy? I'm afraid I'm going to lose you. Is there anyone I can call for you? If we get disconnected, we may . . . better signal at night. Try at the same time AM on this channel, okay? Do you copy?"

"I hear you," said Magda, setting an alarm on her watch. "I'll find you on channel sixty-eight."

She'd have to try to get higher. Out on the balcony, maybe even, although the thought of going out there, exposed to the wind, was terrifying.

There was a long bar of ominous static. "—one I can call for you?"

"I'm just—I'm wondering about my friend Bryce Delgado on the *Dauntless*," said Magda. "I forget the ship number, though. I'm wondering if he made it to Fort Myers. Do you have a way to confirm?"

"H . . . got a whole array . . . hell I've got a SAT phone . . . If you want to reach . . . one, I can try."

"I just want to know if he made it," said Magda. "Hello?"

There was static, then silence. Then: ". . . say Delgado?"

"Yes! I'm wondering about a ship that sailed to Fort Myers right before the storm." But there was no response.

"Hello?"

Magda waited, holding her breath every time the radio crackled. The power had to be running low at this point, and she didn't have any other batteries this size.

"Francis?"

Nothing. This wasn't going to work until she improved the signal. Magda resigned herself to waiting for the less chaotic nighttime signal. It wasn't like they were on a regular schedule anymore anyway. After a few more minutes of fruitless silence, she turned off the radio.

At the moment, she was feeling about as fit as she could expect; her illness seemed to be giving her a break, no doubt due in part to the pills from the med kit—of which there was only a limited supply. She stared out the window and reflected that the stairs where she'd hidden the trunk were just around the corner. She could unlock the door, open the shutters, and bring the bones inside. Take a better look. Prove once and for all it wasn't Isobel.

She checked her watch again. Everybody else was asleep.

Just enough time for a little investigation.

# 12

Thursday, October 10ᵗʰ
3:00 PM

THE TRUNK WAS still stashed out on the porch outside Isobel's room; it wasn't difficult to carry it in, still resting on the piece of plywood and wrapped in a rug. Magda was once again soaked in the storm, which was continuing to batter fruitlessly against the windows. But it was worth it to have the time to reexamine the body, when she finally got the lantern set up and opened the box.

This time she focused on the remains.

Kneeling over the trunk with the rain hammering to get in, Magda felt all the responsibility of her position and the loyalty of her lifelong scholarship—but no revulsion, only mingled sympathy and respect for the diminutive figure in the trunk.

She tried to judge if the hair was the right color. Isobel's hair had been very dark. What was left seemed paler, but it might just be the effect of exposure. Hard to say. Out of respect Magda did not immediately move it away from the face. It had been easier to be objective about the mystery—who was this woman, and how had she gotten

into this box?—when she wasn't staring into the empty eye
sockets of who might have been Isobel Reyes. The woman
who had been her constant companion through school and
for the last twenty years; the subject of her undergraduate
thesis as well as her abandoned dissertation (*The Essential
Place-Making of the Botanical Poetry of Isobel Reyes*), the
focus of every tour she had given twice a day for the last
decade.

If it was her, it was true what Magda told all her visitors: Isobel had never left Whimbrel House.

"What are you looking at?"

Startled, Magda turned to find Emily, leaning heavily
on the doorframe, watching her from the hallway.

Embarrassed to have been caught unawares, and conscious that what she was doing was difficult to explain, she
automatically inched back away from the box.

"Emily! You're up! We've been so worried about you.
How are you feeling?"

Emily seemed to be wavering on her feet, but her face
had better color than Magda had yet seen. "Okay, I guess."

"Hank is just taking a nap, I think. Do you want me
to go fetch him?"

"No—no, don't wake him." Magda understood; in
similar circumstances she wouldn't have wanted to worry
her own father either.

"Does your head hurt? It looks like you took a nasty
blow there."

"Yes." Emily raised a hand to her forehead. "Yes, my—
my head hurts so much."

"I'm sorry we don't have more supplies," said Magda.
"We're running low on everything. Do you want water?
Tylenol?" She didn't think purslane was going to cut it.

"I'm okay."

"You've really been in and out of it. Do you remember walking around before?"

Emily's eyes were unfocused. Magda was pretty sure that was the sign of a concussion. Maybe it was better not to push any drugs. "I don't know—maybe. I remember—dark. Everything is so dark in here. How bad is this storm?"

Magda decided in favor of honesty. "It's pretty bad. I hope we're safe here, but the water's rising. You can hear it out there. It's not letting up."

"Are we—trapped?"

"We're up on the second floor now," said Magda, declining to answer. "This storm has got to blow over eventually, or head away from the island. We're probably okay."

Emily nodded, her hand still on her belly. Magda wanted to ask if there was any sign of life in there, but it seemed impolitic—and what was she going to do differently, whether there was or there wasn't? For the immediate future, as far as any of them were concerned, it didn't really matter.

"Come sit down," she suggested instead.

Emily eased down awkwardly. "This was easier before—ya know," she said, waving her hand at her midsection.

"Did I hear you're having a boy?" asked Magda.

"It's not certain," said Emily, looking down. "I wanted it to be a surprise."

It seemed to Magda that having a baby as a teenager was probably sufficiently eventful without the added suspense, but she nodded encouragingly. She wanted to keep Emily awake and talking; it wasn't time for sex ed.

"So what is that? That box?" asked Emily.

"It's—well—it's something I found in the storm. I've been doing a little bit of, uh, investigating." It sounded a little stupid, saying it out loud. They certainly had bigger problems to deal with, like their survival.

But if she had a similar thought, Emily didn't voice it. "What's in it?"

"Um, well, it's a body. An old body, I mean, from a long time ago. It's just a skeleton now."

*"Really?"* Emily sat up the rest of the way, losing color, but not seeming to let that stop her. "Can I see?"

"Well, I guess." Magda helped her scoot closer on the tile floor so she could lean over to peer inside. "I think it's . . . a woman. Look at the boots. See how tiny?"

"How long do you think she's been in there?"

"Well, the clasp on the box has a date, 1912, so I suppose it can't have been any earlier than that. But she—she must have been an old-fashioned girl. See what's left of her these heels? They wouldn't have been the style in Florida at the time."

"I guess you're a historian, you'd know," said Emily, running her finger over the lock. "Who do you think killed her?"

"Well, we don't know that she *was* killed. Perhaps . . . perhaps her family just decided to bury her in an unusual way."

Emily didn't look convinced. "Where did you find her?"

"In an old cistern that was filled in sometime before the house was sold in 1920."

Emily was silent. "You think it's that sea witch, don't you. The poet."

"You know about Isobel?"

"We had a poetry thing in school. My teacher was all about her. Did she die between the date of the box and when the house was sold?"

"Yes—in 1918. But remember, the official story is that Isobel drowned herself. As far as we know, her body was never recovered. So it really doesn't make sense—oh! What are you doing?" Emily had reached into the box. "Don't touch anything," warned Magda. "We really ought to be wearing gloves."

Emily ignored her, using a finger to push aside the fabric bundled around the skeleton's ribs. There was some dark matter still left there, protected by the cage of bones and the material of the tarpaulin, but it didn't seem repulsive to Magda somehow, after hundred years.

"What are you looking for?"

"What killed her," said Emily. "I guess we wouldn't know if she was strangled, or stabbed, not like on TV. Crap!"

At her touch, shifting the bones, the skull lost its connection to the spine and rolled forward. The motion was somehow lifelike, as if in response to her questing fingers. In the back, the wisps of hair had dissolved away completely, and the bright white of the skull peered through like a face at a window.

"My God," breathed Magda.

At the back of the skull, the bones were cracked and crumbled away around a hole about the size of Emily's finger.

Magda reached to gently cradle the small skull and turn it to one side, so that the skeleton was looking back over one shoulder. The tissue that would have connected the joints was gone, no doubt sloshing around in the fetid water at the bottom of the cistern, or oozing through the rocks now and back in the ocean where it belonged. The skull turned loose on the head, nothing keeping it all together now but habit.

Around the central hole, the back of the skull was fractured, pieces missing, in a starburst. The skull had cracked on a rounded edge, like the seashells that washed up on the beach, broken along the hinges.

The skull pieces that had fragmented were still scattered in the muck, bright washed-clean flecks of bone like chips of paint.

"Look," said Emily, pointing.

Rolling around in the bottom of the trunk—a fat round cylinder with a flattened end, like a cigar stub or a crushed cigarette. Magda stared at it, barely able to understand what she was seeing. It was—was it a bullet?

"Yeah, I don't think she died of drowning," said Emily. "Unless the ocean shot her in the back of the head."

"I wish I had my phone. We could take pictures," said Magda. If there was some way to cue up an email to some of her colleagues, at least there would be some chance of a record of this—no matter what happened.

"I dunno—who really cares anyway?" asked Emily. "Does it matter? She's been dead for a hundred years. We're alive *now*."

"You don't understand," said Magda, wiping a streak of muddy hair out of her face. "A story like that, like the one they told about Isobel—it has *power*. The first thing I do every morning when I come into work is check the dock to see if there are any bodies out there. In the time I've worked here, there have been so many—and those are only the ones caught in the mangroves. We'll never know how many more floated out to sea. People come here because it's a place synonymous with suicide. But it wasn't real! It was never real. Isobel didn't drown herself because she believed she could never write a better poem than "Blood-Root"— in fact she had already started several poems that were probably better. She was murdered, and then her body was hidden in the cistern."

Magda paused to cough. Her chest was burning.

Emily was watching her. "Are you okay?"

Magda waived her off. The Tylenol was only good for four to six hours. It must be wearing off.

"How we talk about Isobel matters," she said. "What we think happened to her matters. It matters if she destroyed herself because there was no place for her—or if someone else got rid of her when she became inconvenient."

Magda rubbed her own head, which suddenly seemed to weigh a thousand pounds. She wondered if Robert Margery had found a way to get the second book despite Isobel's resistance. Had he really murdered her in order to take the final draft? It was hard to imagine, but he had clearly falsified the account of her suicide. Had he fabricated the September letter himself, from whole cloth? If so, how had he prevented Charles from disputing his account? Those angry letters in the Smithsonian—had Charles been paid to keep quiet, or had Margery fooled him too? How could there have been no investigation, no follow-up?

To be fair, it had been a strange time. By 1918, World War was ending, and the Keys would soon be wild with Navy men returning home. The first cases of what was then called the Spanish influenza were racing through Florida. In the midst of such confusion, there wouldn't have been much local appetite for a large investigation into the death of a troubled woman.

If Margery had been behind it, his gamble had certainly paid off: after Isobel's death Charles, heartbroken, had settled with him for only a fraction of what the combined books had eventually sold for.

Emily turned and began to cough too, into her hand, as if Magda had reminded her of it; Magda realized how foolish she was being, keeping the girl up and crouching over a musty old trunk when she had seemed to be at death's door only the day before. "Sit, sit down," she said, pushing the girl back down to the tile and up against the wall.

"I'm okay," said Emily, but she had begun to wheeze. "Magda, I—I need to tell you something. It's important."

"Take a deep breath first," said Magda. "I'm going to get you some water."

They both paused at the sound of heavy footfalls on the stairs. "What the hell is going on," said Hank. "Emily, why aren't you in bed? You shouldn't be down here."

Magda slipped the bullet into her pocket. At least one part of the evidence was portable. Then she closed the lid of the box. She had the feeling Hank wouldn't be thrilled to know his dangerously unwell daughter had spent the afternoon poking at a corpse.

"Sorry, my fault," she said. "We were doing a little historical exploration. You know, to keep us occupied." She wished she was standing in front of the box. She felt protective of it, like she didn't even want anyone else to look at it.

"Uh-huh," said Hank. "Well, glad you girls, uh, enjoyed yourselves, I guess."

"Oh! I do have one good piece of news," she said. "I managed to get a hold of someone on the radio."

"On the—what the hell are you talking about?" said Hank.

"The marine radio. I messed around with it and got it working. I even got a hold of someone," she said. "Some CB operator down at the Navy base. The signal wasn't great—he could barely make out what I was saying, but we're going to try again tonight when the signal is better."

"Slow down," said Hank. "You really talked to someone? You're sure?"

"Definitely. I talked to a person, told him we were here. Figured if anyone's worried about you, at least they'll know you made it this far."

"That's great," said Hank. "That's a real relief."

"Isn't it wonderful? Maybe they can send help for Emily!"

Of course, even if they could get an emergency crew out, Magda didn't actually plan to leave herself—she had sworn she wouldn't impose on the rescue services—but if she knew Emily was safe, it would be a huge weight off her mind. And obviously Hank would need to go with his daughter.

It would be strange to be alone in the house again. But of course, with more supplies and an update on the coming weather, it wouldn't be so bad. At least she had a better sense of what to expect.

"And you're sure he heard you?"

"He definitely heard parts of it," said Magda. "They know we're here."

"Well, that's really something," said Hank. He seemed almost dazed by the news, which made sense—Magda was so used to thinking of Whimbrel House as a tiny island of their own, its own country really, that it was easy to forget there was still a whole world out there.

Hank checked his watch. "He said he'd be back during the night? That's usually a better signal."

"Yeah. I set an alarm. We need to find a better spot, though; this room barely had a connection. I wonder if the front room would be better? I hate to think of going out on the balcony or up on the roof. And I don't know how good the batteries are. I brought a backup phone charger, not backup triple A's—I didn't think I'd need them."

"Well, great, let's give it a try," said Hank. He shook his head. "It's too bad you didn't pick a sooner time to try because I'm not sure how we'll be looking tonight. I came up to tell you we've got a different problem: the tide is coming in like nothing I've ever seen. I just checked the front. That water out there's still rising, and it's getting worse. We need to make a plan here."

Magda had almost forgotten about the surge danger. But now, looking out through the gap in the shutters, she could see he was right. The water level, which had been steadily increasing all day, was now closing in on the porch.

"This is it," said Hank, standing behind Magda at the window. "I guess it finally caught us."

*       *       *

It came on in waves that didn't ever seem to go back out: they swept all the way up over the garden, and behind one was another, and behind it, another. Neither the rain nor the wind seemed worse than they had been, but still the water kept coming. Almost right before her eyes, the ocean was beginning to measurably rise.

It didn't happen like she'd pictured when she'd imagined the storm: howling like the tornadoes of the plains, like a bomb, all the fury of God and nature. Like that storm she'd seen with her father, once the sky turned green and all the hair stood up on her arms: "High Winds from Goshen."

This was nothing like that. It wasn't fast, it wasn't flashy. It was as slow and inexorable as old age. And once it started, it was relentless.

"But—what are we going to do?" asked Emily as Hank ushered her back to bed. "Are we going to die here?"

Hank cleared his throat. "Of course not, babe. We'll be fine. We've only got to get through the high tide. It's not going to last forever. Then we can see about getting out of here."

Unless they couldn't—who knew what would be left after the water drained? Even after indirect hits, Magda had heard the stories—the power out for weeks, the rescue crews unable to get down, people running out of supplies. Folks started getting sick from the water or died from generator fumes or in chainsaw accidents. And this didn't feel like just another hurricane—it felt like the end of the world.

But she knew when to keep her thoughts to herself.

*　*　*

It took no time for the water to travel up to the porch, then lick its edges, and then, more slowly, for it to begin to climb. Like a lady gathering her skirts, it took each step carefully. No rush.

Magda was standing in the dining room as the water moved over the porch toward the front door. She straightened the edge of the sisal rug. A thousand times she had swept it out. She set up the candlesticks on the dining room table and, although the candles were broken, set them in the center of the table. Then she took the cane-backed chairs and, one by one, tucked them in, neat and tidy.

As far as she knew, the water had never come up this high before in nearly two hundred years. The floors, the foundation, the interior beams—it was hard to know how any of it would react to saltwater. She had a moment to be grateful that Isobel's notebooks were still in the library archive at the Smithsonian. Thank God she had never been successful in lobbying for them to be returned. Or maybe the storm, which had been a monster on the satellite, was already stretching all the way there too. Maybe this was the end of everything Isobel had ever touched.

Hank was laying the sandbags on the inside of all the doors. Magda slipped upstairs to re-wrap the trunk, the best protection she could offer it now.

"So, you gonna tell me what that thing is now?" he asked, coming back to find her trying to wrap it in plastic she'd pillaged from the downstairs shower curtain, held together with an extension cord.

Magda coughed into her sleeve, rubbing her chest. Ah, what the heck. Mutely she opened the top to show him the skeleton inside.

"Jesus Christ," he said, peering in. "Well, that looks old, though. That's been here for years, don't you think? To be picked clean like that? And look at those boots— that ain't a recent corpse." Before she could stop him, he reached in to pluck one out and hold it up.

"I'm inclined to agree," said Magda, reaching to take it back from him before it disintegrated.

"Well then, it's none of our problem here. Throw it out, I guess."

"Throw it out? Do you know what I went through to get it in here? This is a piece of history. I think—I haven't proved it yet, but I believe this is the remains of Isobel herself."

Magda looked down at the shoe in her hands. There was something driven through one of the rivets, she noticed for the first time. Carefully she worked it loose.

"Look, we don't have time for that kind of stuff," said Hank. "This ain't the History Channel. We're almost completely out of supplies, and the food we've got won't last but another two days, even if we all take it easy. That ocean's gonna come right in your front door. You think maybe that's more important than an old heap of bones? We're going to end up skeletons ourselves if you don't pull yourself together—you're going to end up just like her."

"You don't understand," said Magda. "I'm a historian. This is what I live for."

It was—it was a twig, thrust right through the eyelet of the shoe. It must have gone into the box that way, to be jammed so deep, but it didn't seem like somebody would walk around long without noticing it.

"There's not going to be any living for anything soon. This damn storm is just squatting over the Keys like a top, turning in circles and never clearing out. That means it's gonna be right up our asses again, and it'll be getting dark again soon. You think this water is an issue now? Wait until it's pitch black. So unless we can eat it, I don't want to hear about it. And I don't think we oughta eat *that*, and don't think it hasn't crossed my mind. So get rid of it. Toss it off one of these railings and listen to the splash. Because we're definitely not keeping it here in the house—even bones that old can still stink."

Magda wanted to push back, tell Hank he didn't have the right to try and take control now. Whimbrel House wasn't his; it was hers—hers and Isobel's. But she couldn't deny, just at the moment, that he might have a point. And practically speaking, the box did smell, not so much of human decay—the skeleton had been in the saltwater too long for that—but of the musty eroding materials the trunk itself was made out of. The straps were decomposing away, the metal parts were all rusting to nothing.

"Go deal with the sandbags," she said. "I'll take care of this, and then I'll come help you, okay?"

He grunted and left. Magda waited until he was out of earshot, then returned to her examination of the twig from the shoe. She was surprised it hadn't degraded away, but no, it was smooth and solid, and . . . tapered.

Not a twig—a *thorn*.

To almost anyone else, surely, it would have meant nothing: merely another piece of detritus caught up with a body, indistinguishable from any other piece of plant material. But to Magda, who had spent patient hours toiling over the young plants, carefully trimming back the dead branches at the end of the growing season, and cutting switches, wrapping them up for transport as the storm swept in, there was something unmistakable about it. It was broken from a branch of the old-fashioned Key limes.

"Magda? Are you done in there?"

She blinked. "Just a minute."

She put the thorn back in the toe of the shoe, the shoe back in the box. Then she knelt to wrap the trunk carefully in the plastic and tie the cord tight. She dragged it back out to its nook out on the balcony, which was at least high enough off the ground that the water wouldn't getting to it anytime soon. There it could be tucked against the corner of the house, sheltered by the overhanging roof and a cement column, swaddled in plastic. By the time the water reached that high, if it did, they'd have bigger problems than decomposition.

Standing out in the stinging rain, Magda could tell she was getting sicker. Her skin felt like it was crawling, the bones misaligned, the joints aching. She was chilled down to her toes. It was the fever, she was sure, that was dragging her down. Ever her fingers hurt, swollen and clumsy.

She imagined for a beat that she could see Isobel in place of the box, standing out on the balcony with her dark hair streaming in the wind. Looking out over the gardens she had loved. The place she had been killed.

Magda forced herself back downstairs to help Hank gather everything they could to take up to the second floor.

# 13

Thursday, October 10<sup>th</sup>
5:00 PM

T HE WATER CAME in under the doors first. It seemed
futile to board them all shut now, when they might
need to get out that way in the end. Hank tried, but that
didn't stop it from coming in around the edges, the seams.
Eventually when the pressure was equal on both sides, the
ocean threw the door open like a guest at a party.

It came down the hall the way Magda herself had
walked a thousand times.

They had moved what they had up to the second floor,
but it seemed obvious the water would eventually follow
them. Hank and Emily caught what sleep they could as
Magda kept heading down the stairs at intermittent peri-
ods to check on the water. The stairs were now definitely
rattling under her weight in a very disconcerting way. The
plaster felt mushier under her shoes, no doubt from the
water that was filling the footwell. There was at least knee-
deep water throughout the first floor.

There was a current through the hallway, eddies in the
corners. There was the risk of being hit by the furniture,

some of which was floating. She made sure not to look, the way soldiers must walk past the fallen on the battlefield, unwilling to be weighed down by the loss.

Everything smelled strongly of salt. Dampness clung to the plaster. The wooden baseboards all along the edges of the floor were clearly ruined.

She wasn't sure how long they'd be safe on the second floor, or the attic, if the foundation was being eroded away from the bottom. Would the whole house eventually collapse?

Magda waded through the dirty, knee-deep water in the kitchen, almost losing her grip on the tile floor more than once. The water was streaming into the cellar, creating a current. She took a minute to appreciate the fact that she was about to be the final member of her family tree to drown in a disaster.

*Hold on, Louis Trudell—I'm coming.*

She caught herself on the doorframe and gripped with her fingernails. This was how it happened, she thought. You were distracted by something else—that morning's mine inspection, say—and you weren't watching as the new shaft neared that lake overhead. You didn't realize the moment was already upon you until it was too late.

She shook herself and carefully started back down toward the stairs.

She needed to get to the library, where there was still one book she wouldn't have bothered to save. It wasn't historic; it was one of her own books of reference for her restorations. It was still on the shelves: *The Glossary of Southern Design*. There was a whole section on the Civil War, which Magda had never really used. Howard Reyes had been too old to fight, and Charles too young.

Having made it, she sat right there in the flooding library to flip through the pages on weaponry. Hank had said the rifle was a Springfield, so Magda started there. She was a historian, not an antiquarian, and these days more of a generalist than her professors would have liked to acknowledge; experts in period furniture didn't often spend their days weeding flower beds or scheduling wedding rehearsals. But she remembered her courses in authentication and restoration well enough to find the illustration of the 1862 Springfield, disassembled on the page like a dissected frog.

There were several pictures of its bullets on the next page—the "Minié ball." It was quite an invention, apparently, in terms of its lethality. There were two photos: first in its intact stage, small and blunt like a cigarette butt, and then one of one that had been impacted. The notation read "taken from a stone wall in Gettysburg, Pennsylvania." Apparently it was common for them to travel straight through bodies, shattering bone.

Magda had fished the bullet out of her pocket to compare. The mushroom head had peeled open around a hollow center, but there was no question in her mind that it was the same type of bullet.

A woman had been killed sometime after 1912 with a bullet that could only be fired by a Civil War–era rifle, and meanwhile Magda had discovered a rifle from that same time period, behind a shelf.

Sometimes it didn't take CSI, Key West.

\* \* \*

Leaving the book behind, she arranged the sandbags around the antiques on the landing but didn't risk the last of her strength to take all them any further. It didn't make sense to try to outrun the whole ocean.

She wondered how much more she could have saved if she had washed her hands right after high-fiving that sick kid from the tour. She wondered if the captain of the *Titanic* had also been suffering from a head cold. Maybe he didn't see that iceberg because his head was all stuffed up and he was running a fever.

Grimly she pushed on, dizzy now. She couldn't let herself think too much about the remaining furniture. Most of it was valuable, but not irreplaceable.

Still, it had been the work of her career so far to pick out every item in the estate. Each chair and table had, one by one, been carefully selected, positioned—never mind fundraised for. Some of it might be covered by their insurance. Someone would have to go back and review the policy when this was over. She was no longer positive it would be her.

She wondered how far into the storm they were. Halfway? Not even? It was impossible for her to tell if it was getting better or worse outside—there was nothing but an endless din. She wasn't sure how long they'd been in the thick of it. More than six hours, but was it more than eight? The last forecast Hank had heard, it had been predicted that the storm would linger over the islands. But for how long? A few days? A week? Was that possible? Or was the water reclaiming the whole island permanently, washing away everything that had once protruded from the ocean's surface? Whimbrel House was the third highest point in Key West. Was there anything else left?

She leaned in to check on Hank and Emily—they were both asleep. But there was still one thing left she could save.

She crept to the hallway and struggled to pull down the ladder to the attic, the handle for which was taller than her head. Who the hell had built this thing—weren't people shorter in the past? Finally, she jumped and caught it, aware at once that she was dangerously ill when her knees almost gave out. But she managed to use her weight to drag it down with a terrible groan. The attic looked dark and foreboding—she didn't have a light—but she was just relieved it was dry. If there had been a leak up here, there would be nothing else to do but wait for the end.

She wasn't sure how she was going to get Isobel's heavy painting up the narrow ladder stairs, so she started with the boxes of books, which were waiting patiently at the top of the staircase. She tried to match her steps up the rungs with the pounding of her heartbeat in her ears.

The sound in the attic was horrific. She was abandoning the security of the stone walls, coming up here, for the uncertain protection of wooden roof beams that were currently being hammered by the wind and rain. It sounded like hail, unless that was the raindrops being whipped into the tiles—Magda wasn't sure. The storm was shrieking, loud enough that she might have clapped her hands over her ears if she thought that would help, although part of her also wondered if she might not be hearing the high pitched whine of her own fever, on top of the racket. Impossible to say. It didn't matter.

She made two trips and then had to pause, trying to figure out how she might be able to transport the heavy oil painting into the attic.

It was hard going, but she managed to lift up one end and rest it on the middle rung, and then sort of slide it upward by pushing with all her waning strength, then bracing it on her own shoulders and clambering up, rung after rung. Several times she wavered, her vision almost whiting out, spots dancing in front of her eyes, her knees trembling.

She wasn't sure what was most likely, that the painting would slide back down and crush her or that she would fall off the ladder and strike the hard ground. But somehow she managed to wedge it sideways through the hole into the attic and heave it up. It fell with a clatter, and she shuddered to think what damage she was doing to something literally priceless; she might have cracked the frame, she might have warped the canvas, the paint might be chipping even now. But it was as high as she was going to be able to get it.

Magda let her head drop back against the wall. At least she had bought more time. Maybe she should try to rescue more of the antiques from the landing, try to get them at least up back in one of the bedrooms, maybe up off the floor, if not in the attic. She wasn't at all sure the stairwell would support more weight, or that the roof would hold, but at least she could try. Maybe after she got a little rest. She was so tired. Chilled through and exhausted. Numb with shock. She'd thought herself prepared, but there was no preparing for something like this. There was only sur- viving, or giving up.

She needed to at least make sure the painting was safe. Magda crawled up slowly behind it and wrapped it care- fully in its plastic shroud. Done, she paused. There was nobody in the hallway that could hear her. Over the sound of the wind, it was impossible.

She nudged a roll of insulation over the entrance with her foot, taking her from gloom to perfect darkness.

The cataclysm outside was so loud that it was almost womb-like. This was the heart of it, she thought: the heart of the storm. She put her head in her hands.

She had lost every member of her family one by one, but it wasn't—it hadn't been like this. It wasn't because of her own failure to save them. They had, each in their own way, chosen to leave her. She had never cried after Bryce left, not really. She had drunk a lot, she had been quieter for a few weeks. But she didn't remember this sense of complete devastation.

There was going to be nothing left of the house to save. Everything she had worked for, wished for, sacrificed for: it was the end of everything. The best she would be able to do was keep the three of them alive—and probably not even that.

Secluded in the temporary shelter of the attic, Magda covered her face and let the tears come.

* * *

She was not sure how much time passed exactly, but after the brief but intense paroxysm she felt surprisingly better. *"Enough fretting, Magpie,"* her father's voice seemed to tell her. *"Don't you have anything else to do?"*

Her whole adult life, Magda had seen her job as trying to preserve Isobel's legacy, exactly the way it had been in life. Every brick of the house Isobel had loved, every plant in the gardens she had walked in, and every perfect word she had written, each lovingly conserved as though in amber. If it hadn't always been a glamorous role, but it had felt important. Because Isobel was important.

And that had failed. It was over. They were never going to be declared a Cultural Heritage Landmark—because most likely Whimbrel House and everything it contained would be wiped from the face of the earth. The exact opposite of a landmark, in fact—the empty place where something was missing.

But now, having been confronted with the bones of her idol, Magda felt the new role rising up out of the water in front of her: to be the person to rewrite the books, the person to tell this new story.

*I can't die here,* she thought. *I can't die until everybody knows what was taken away from us.*

She put the precious books—all except one—and the wrapped painting in a dry corner, then felt her way out of the trapdoor and descended the stairs.

The one book in her hand was the household ledger from 1918. The ledgers were among the books she had rescued in her first salvo, packed into boxes and carried to the second floor. The early books were written in pencil and mostly faded; the later ones had darker spines and were written in ink.

Now Magda carefully turned the brittle pages covered in Charles's irritable scrawl. He kept no diary, but he did keep meticulous track of the household accounts, especially in the years after 1910 as the family fortunes started to turn. Most of the entries were dedicated to what supplies had been purchased and which had already been paid for.

The year of 1918, the meal accounts were studded with appearances of "Rob't Mgry." According to the household records, he had been a not-infrequent guest at Whimbrel House during the final year of Isobel's life, often staying overnight and returning to Miami in the morning. But the final overnight visit was noted as occurring on September 7th and 8th, two weeks before Isobel's death. The following week there were only modest provisions, presumably for only Charles and Isobel. It didn't appear as if any guests had been eating meals at the house.

Of course, that was just what had been written down.

Magda was confident she had read just about every piece of recorded history relating to the last months of Isobel's life. Assuming the reported date of her suicide (September 20th) was around the actual date of her death, she had been preoccupied with the publication of her second book of poems.

It was well known that she was considering not publishing again, which she had written about several times to her mother's family in New Orleans. She hadn't enjoyed the attention brought on by the first book, and despite the promises of the publisher, the money that was owed to her was still held up by the time she finished the second volume. By then, Whimbrel House had debts related to Charles's business affairs, and it must have seemed like a needless drain of her health and energy.

Magda wrapped the ledger in a plastic bag and, with the last of her strength, added it back into the box with the others, leaving the ladder down after she had descended because, at this point, they'd end up needing to use it. That old cliché—heading up to the attic with an axe—didn't seem outside the realm of possibility now.

As far as she could recall, the house didn't even have an axe. There had been a chainsaw in the shed, but it was unreachable now.

She wiped her burning cheeks and pressed on.

\*   \*   \*

Emily was awake when she got back to the bedroom they were currently camped out in, which was Charles's, on the higher, drier side of the house. "Hey, honey," said Magda, "how are you holding up?"

"My head hurts, and I need to pee."

The second-floor bathroom wasn't functional—Magda was not volunteering to try and fix the old rainwater system from the roof—but there was a bucket. Magda nodded and helped her up, and together they made their way down the hall.

"I'm sorry about your house, and stuff," said Emily.

"Thanks," said Magda. "I appreciate that." They got to the bathroom, and Magda let Emily take more of her own weight. "I'll wait out here. You do your business and I'll help you back, okay?"

"Thanks."

Standing in the hallway, Magda reflected on just how crappy she was feeling now. Maybe she ought to give in and take that second-to-last Tylenol; at this point, she would need her strength to get them through the night. Her fever seemed to be higher, if the whine in her skull was any indication, and her fingers and toes had begun to tingle and cramp.

The sound of a door opening made her turn; it wasn't the bathroom door or the bedroom behind her. It was the door to Isobel's room.

Well, the house was rattling, it made sense that it had knocked the door loose. Magda went to close it again, fumbling with the old brass handle.

She could see her own shadow against the door, but the shape of it seemed to waver; she was shrinking down, and her hair was long, longer than it really was, all the way down to her waist. She could smell citrus flowers and saltwater.

Magda put her hand out, imagining she could see the glossy leaves of the lime trees overhead, their round bitter fruit.

"Magda?"

"Em, everything okay?" Magda turned; it was Hank, poking his head out the doorframe of the other bedroom.

"Magda?" It was Emily, standing in the hallway, looking frightened. "Where were you? I've been calling you. Why didn't you answer?"

"What? I've been—I've been right here the whole time."

Emily shook her head. "You were in that other bedroom," she said. "Were you looking out the window again? You said you'd wait for me here."

"I didn't—I didn't even leave the hallway," said Magda, confused. She hadn't—had she? She'd never even gone into Isobel's room. Although—she looked again—although someone had opened the bolt of the big double doors out onto the balcony. And they'd been locked the last time she'd checked.

"I want to go back and lie down," said Emily, impatient. "Will you help me get back to the room?" She was resting her hand on her swollen belly, rubbing it as if it hurt her.

"Of—of course. I'm sorry. Here, let's get you back to the room."

"I've got her," said Hank, coming to take his daughter under the arm. "Are you okay, darlin'?" He looked at Magda. "You don't—pardon me for saying it—but you don't look so hot."

"I don't feel great," Magda admitted. Her hands felt superheated against her forehead. She couldn't get warm. It felt like the cold was inside her. No amount of blankets would be enough, and neither would a day spent soaking in the hot tub on the deck of Bryce's condo building. She had the feeling if she got into it now, it would freeze over, radiating outward from her body.

"Alright, you try to rest," said Hank, patting her shoulder. "I'm going to try to shore up the stairs so we're not stuck up here."

"Be careful," she reminded him.

Emily pressed close against her shoulder. "I'm so scared, Magda," she whispered. "I've been so scared for so long."

"It'll be okay, honey," murmured Magda. "We'll be alright." That's what her father had always done in these circumstances: lied. She thought about that tornado, the terrible train engine scream of it, and her father's steady voice saying, *Wow, ain't it something, Magpie? Look quickly now—it'll be gone in a flash. You don't want to miss this.*

Magda shifted to put her hand over Emily's. She couldn't touch her chin to her chest, she realized dazedly. Perhaps her throat was swollen. Her neck didn't quite seem to bend that far anymore, although it had once, surely?

"Magda, I really need to talk to you," said Emily, shivering. "I need to tell you something."

"Honey, just let her rest," said Hank, appearing in the doorframe. "The most important thing is that you both save your strength, okay? I don't know what's going to happen on this call, but this could be our last chance to rest up. Come sit with me now, and let Magda sleep."

Emily fell silent, shrinking back. Hank dropped a hand on Magda's forehead and sighed. He had brought up the med kit, which was looking sadly depleted. "Okay, I got some more Tylenol for you, and here—there's Dramamine, and it's not expired. Take this."

"Seasickness pills? Why would I want those?"

"Because they make you drowsy. Sleep might be the best thing you can do for yourself right now."

Magda had to admit that unconsciousness sounded pretty appealing right this minute. She watched Hank grind the pills into powder and add it to a bottle of water. "Bottoms up."

"Are you sure?"

"A couple hours' rest can make all the difference."

Magda took it and drank deeply.

"Just try to get some sleep," he said.

"The radio," managed Magda. "Don't let me sleep through the check-in." The pills worked fast; within a few minutes she felt vaguely like she was spinning.

"I'll wake you up, okay? I'll set an alarm. Where did you leave the handset? Do you have it?" But Magda was already past speaking. She managed a cough, the sound grating. She felt as though she was carrying a ball of fire in her chest, and it was burning outward through her throat.

She dragged her damp sweater over her shoulders and dozed with her head against the plaster, murmuring to herself every time another rattle of wind or rain shook the house down to its bones.

# 14

Friday, October 11th
2:00 AM

*Day Five*

MAGDA WOKE UP from a dream. Something had shaken her foot, like a hand on her ankle.

She sat up. She felt god-awful but she accepted that. Why was she alone in the room? She had no idea what time it was, and at this point was having trouble tracking the days—was it Thursday? Was it time to check the radio? Had she slept through the alarm?

That some time had passed she accepted on faith because the light outside seemed to have stayed the same unrelenting gloom since the hurricane had moved onshore.

She had fallen asleep next to Emily, but now there was nothing but the water bottle lying open on its side, with an inch of water still inside.

In the gray shadow of the room, she felt she could hear someone breathing softly, and yet there was nothing. *Stress,* she reminded herself.

She put both feet on the floor. She felt terribly dizzy.

"Hank? Emily?" Slowly and painfully she made her way down the hallway. The doors of both other bedrooms were open, but the rooms seemed to be empty.

There was water lapping at the base of the stairs, sloshing gently.

The light seemed to be flickering, like a strobe, slowing down each moment to a beat. Beat. Beat.

There was a shape at the bottom of the stairs.

Magda blinked.

Emily was lying on her side on the landing, unmoving. Her skin was pale blue.

*　*　*

"Oh God." Magda started down the stairs, swayed, and had to catch herself on the railing. "*Hank!* Hank, where are you?"

She used the wall to brace herself on the way down, reaching with both hands to roll the girl onto her back. Emily was soaked, having clearly been fully immersed in the water at some point. Her chest wasn't moving. Magda fumbled at her neck but couldn't feel a pulse. "*HANK!* Oh God, oh God, please . . ."

Magda didn't have more than basic first-aid training, required to host school groups. She had always figured she had a fifty–fifty chance with the Heimlich maneuver and even odds with an allergy attack. She had half a recollection of CPR from a video she'd seen at the physical therapist's office she'd taken her grandmother to after her broken hip.

She didn't know how long Emily had been like this. Her body was chilled, perhaps from the water; but that could give them a chance; wasn't cold preserving? Magda knew from Ishpeming that nobody was dead until they were warm and dead. "Come on, little girl," said Magda, heaving her back onto her side, pointing her face down and thumping her on the back. "You probably swallowed a lot of water, but go ahead and cough it out now."

Emily did not react. Didn't move, didn't inhale.

"Okay, okay, don't panic," said Magda, who was panicking. "*HANK!* Let's not make me try CPR, okay? I don't really know CPR. Do you hear me? I don't know how to do it."

"Good Lord," said Hank from behind her. "Emily? Oh God, Emily!"

"I just found her like this," said Magda, teeth chattering. "She's not breathing. Do you know CPR?"

"I—no," said Hank. "No, I don't know how to do it."

"We'll do it together," said Magda. "I saw it explained once. It's easier with two people. You do the breaths, and I'll do the compressions, okay? I'll count you off. You start with two." She didn't know if two was the right number. Maybe they didn't do breaths anymore—had she read that somewhere? Or maybe that wasn't right. Her brain was numb, frozen.

There was no way this was going to work. But how could they not try? Every second they waited was another second that Emily drifted further out of reach.

"I don't know how to do it," Hank repeated, shaking his head. It would be any parent's nightmare, thought Magda, to find their child like this.

"You do know how," she said. "Come on now—it's just like on TV, okay? You have the easy part. Give it a try, or else I'm just going to have to do both parts, and I can hardly take in a full breath as it is."

Hank moved to his daughter's head. They were crammed in on the landing, which wasn't wide enough for all of them; Emily's legs were on the lower stairs, Hank was kneeling on her hair. "Lift her chin up," said Magda, trying to remember. Something about the position of the tongue, or—who knew. But they had to try. "Okay, give her the breaths."

Magda moved to the girl's thin chest, putting the heels of her palms down over her ribcage like she was going to knead a loaf of bread. No doubt there was a whole art to the right position that she couldn't remember, but she took the chance of putting her hands right over the sternum, avoiding the sight of her rounded belly. She couldn't think about the baby right now.

The breaths that Hank delivered seemed feeble and poorly aligned, but Magda couldn't fault him for being short of breath in a crisis. She felt the same way herself, like she wasn't getting air.

"Okay, one and two and three and . . ." How many to give? Magda didn't know. It probably didn't matter. More seemed better. She should keep going until she couldn't anymore.

"Okay, you go again," she said, after what might have been twenty or twenty-five compressions. She hadn't been counting. Her shoulders ached, her locked elbows and wrists.

Hank bent over again as Magda, ironically, caught her breath. He gave two exhales and paused, examining his daughter's face.

"Anything?" asked Magda.

He shook his head, his face white, eyes blown wide. He might be going into shock.

"Then we go again," she said, getting back up on her knees.

For how long? In the movies, the victims came obviously back to life, sputtering and lurching up. Was that real, or just Hollywood drama?

"One and two and . . ."

They traded places again and again. Magda couldn't tell that it was working. On the TV shows, one of the gowned figures would tell the other when it was time to stop. With only the two of them left, there was no stopping. How long had it been?

Hank was doing his ineffectual breaths again and had just sat back when Magda saw it—something white, sliding down Emily's cheek. "She's throwing up," she said. "Roll her onto her side." Corpses did such things, in Magda's recollection—they frothed, they shat.

Hank took her under her shoulders and heaved her over—and Emily coughed weakly, still dribbling sputum and water onto the floorboards.

"Oh my God," said Magda, as Hank bowed his head and covered his face. "Oh my God, we did it, we—we did it. She's alive."

"Emily! Emily, can you hear me, honey?" Hank bent and cupped her sallow cheek in his palm. "Emily?"

Her eye flickered, opened. She drew another shaky breath. Her lips moved once; then she turned her face in his hand and her eyes closed again. Her breathing seemed normal.

Magda let out her own breath slowly, trying not to choke on the relief.

"What the hell happened?" said Hank, still feeling for her pulse. "I thought she was upstairs. How did she even get down here?"

"I don't know. I just woke up and found her like this."

"Maybe she was feverish again," said Hank. "She might have come down here, fallen in the water—maybe she was able to crawl out up to the landing before she . . ." He trailed off.

"Yeah, maybe," said Magda.

Hank raked his hair out of his face. "We need to get her back to the room, get her dry again."

"Take her up," said Magda, "I'll be right behind you, I just—I need a minute. Just one minute."

So Hank gathered Emily in still-shaking hands and scooped her up into his arms, carrying her up away from the greedy water. Magda closed her eyes and tried to breathe, tried to slow her pounding heart. Then she heaved herself up.

There couldn't be more than a foot at the base of the stairs. It was lousy luck to almost drown in such shallow water.

It seemed to take an eternity to get up the hellish stairs, with her vision sliding in and out of sepia tones, like walking through an old-fashioned photograph. She had to stop at one point to lean over and try to catch her breath, seriously expecting that she would throw up herself. But finally they were all safely ensconced in Charles's bedroom again.

Magda observed the two of them were taking turns with the cot. Apparently it was Emily's turn again.

Hank bowed his head over Emily's wet hair, stroking it off her face with his calloused hands. Magda could feel the terrible love in the gesture. Imagine watching your only child suffer, knowing there was nothing you could do to make it better. "I was downstairs trying to deal with the boat," said Hank. "I was futzing with half hitches a hundred feet away while she—while she . . ." He dropped his hands. "Damn, I need a drink."

"You need to rest," said Magda. "Did you even get any sleep last night?"

He rubbed his face. "Naw."

"This is your chance. There's still an hour before the radio check-in, by my watch. I'm not going back to sleep, so I'll sit with her. I won't let her out of my sight. If anything happens, I'll wake you up."

"Wake me up if she's coming to," said Hank. "Please, I—I need to know if she's gonna be alright. As soon as she's waking up, I want to know. Promise me."

"I will," said Magda.

So Hank curled himself into a ball in the corner, wrapped in his raincoat.

Emily slept like the dead, bundled up in the warmest layers they had. Magda felt her pulse—slow and steady— and watched her breaths. Her skin was still chilly and pale.

She sat on the edge of the cot. "Gave us quite a scare, you know," she whispered, rubbing her eyes. "What happened to you, huh? Why can't you just stay where it's safe?"

Emily's eyelids quivered, face flickering with expression, but she didn't move.

Magda tried to think of something to say, if only to keep herself awake.

"You know, when I was your age, I was living with my grandmother in Ishpeming. My dad—my dad was a great musician and a cool guy, but he—there were things he didn't care about. And when my grandmother offered me the chance to stay in one high school, he couldn't—he couldn't understand why that was important. He said he would come visit, but . . . but he never did. And then one day he was gone, forever."

Emily stirred but didn't wake.

"I barely have anything left of him. He didn't like to record his songs. But my grandmother used to say singing them was the best way to remember him." Magda herself was named after "Magdalena with the Lamp," his favorite deep-cut track. "Maybe I'll sing you one when you wake up."

She checked to see if Emily was responding at all, but there was nothing. Magda sighed.

"My dad hated Ishpeming, and he got the hell out of there as soon as he could, but . . . I guess I always wanted to find a place to *stay*, you know? I guess . . . I guess that's what Whimbrel House became to me. What I wanted it to be for everyone."

Emily sighed.

"Emily? Emily, honey, can you hear me? Can you open your eyes?" She ought to get Hank, but he'd barely gotten to sleep. She hated to wake him up until she was sure.

The girl coughed and her eyes fluttered open, then fixed on Magda. "Where's . . . Hank?" she asked weakly, voice cracking.

"He's right there, honey, asleep. Let me get him for you."

"No!" said Emily, trying to sit up slowly with a hand at the small of her back. It seemed to cost her great effort. Lord, they were doomed. Magda could barely climb stairs, and Emily couldn't sit. The storm was only getting worse. "No, give me—give me a minute." She gripped Magda's sleeve.

Something hit the side of the house, hard, and both of them flinched; whatever it was, it dragged all down the side of the wall as it slid down to land with a crash in the garden. The wind was howling again, sharp like a woman screaming.

"Your father wanted to know as soon as you woke up. Let me get him."

Emily's colorless eyes darted back to the window. When she spoke, her voice was very faint; Magda had to lean close to hear.

"He's not my father," she said.

Friday, October 11<sup>th</sup>
3:00 AM

"WHAT ARE YOU—WHAT are you talking about?" said Magda. Was Emily still raving, perhaps from the fever? "Emily, of course he's—"

"You don't understand," said Emily, her voice cracking. She raised a shaking hand to her head, wincing. "He was my mom's boyfriend, but she kicked him out ages ago. And the baby—the baby was his."

Magda could barely hear her over the sudden roaring in her ears. "What do you—Emily, I don't understand—wait—'*was*'?"

"Keep your voice down," whispered Emily. "He's asleep." She turned her head painfully to look over at the corner, biting her lip. Magda was worried about Emily's lungs, about her heart, but didn't stop her from continuing. "The baby is already dead. It was dead before we got to the house. When we were in the hotel, I had real bad cramps, and—it came out. It was all gray. You know? Like, green-gray."

Magda did indeed remember the skin of the old corpses that had washed up on shore. "But what did—what did you do with it?"

"I couldn't let him know," said Emily. "He would have been so mad. I put it in my backpack. Then I waited until the water came up, and I—I let it go."

Maybe someone would find it in the next hurricane, thought Magda hysterically.

"It was a girl," said Emily. "He wanted a boy anyway." She shook her head. "I felt so grown up, when he—when it started. And when I got pregnant, he convinced me to keep it." Her voice was rasping and weak, but she persevered: "We kept it a secret until we couldn't anymore. He said he would take care of us, that I just needed to get away from my mom back in Tampa. So we left together. But— but it wasn't like I thought it would be. He's not like I thought he would be." She sniffled. "I tried to get away, run to my friend's place, but with the storm and every-thing—he found me, and I—I promised I'd be good. So I couldn't—I couldn't tell him the baby was gone."

Magda closed her eyes, her heart pounding. "It's okay, honey," she whispered. "It wasn't your fault. None of this is your fault, okay?"

"You have to be careful," said Emily. "He knew I was going to tell you, and then I woke up on the stairs. He gave me his water bottle to drank from, and then . . ."

Magda shuddered. "It's all right, now. It'll be alright, sweetheart."

She shook her head. "He thinks I'm too much trouble now," she whispered.

Magda remembered the sight of Emily lying at the base of the stairwell. Obviously drowned, with no marks on her. Had Hank tried to drown Emily because he thought Magda was about to learn the truth?

He had been nowhere nearby when it happened. *Was it possible?* Had he carried her to the water? Held her down? Perhaps she had crawled out after he had—what, left her for Magda to find?

How could a man do that to a defenseless teenager?

But Hank was the one—Hank had said she must have gotten out of bed, and it made enough sense at the time. Magda had no reason to doubt him, so she had—she accepted the story because—because he was her father.

*Just like everybody would have believed the story of Isobel's suicide if it came from a trusted source,* said the part of Magda's brain that never shut off. Someone who would never hurt her, someone who loved her.

*Focus, Magda. What are we going to do about Hank?*

But her mind was spinning.

Isobel hadn't wanted to publish the second book of poetry, she remembered suddenly. *Focus, Magda.* But she couldn't stop. Isobel had been delaying the final poems for months. Maybe it wasn't just the publisher who wanted the book. Charles had already met Amelia Whitehead at that time, his future wife. Whimbrel House was in debt. And Charles needed the funds to start a new family, a new life.

But . . . but Charles had demonstrably adored his daughter. He'd supported her all his life, defended her against detractors from town who suggested she would be better off in an institution, and encouraged her literary pursuits. It made no sense that he would have killed her, right on the eve of all of her success.

And yet there was only one person who could have buried Isobel in the cistern without anybody noticing, without attracting any suspicion. A person, perhaps, who kept a Springfield rifle over his fireplace. Not the publisher, who hadn't even been in town at the time. Charles.

*He killed her,* thought Magda.

Had he simply run out of space for her in his life—did he need his eccentric daughter out of the way before he could marry a respectable woman? But then why would he send the book of poems to be published? He could have easily gotten rid of them if he didn't want the notoriety.

Her eyes flicked back to Emily. Maybe in the end, Charles just couldn't stand for Isobel to outgrow him. She was making her own decisions, about the book, about her own fame. So he had taken back control. And once she was gone, he had sent her book of poems to the publisher. And nobody would ever have known until the hurricane destroyed all of Magda's hard work, her careful cultivation, her recreations. It was all gone now—but the truth came up, bright as a penny, from out of the mud.

"What are we going to do?" asked Emily.

*Pay attention, Magda!*

Magda couldn't imagine her own father touching a hair on her head, never mind . . . blowing it open. Of course, Charles Reyes wasn't anything like her laid-back father. Charles had been a skilled businessman in his day and was known to drive a shrewd bargain with the merchants in town.

And Hank. What kind of man was Hank?

Was there a chance that Emily was lying, making the story up for some reason?

Looking into her small, upturned face, Magda didn't think so.

"Alright," whispered Magda. "Okay, honey. It's almost time for the radio call. I can—I can try to dial in early. You stay here for now, pretend to be asleep. Don't let him know you woke up. I'll try—I'm going to try to send a message out, get help."

Numbly, some part of her was now wondering what Isobel's life would have been like if she had lived. Would she have become a war expat like Pound, Eliot, and H.D.? Would she have stayed through the storm of 1932 with Hemingway, assisting in the cleanup? Debated poetic styles with Robert Frost (who stayed in Key West for sixteen consecutive winters)? What poetry would she have written if she'd lived to see the fifties, the sixties? How else would she have changed the world?

"No," said Emily. "No, don't go. I'm scared."

"I have to, sweetheart. It's our best chance." Magda slipped her fingers into Emily's limp ones and squeezed. "Be brave, okay? We can do this. I'll be back as soon as I can."

Hank was still asleep in the corner. Magda held her breath as she inched past him and crept out into the hall and across to Isobel's room, where she'd left the radio tucked away in the window frame. God, it looked terrible out there—the sea was churning, the winds fierce and swirling.

She had to try to reach someone—to at least try to send a message, tell them what was going on.

Her hand brushed over the plaster wall, and she leaned on it for support; for a second she imagined she could see another hand, stretching toward her—but it was probably the shadows playing tricks on her. There was no reason to believe that there were fingers reaching to interlock with hers, although she could swear she felt them, real as life.

There was a heavy *thunk* behind her; Magda turned and saw the shadow of a large man advancing down the hallway toward her, and she stepped back with a startled gasp. In a second, it was gone, and she put her hands on her chest, her heart pounding.

"Magda?" That was Hank's heavy footsteps in the doorframe; it hadn't been him at the opposite end of the hall. "Was that you knocking? You need something?"

"No—what? I didn't—I didn't knock."

"I thought I heard someone knocking on the door." Hank looked rumpled and ordinary, his face creased from sleep. He looked her up and down, clearly confused by her presence in the hall. "Is it time already? I didn't hear an alarm."

"I think it's a little early yet," said Magda, praying her voice came out steady. Her heart was pounding. She needed to concentrate, not be distracted by her own imagination. Would Hank be able to tell that she knew, just from looking at her? How good of an actress was she, really? She doubted she was great. "I was just afraid to miss it. You don't have to wait, if you can get more sleep."

Hank glanced at his watch. "Nah, it's almost time. Let's just go ahead and get started now."

Magda couldn't think of any way to get rid of him that wouldn't be obvious. Numbly she picked up the radio and checked that the batteries were in. The piece that held them in place was broken, so she had to brace it with her thumb. "I thought this room might get a better signal," she said. "I could barely make contact last time."

"That thing was always a piece of crap," said Hank gloomily. Magda turned it on to static. Hopelessly she flipped it through the main stations, just in case she suddenly had connection—but there was nothing.

"You sure it's working?" asked Hank.

"He said station sixty-eight. What time is it?"

"Five till. Maybe I should be the one to talk to them," said Hank.

"I've got it," said Magda. With shaking hands, she turned the radio to the conversation frequency. The static cut out and there was silence.

Magda pressed the "Talk" button. "Francis? Do you copy? This is Magda."

"I'm not sure it's working," said Hank.

*You'd like that, wouldn't you?* thought Magda.

There was a crackle. "Francis? Francis, can you read me?"

A jangle of broken syllables, heavily interspersed with static—Magda's heart sank. It didn't seem like the connection had improved at all.

"We need to get higher," she said, already reaching for the shutters—but then there was a sudden ringing, and then sudden, sparkling silence as he spoke.

"Magda? This is Francis. How's this signal?"

"It's wonderful!" said Magda, her joy and relief obvious in her tone. "I can hear you fine. Can you hear me?"

"Mm, it's a little rough, but I think I've got you. I'm boosting my transmission so you'll receive better than you're sending. Now, I wasn't able to get the authorities on this call in all this chaos, but I've even got a little surprise here—stand by."

Magda, who had been preoccupied with exactly what she could say within Hank's earshot, paused at that. A surprise? Hank caught her gaze, eyebrows raised, and she forced herself to hold his eye contact with a shrug.

"Alright, hold on Miss Magda, I'm patching someone through. Here we go. How's this?"

"Maggie?"

Magda almost choked on her own spit. "*Bryce?* Bryce, is that you? Can you hear me?"

"Who the hell is Bryce?" asked Hank, aside.

"Magda? You're cutting out a little. And I don't know how the hell you got on a marine channel, but I don't care. How are you doing—are you alright?"

"We need help," said Hank loudly.

The radio crackled.

"There are people here with me," said Magda eagerly. Hank opened his mouth, but she pressed on; "Hank McGrath, the handyman, and a teenage girl, Emily." Damn, she didn't know if McGrath was Emily's last name. She didn't even know for sure that Emily was really her *first* name. "We're on the second floor of the house, all three of us."

Hank cleared his throat loudly, and she pulled the radio away. How could she warn them of the danger? What could she say that would put them on alert?

"Say again? Magda, it's going to get so much worse. Have you seen the satellite?"

"No, we don't have a way to get the forecast," she said, her mind still racing. "But I said I'm not alone here, Bryce—"

There was a buzz of static and she jumped, almost dropping the radio.

". . . few days," Bryce was saying, his voice suddenly louder. "Look, I called your location into the County, okay? They're going to call the Coast Guard about your location—they know you're there."

"Thank God," said Magda. "Bryce, can you hear me?"

"I think I convinced them to try and do a flyover today, okay? If you need help, put some kind of light on. Just light whatever you've got. Flashlight, flare—whatever you can get to. Let them know you're still there. Hopefully they'll see it and—Christ, I don't know, maybe they can get back there, send someone, okay?"

The radio crackled in Magda's hand.

"Bryce, I think I'm losing you," she said. "Francis, can you read? Maybe if we go to a different window," she said to Hank. "Hello? I'm not alone here," she said into the radio. "Hello?"

"Here, let me try," said Hank, taking it from her as she turned. "The tuning was always kind of shitty on this thing."

"No, I've—careful, you have to hold on the battery case," said Magda, reaching for it—

Hank fumbled with it, his bad hand clumsy. The batteries fell out, hitting the floor with a clatter and the line went dead. "Oops."

Magda dropped to her hands and knees to collect them as they rolled in all directions. With shaking hands she replaced them in the case and checked it over, clicking it on and off. It wasn't picking up. "Bryce? Francis?" It wasn't working. The radio wasn't even connecting, as far as she could tell.

To have had Bryce on the line, to have been so close to being able to tell him—and to have lost him. Again. To not be able to send a signal at all, for the words to go only one way . . . She was voiceless and adrift. Mute.

"Sorry," said Hank. "Old butterfingers."

Magda knew better than to mention that she'd fixed it once before. Maybe if she could get time alone with it, out of sight . . .

"A flyover," said Hank, rubbing his hands. "What luck! You've got friends in the right places, darlin'. God, a helicopter, that's what we need."

Magda looked out the window at the driving rain. "Hard to believe they can fly in this," she said. "Maybe we shouldn't get our hopes up." She slipped the broken radio in her pocket, hoping it was unobtrusive. She needed to find a time he wasn't around and try again.

"They've got planes that can fly right into the eye of a hurricane, right? Like on TV. We just need to have something to signal them. We need to be ready. What do we have to send a signal?"

"Well—they said a flare, but we don't have one of those. And we don't have enough batteries to try to keep a flashlight going all night, even if it was bright enough. Maybe the big lantern?"

"That could work. Or maybe a fire," said Hank. "I bet we could rig something up. A light on every side of the house."

"We can try," said Magda. As much as she wanted to avoid him, the most important thing was to keep him away from Emily. If he had tried to kill her once, he might try again. In fact, this new chance of rescue might make him more determined. If only she'd been able to make the radio call in secret!

"Let's go through our supplies, see what we've got left," she suggested. "I don't know how good our odds are, but I guess it doesn't hurt to be prepared."

"That's the spirit!" He bumped her shoulder, full of enthusiasm; Magda flinched.

Hank squinted at her. "You okay?"

"Oh! Yes, fine. Just—overwhelmed, I guess. It's a lot to take in."

He peered back at the hall. "You think Emily is asleep?"

"Yes. She looked exhausted; I'm sure she's resting."

"Did she wake up at all?" asked Hank.

It was a natural question to ask, thought Magda, a perfectly normal question for a father to have about his sick and injured daughter—and yet now with Emily's words rattling around in her mind, it took on a new, sinister edge. Perhaps he wanted to know if Emily had said anything, wanted to make sure she hadn't told Magda the truth.

"No," Magda lied. "Not really. Tossed and turned a little, is all. I'm sure she'll—I'm sure she'll pull through, though. She probably just needs to rest. Don't you want to go see about setting up a signal?" She forced herself to speak casually.

Hank glanced around the room. "Gimme a kiss first, for luck," he said, his voice low.

Magda made a fist in the pocket of her raincoat, digging the nails into the flesh of her palm. She forced herself to laugh. "Not exactly in the mood," she said truthfully.

"Aw c'mon, a man's got to have some inspiration in these times of trouble, don't he?" Of course he would feel, having had sex once, that it might be on the table again.

Magda offered a smile that felt watery, even to her.

"What's wrong? You look like you've seen a ghost."

Magda tried not to grit her teeth. "No, no—ghost." She leaned forward and brushed a dry kiss to his stubbled cheek. "That's all you're getting," she said with forced lightness, sliding past him.

He caught her wrist. "Later though, right?" he grinned.

Magda snorted, tugging free. She felt clammy and sick, and this time it wasn't just the fever. *Did he know? Could he tell?* "We'll see."

"I'll be waiting!" he called after her.

Magda took a few deep breaths. If they were going to try to send out a signal, they should probably put the large lantern in Charles's window; maybe one of the hurricane lamps on the other side of the house. She wished they could set something up on the front porch, but it would be hard to even get downstairs. How much water was on the first floor, anyway?

She needed to go down the hallway and check, but when she took a step, she almost lost her footing. Her breath felt trapped in her lungs. Was this sickness, or panic? She needed to keep moving. She needed to make sure to keep Hank in sight.

The room began to spin slowly.

She almost lost her balance, grabbing for the banister to hold herself up. Her legs wouldn't stay locked, she was dipping and spinning like a tile-a-whirl, like the first time she'd read "Antigone"—*Focus, Magda*—

"I think I'm—"

There was a roaring sound that came up from her feet, and the world wavered and went gray.

It felt to Magda, in that moment, as if a pair of burning palms pressed against her shoulders—and *pushed*. She lost her grip on the railing and slid sideways, her shoulder glancing off the wall and then sending her tumbling down the stairs.

No doubt Isobel, in the fatal moment, had some perfect distillation of phrase—but Magda, who was only mortal, was left with *Shit, fuck, shit.*

She didn't remember the descent. Just the sense of a tall man's shape, looming over her; a man with a mustache and dark hair.

"Magda!" At some point she came back to herself with a crash and managed to at least stop sliding.

"*Magda!* Are you alright?" Emily's voice was high and pinched.

"Oh yes," she called back, trying to straighten up. "How funny, I guess I just—"

She put too much weight on her back foot and slid backward off the stair. The old wood under her foot collapsed, and she fell forward with a screech as the hooked edges of the broken boards embedded themselves in the flesh behind her knee.

It didn't hurt at all, although she could feel the scrape of something against what must have been her own bone. The stairs creaked ominously, and she pictured how they would collapse in on themselves, rotted away from the bottom, and how she would fall down with them. It seemed almost inevitable, in a way, that this would happen; they had been too lucky until now; she had taken so many risks, hazard after hazard: it seemed like this was the only thing that could happen, really.

She was still holding on to a broken-off spike of railing. She kept hold of it because she might still need it.

"Jee-sus Christ," said Hank, making his way cautiously down the stairs to reach for her. Emily's pale face was peering over the railing down at her.

For Magda, whose vision was currently going haywire, it appeared as though a second face, sharp and pointed, slid in and out of focus overtop of it, like images in a lens. She blinked and her vision cleared.

"Careful, they might all collapse," she gasped to Hank, who was making his way closer. "Wait—don't. It's not safe."

"Darlin', we can't just leave you there, so just hush up and try not to move too much. It won't take but a second."

It seemed that his luck—and the staircase—held. He got to the step above her and squatted awkwardly, trying to spread his weight around. Having him close enough to touch was not reassuring, especially when she was injured, but she had no choice but to act as normally as she could. *Don't shrink away. Don't let on that you know.*

Below the knee Magda felt a spreading cold that might have been blood, or perhaps just the loss of sensation. It was not exactly pain. The body had ways, she assumed, of handling what would otherwise be unendurable.

He reached to take her under the armpits and haul her up. Magda hissed—the wood of the broken stairs was scraping along her leg. Hank cursed and tried to push the edges away with the toe of his boot. "Hold on, now."

"There's nothing else for it," said Magda evenly. "Just pull me out."

So Hank pulled, and Magda closed her eyes and pretended not to feel the broken edges of the stairs scoring her damaged skin.

"Emily, toss me a shirt or something. Is there still a tube of disinfectant in the med kit?" Hank got her sitting on the landing, which Magda didn't actually trust to hold, and examined the place where the worst piece of the wood had gone in. She was glad she couldn't feel his hands touching her. "That's deep," he said, rubbing his chin. "Hard to keep a wound like that clean in a place like this."

"Just wrap it up," said Magda. She could tell the muscle itself was damaged. She would probably have a limp, possibly for the rest of her life, just like Isobel. She had already been electrocuted—by the end she would probably end up mute and half deaf too—and then dead.

Time grayed out for a second; at some point Hank came back with an old T-shirt from his duffle and the tube of cream. "Easy, now," he said. He used the clean bottle of drinking water to rinse the wounds, his hands steady and competent. Pain was creeping back in, startling with a tingling like frostbite. Magda closed her eyes so as not to have to look at him, or her mangled lower limb.

"Can you move it?" He asked. "Go on, try, just a little. Try to wiggle your toes maybe."

She tried to flex her knee but stopped immediately at the warning spike of pain. It felt as though her bones would grind together. Staring fixedly at her toes and nothing else, Magda saw them move, although she wasn't sure how it was possible.

"Probably gonna swell up something awful," said Hank, observing.

"I'm more worried about infection," she said, brushing a hand down her calf to knock loose the remaining splinters. Hank made a face and picked out a few more carefully. She hoped it was subtle when she moved away.

"I'll give you the very cleanest part of this old shirt," he told her, tearing it into strips with his teeth. He wrapped the puncture wound first, carefully coated with the cream, and for whatever reason that was the touch that caused the pain to ignite. Magda gritted her teeth. It was only one more out of a thousand aches, at this point.

Hank did what he could for the rest of the places the splinters had broken the skin, but Magda doubted she'd be able to keep her whole lower leg wrapped for long. He tied off the fabric around her ankle and wiped his hands. "I guess that's the best we can do for now. I sure wish we had more supplies."

"It's fine," said Magda, swallowing down the pain. She imagined absorbing it into her skin, keeping it locked away inside her. Anything to get him to move away. "It will have to be fine."

"Do you hear that?" called Emily, from the top of the stairs.

The inside of Magda's head was awash with sound, but she had not assumed it was audible to others. "What?"

"I hear it," said Hank. "Come on, Magda. Up, up the stairs."

"What is it?"

"Up you get," he said, taking her under one arm. She gasped and jerked away, unable to conceal it—it was too much, after letting him touch the wounds, letting him hunch over her in the stairwell when she was dizzy and sick.

"Jeez," he said, backing off with his hands up. "What's your problem?"

Magda stared at him, unable to answer, her mind slack with dread.

"What's your problem?" he repeated, his hand gripping her arm.

"It's getting closer!" called Emily.

Magda forced herself to concentrate, listening: low humming, a drone that stood apart from the wind and the rain.

"Oh God, the helicopter," said Magda. "A signal—we have to set up a signal—hurry!"

Without a word, Hank half dragged her up to the top of the stairs, as she scrambled to keep the weight off her bad leg, which was heavy and numb.

"What do we have?" he said, disappearing into the room. "We need something for each window. What can we use?"

Magda's mind was a blur of pain and panic. "The big lantern and the lamp," she stuttered, looking around. "There's another oil lamp around here somewhere, or there was. It should still have oil. Here. It's here. I have—I have a lighter."

"Emily, deal with the lantern," said Hank, coming back. The engine sound was distinct now, coming closer.

Magda's hands were shaking as she lifted the glass chimney from the base of the lamp. She fumbled for the butane lighter in her pocket and flicked the tip over the wick. It didn't strike and she tried again, afraid to exhale. This time it caught—and held.

The wick turned brown under the flame, threads curling. The air was too damp.

"C'mon, c'mon," said Magda.

They could deal with everything else later, she thought; if they could get back to civilization, she'd find a way to keep Emily and herself safe from Hank. She just needed help. There were some things a historian just wasn't equipped to handle.

"Steady now," said Hank.

The sound of the helicopter was getting louder, cutting through the storm.

On the next pass, the wick caught with a puff of black smoke. Magda adjusted the flame with the knob, still holding her breath. She replaced the chimney and they all watched the weaving, unsteady light. "We need to get it to the window in Isobel's room," said Magda, forgetting that he probably didn't know what room that was.

The rumbling was getting closer, the puttering of rotor blades like a promise of safety.

"I've got it," said Hank.

He picked it the lamp around the base; it was top-heavy and started to swing. Magda darted out a hand to right it.

"Hurry!" she said. "Go!"

Would a helicopter be able to land in the middle of a storm like this? Or send down a basket like in the movies, maybe? How soon could they be back in the world—an hour? A day? She pictured the sheer relief of a shower and a hot meal: the first cup of strong Cuban coffee or, better, rum.

Hank was still standing, listening too.

"Hurry, go!"

She looked up at him. The bouncing light of the lamp cast grotesque shadows over the walls. His face seemed to waver; a man with a mustache. He looked directly at her and smiled, his expression stretched like the gaping of a skull. Magda gasped, but in the next moment he was turning to disappear into Isobel's room.

*Almost over,* she promised herself. *It's almost over now.* "Emily," she called, her voice raw.

The girl appeared, clinging to the doorframe. At least she was back on her feet. But the room behind her was dark.

"Emily, didn't you get the lantern?"

"He knows," whispered Emily. "Magda, he *knows.*"

Magda shook her head, biting down hard on her lip. "Where is the lantern? We need to hurry." The engine sounded like it was right on top of them now. She braced on the wall and dragged herself, mostly crawling. "Help me up," she said, reaching for Emily when she was close enough. "Hank, did you get to the window?"

There was no answer.

Emily bolstered her onto her feet. Neither of them were steady. Hank was the only one still standing.

"Give me the lantern, we can flash it on and off— Hank," she shouted, "They're almost on top of us!"

"The battery is gone," said Emily.

"What? It was there a minute ago." The big lantern had a massive power cell, not the little AAAs.

But Emily held it up and the battery case was empty.

*"Hank!"*

There was no answer.

Had Hank—had Hank taken it out? Why? Just to make sure that he was the only one who could control the light?

"Magda, what are we going to *do*?"

The sound of the helicopter was so loud; they must be right overhead.

"Hand me the little flashlight," said Magda, desperate now. "I've got the radio batteries, we can put them back in. Maybe it'll be enough."

"He doesn't want anyone to know about us," said Emily, sobbing.

"Emily, *the flashlight*. Hank, they're on top of us! Please!"

Emily brought the little flashlight over, and Magda loaded it with shaking hands.

"Go see what he's doing," she said. "He's got to get the lamp to the window!"

Emily staggered into the hallway to peek. "He's standing against the wall," she reported, shrinking back.

It was on purpose, Magda realized. He didn't want them to be rescued. Why? Surely he wanted to live as much as she did. Didn't he realize they were all going to drown here?

She clicked the flashlight; the light came on, reedy and unsteady. "Take it to the window," she told Emily, shoving it into her hands. "Flick it on and off."

The sound of the engine was moving farther away.

Emily rushed to do it, but the light was feeble, not nearly enough to send a signal amid all the noise and confusion of the storm, surely. "It's not going to work," she said, sobbing.

"It has to work," said Magda. The alternative was unthinkable.

There had to be something: *Think Magda, think!* The oil lamp from Isobel's room was out of oil, and she didn't

have the lighter—was there a mirror, a phone, a flame anywhere . . .?

There was a sudden crash—it sounded like the noise a
glass lamp might make hitting a plaster wall. Magda could
picture the precious oil sinking into the hardwood floor.
She wondered if there was any chance she could get in
there and light it up. Better to let the house burn down
around them than lose this only chance to escape.

The drone of the engines was fading. Magda swallowed a sob. "Keep trying," she told Emily. "Don't stop."

Emily was already weeping; Magda would have liked
to join her, but forced it back.

The sound moved off, wavered, and disappeared.

"They're gone," said Magda, hollowed out. "We missed
them."

Maybe they would try again, she thought hopelessly.
Bryce knew someone was here. Whimbrel House was not
exactly hard to find.

But they might assume no lights and nobody outside meant
there was nothing worth taking the risk of coming closer.

*They were trapped.*

She sank down on the camping cot, bad leg extended,
and put her hands over her eyes.

"I don't think they could see us," said Hank, bursting
back into the room. "I'm not even sure that was a rescue
copter anyway. Damn hard to tell where anything is, echoing like that in all this confusion. Could've been further
out than it sounded, whatever it was."

Magda didn't bother to ask about the battery, or the
lamp. There was no point. "I need—I need to lie down for
a while," she said faintly. She felt like a guttering candle,
almost out. "Emily, you must be exhausted too. Come here
and lie down with me."

She had to get back in touch with Frances, tell him what had happened. Without Hank standing over her.

"You're going to sleep?" Hank raised his eyebrow, suspicious as Emily scooted in under her arm, huddled up close. Magda covered her in her jacket, tucking it in.

"My leg is killing me, I'm worn out," said Magda truthfully, lying back. "What else is there anyway? We're just waiting now."

"I . . . guess so," said Hank, clearly suspicious. "Well, I suppose I could use a break."

"Can we sleep in shifts?" asked Magda, closing her eyes. Emily pressed closer. Magda wrapped an arm around her tightly. There wasn't enough space for both of them on the cot, but neither moved.

"Hey, I'm tired too, you know."

Magda counted her breaths, very slowly. In and out.

Hank muttered to himself, digging through the duffel bag, seemingly not attempting to be quiet. When he stood still, Magda imagined she could feel his gaze roving over their bodies, and she fought not to shudder.

Finally he went out into the hall, shutting the door ungently behind him.

"Magda," Emily breathed, "what are we going to do?"

"Give me the flashlight. I've still got the radio. We can put the batteries back. We just need to be very, very quiet."

"He's never going to let us leave," whispered Emily. "Not alive."

Magda closed her eyes and didn't respond. She counted to ten, slowly. "Come on, sweetheart. Get me the batteries."

In the perfect darkness, Magda did what she could to repeat her previous trick, cleaning the contacts. She slipped the batteries back in, but this time she suspected some wire was loose somewhere. She was fumbling, trying to jiggle the places where they might have lost contact—the switch, the battery wires, hoping that jostling them might make a difference.

At one point, there was a crackle of static that had them both gasping.

"I won't be able to get a signal in here, even if it's working," Magda whispered.

Her best option was the balcony. It was convenient sometimes, to live in a house that was entirely made of doors.

"He'll hear you," said Emily, holding her tighter.

"What else can I do?"

"We have to wait. He'll have to pee, or he'll get bored sitting out there. Just wait till he moves."

So they lay in silence, listening for the creak of floorboards. But there was nothing. Had he fallen asleep out there?

"I have to try," said Magda.

One leg was almost useless as she maneuvered herself up and out of bed. She dragged it behind her to the double doors that led out to the balcony, clutching the radio.

It would be impossible to open both the door and the shutters without making a sound. Magda paused with her hand on the knob, coughed once and turned it in the same second. But the hinges would still groan at the very least.

"Magda, I think he's going to the bathroom," whispered Emily. "Wait."

When the creak from the hallway was evident, Magda hurried to pull open the inner doors, flinching at every sound, and then scrabbled at the hurricane shutters, pushing them open. The wind and rain, triumphant, streamed in.

CHAPTER

# 16

Friday, October 11th
8:00 AM

IMMEDIATELY HER HEART started racing at the sheer power of the storm, which blasted her back—standing out in it, even under the relative protection of the overhanging roof, seemed insane. The water hammered down like it was being shot from a nail gun. Still Magda crept out onto the balcony, holding tight to the railing. Pressed up against the wall, she was able to keep at least the radio relatively dry.

Magda turned on the radio, hearing nothing at first above the storm. She suspected the speaker wasn't working, but she checked that the light came on and carefully turned the whole thing on and off a couple times in a deliberate pattern. Three long, three short.

A crackle of something. She held the radio, tinny, to her ear. Nothing. Was she on the right channel? She could hardly tune it in the dark. It was impossible to hear over the wind and rain.

On, off, on, off, on, off. *Mayday, Mayday.*

She imagined Bryce on the other hand, asking her questions: *"Is that you, Magda? Are you okay?"* But she couldn't hear.

She just clicked the radio on and off.

*People know we're here,* she reminded herself. *They will come looking.*

Eventually.

There was a sputtering cackle, but the signal was lost. No matter what Magda tried to do, nothing brought it back to life.

Standing on the balcony outside of Charles's bedroom, Magda realized for the first time that the big window overlooked the place that had been Isobel's grave.

*Click, click, click.* It wasn't working.

She imagined him slipping down the dark stairs, the rifle in his hand. He would have picked a day when the house was empty, the servant's day off. He would have had as many hours as he needed, uninterrupted.

According to the book, the Springfield rifle took time to reload—he would have only had one chance. Had he been a good shot? He had been raised hunting fowl in the Keys; he might well have been. That she had died instantly on impact seemed certain, given the size of the hole in her skull. Somehow Magda was certain she hadn't merely turned her back and let him take aim. No, it had been a surprise—while she was looking away, standing, perhaps, under one of the Key limes, looking up at the crop. She had died in September. The fruit would have still been ripe on the branches; they bore all year long in frostless islands.

Or perhaps she was looking out over the water, watching the birds, as Magda had done a thousand times in the same spot.

The cistern was already partially filled in. When it was done he would have carried her here, opened the trunk which had been left or borrowed from Robert Margery, tucked her in one last time. Cleared out the space, then covered it over.

She kept pressing the switch, on and off. On and off.

*I'm sorry, Bryce. You did your best.*

*Click, click, click.*

The door shut. "What the hell are you doing out here?" asked Hank, coming over. "Why did you leave Emily?"

"She's asleep," said Magda. "She's—she's fine. Leave her be."

Hank studied her, his face perfectly expressionless. Magda took an involuntary step back. He looked like an empty shell like that, like a container waiting to be filled.

"You're right," he said at last with a smile. "I'm sure she'll be fine." He stepped in front of the door, blocking it with his body. "If it wasn't for this storm, it'd be a nice thing, these big windows being doors to the balcony. Hard to see much through the shutters, though." He inspected the open door. "This doesn't look like old glass."

"No, the original panes upstairs were broken long ago. This was all replaced with hurricane glass, although we did restore the frames and the lead panels downstairs."

Sometimes Magda could hear herself talk and almost rolled her own eyes.

The rain was furious now, slamming into the side of the house like a wall of water. How was it possible for there to be any water *left* in the sky? It had been dumping swimming pools for days. She supposed the storm had the whole of the ocean to work with.

She didn't have any kind of weapon. She had left her jacket—the penknife—with Emily, who didn't even know it was there. The closest she could think of was the useless, rusted rifle—which didn't even fire.

Magda stepped to the side. "I should go back to Emily," she said. "Back to bed."

"It's quite a view, ain't it?" he said, ignoring her. "This balcony is holding up pretty good, long as you don't get too close to the edge. But who would do that, right?"

Magda started to stagger around the side of the house—there were other doors in. But her leg was useless and Hank easily overtook her, reaching to snag her arm. He closed around her like a trap, bracing himself against the corner railing. His hands were burning hot against her skin; she remembered thinking, when they'd been together, that he ran so much hotter than her.

"Don't you want to look at it?" he asked. He dragged her out from under the roof. With the state of her left leg, she had almost no chance of resisting him. Instantly she was soaked by the water streaming off the gutters.

"It's almost pretty, don't you think?" he shouted, still looking out. "In a weird kind of way?"

"Hank, no," she said, turning her body away from the railing of the balcony. They were high enough that the drop made her heart lurch sickly. The water outside was so murky and dark, swirling with debris, and it looked—it looked *hungry*.

"Sorry, darlin'," he said, and the thing was, he really did sound kind of sorry. But Magda could tell she was becoming only a thing to him, an inconvenience. He was deleting her. She was watching it happen in his face. He must have done the same thing to Emily when he'd decided to drown her, deciding she'd become too much of a nuisance.

Magda had wondered how it was possible for Charles to kill his own daughter—the child he'd raised from

infancy, who by all accounts he'd been anxiously guarding
for years, protective, loving. But she was beginning to
understand.

"This fucking house," he said. "We never should have
come here."

"Hank, *don't*," she said, as he tightened his grip on
her arm. She was trying to keep her balance, keeping her
weight on her one good leg, trying to keep away from the
edge—

He swung her around without a warning, and Magda
had no chance to brace before she felt herself thrown hard
against the iron railing. She would have screamed, if she
could have caught her breath, but there was not time even
for that, before there were hands on her shoulders—and
then she was falling, her arms flailing wildly, trying to grab
hold of nothing. The walls of her beloved house flew past
her, and then she was plunged into the icy arms of the water.

She surfaced. Thrashed, went back down, and then
surfaced again.

*There was a man standing on the porch. Magda shoved
her wet hair out of her eyes, trying to call out, but her voice
was gone—and yet she could see him watching, coolly apprais-
ing her. A man in a brown three-piece suit, his edges blurring,
a brown bowler hat and a dark mustache—no, it was a black
ballcap and a brown camo jacket, it was Hank, it was
Hank—and he watched as the wave swept over her and
pulled her down, covering over her head, dragging her out
away from the house.*

*       *       *

There were waves pulling her in all directions—from off
the ocean and from off the land. Magda tumbled in the
surf, unable to put her feet down. One of her legs, the

useless one, was alight with pain from the saltwater, but she couldn't concentrate on it. She wasn't sure where she was or which way the water was carrying her. It was as much as she could do to tilt her head and breathe when her face found the air. Her loose hair streaming in her face and the lashing rain obscured her sight above water.

She felt the leaves of what might have been a lime tree skating along her sides—then a piece of flotsam, perhaps from the wreck of the lemur garden, careened straight into her and she went under again, all the air knocked out of her lungs, disoriented—and then the long grass down at the shore, through her fingers like hair. Then she felt something under her fingertips, and as she rolled, bumping her knees.

Oh God, it was the *dock*—she was feeling the battered wood of the dock skimming along her bare legs as the water dragged her farther out—just like so many people who had lost their lives here, she thought in the last seconds as she was swept all the way off the end and out into endless dark of the open ocean.

*   *   *

It was a hot day in the back seat of a crosstown bus. Magda's thighs were sticking to the pleather seats. They had just come from playing four days at a festival and were going to catch a train to El Paso for a gig that might last anywhere from ten days to two weeks. This was after the car had broken down while her dad was still saving up to buy the van.

Magda cleared her throat. "I want to move in with Gramma in Ishpeming," she said. The words she had practiced saying in a thousand cracked and cloudy motel mirrors.

Her dad grunted. "No one wants to move to Ishpeming," he said. "Do you know how hard I worked to get the hell out of Ishpeming? Do you know how many generations of Trudells are frozen into that godforsaken rock?"

"But I can stay there until I finish high school. I want to go to college."

He sighed. "Mags, school is fine, but it's not real life, you know? This is real life." He motioned to the hunched passengers of the bus, the streaming sunshine outside, the gritty road rolling under the tires. "You're not going to learn anything from those books that you can't learn out here."

"I want to study Isobel's poetry," said Magda.

"Jeez, not this again."

"I want to become an expert in everything about her life."

"C'mon, you've read every poem, what else do you think there is to know? You think she sat in a classroom to learn to write like that? Those poems aren't about a bunch of—dusty research, or whatever. You don't have to move to the literal end of the world to read poems."

*It's not the end of the world, but you can see it from here:* an old Upper Peninsula joke.

"It's only two years," said Magda, as if two years was not an unimaginably long time for either of them to stay in one place.

"Did your gran put you up to this?"

"No, I wrote to her. I asked her."

He lit a cigarette and smoked it thoughtfully. That was back in the days when smoking on a bus was still possible.

Magda had expected a fight, had a plan to take the go-bag and disappear if she had to. They'd had a similar discussion a year ago when they went home for a Christmas, and she hadn't won then.

Maybe it was because they'd lost the car; maybe it was because their finances were even worse than usual; maybe it was because he was still thinking of the festival in Reno, a bad city to leave a sixteen-year-old girl alone in for weeks at a time.

"Look, Magpie," he said at last. "It was my dream to get away from Ishpeming. I wanted to sing songs, tell stories. And that's not your dream. I get that. If you say you want to go back now and *read* stories—I mean, I don't understand that, but . . . maybe I don't need to understand, you know?"

He took a long drag, held it in.

"I know whatever you do, it's going to be something special."

He offered her the cigarette, and she smoked the rest of it.

"Listen, we get to El Paso, we'll scrape together the cash for a plane ticket, okay? And, uh, maybe a winter coat. Or like three. Some ice skates, maybe."

Her grandmother sent the money for the ticket in the end, and two weeks later Magda was studying the parts of speech in a classroom that smelled like mold and wet cement. *This is real life too,* she'd written then. One of the thousands of letters he hadn't answered.

But the year she graduated, he'd sent her a roll of two dollar coins and a note that said, *Don't forget to pick your head up sometimes, okay?*

That was less than a year before the crash.

*   *   *

Magda coughed and vomited saltwater, feeling like she had swallowed the entire ocean. The churning mass was full of debris, what she assumed was the wreck of the whole neighborhood and all her own efforts of the last ten years. Sometimes it sliced the skin of her legs and feet, sometimes it bobbed harmlessly past her. It should have been impossible to keep her chin above the chopping waves, but in the saltwater she was surprisingly buoyant.

Something bumped into her chest, and she grabbed it—it was floating, a milk jug perhaps. She felt as if she must be in the middle of the ocean now, and there was not another living thing for miles—just herself, bobbing with the empty plastic bottle in her arms.

Her mind was perfectly blank and still. She was impossibly small. She felt she could see, as if by drone footage, her perspective rising up above the waves, zooming out over the whole of the inlet, over the empty deserted isle— the hundreds of perilous miles of storm-tossed ocean.

But she was tethered by the knowledge of Isobel's skeleton tucked under the stairs on the balcony, of Emily lying with her arms wrapped around her knees on the cot. Would anybody ever know what happened to either of them? Or would they disappear and be erased from history, together. Maybe all three of their bones would end up in the water stretching across centuries to mingle their knuckles and ribs together on the ocean floor.

She wished she had found a way to get a message to Merrick, the only person she could think of who would be as fervent about Isobel as she was. Sent him the sketch of the rifle, a description of the thorn in the shoe, and her notes about the bones. At least someone would have *known*, would have cared. It wouldn't have all been for nothing.

A wave swept over her head, abruptly, from behind. Magda hadn't been trying to swim, completely disoriented as to even which way was back toward shore. Another wave swamped her, and she lost the plastic jug and flailed, slipping under. It was perfectly dark and still beneath the water. Her own gasp didn't even release bubbles.

She came back up from sheer buoyancy, having barely offered a kick to help, and instinctively lay backward as soon as she broke the surface, letting the water hold her up. She watched her own chest fill, her feet rising alongside her abdomen. Another wave would be her last.

The ocean water felt cold, but not as bad as it could have been in October—or else she was just so used to living soaked to the skin that she had forgotten the temperature of dry air. At least she was fully dressed. Even her shoes were still on her feet, although she was sure she'd heard it was better to kick them off in the water. She was lucky everything she was wearing was light. Isobel's gray dress had been said to drag her down, sodden, heavy wool—but of course that had never been true. The whole story was fabricated. There was little chance she had died like this, like Magda was in the process of doing.

Maybe it wouldn't be so bad to turn into the coral and the sea. Maybe she would come back as a bird, like Isobel said.

Something—something wooden—bobbed against her outstretched fingers, and she slowly rolled over on top of it, pulling it in underneath her breasts. Clinging to what might have been an old shutter, Magda bobbed and lost track of all time.

She wondered how far she had been swept out, how long she had been dragged and floated. Was she miles off the coast? Was she all the way out past the end of the Key? Would she wash up on the Dry Tortugas, where she had spent the happiest days of her life snorkeling with Bryce— or circle around south and end up in Cuba, perhaps. She wondered if a hurricane would drive away sharks, if they'd avoid debris-strewn water and clamor. Thrashing was said to attract them, and she wasn't thrashing. Just bobbing along, a piece of jetsam.

It could have been hours or days—it felt like years. She kept waiting for the end, either from some toothed inhabitant of the ocean, or from a wave that finally succeeded in breaking right over her head and dragging her down. But the end didn't come. Only the endless crash of the water and the howling of the storm. She began to feel disconnected from herself, almost sleepy. The worst that could happen had already happened—the destruction of the house, realizing Isobel had been murdered and the murderer had gotten away with it all these years—and now her complete failure to protect Emily, Hank's betrayal, and likely now her own death. It had all taken on a dreamlike tone as she was rocked by the waves.

It seemed to her, as she floated, that it *was* all a dream. Maybe—most likely, in fact—she had been lying on the ground behind the house ever since the electrical surge had knocked her off her feet, that first night. Perhaps she was still lying there in the electrical shed. Or perhaps she had died there, electrocuted just like Abigail Reyes. Perhaps this was the afterlife, a world where nothing made sense.

Whimbrel House had always been haunted, she thought dizzily, but *she* was the ghost.

Another wave swept over her, and Magda was taken totally off guard, sputtering and gasping as she sank down into the trough—and her feet brushed against something underneath her. She gasped and pulled them away, thinking irrationally that it might be something living, and then more rationally that it might be debris that would cut her to ribbons—but in the next drop she was pressed down into it, first lightly, then again so hard that her knees folded. And it was sand. The sandy bottom of the beach. The next wave picked her up and off it again, pulling her backward.

She could barely swim with one good leg, but still she scrambled forward, aware she could be about to step onto sharp reef or lose her footing entirely and be swept out to sea. She was making progress until she started to feel resistance in the current—it was getting harder to advance. *Don't panic, Magda. Keep calm.* She could manage a front crawl that was mostly arm. Maybe if she tried swimming parallel to shore like someone stuck in a riptide . . .

There—under her feet, her bad leg, *ow*—land.

Somehow she had been washed back to shore.

These were Isobel's waters, she thought dizzily. They had swept her out, and now they were bringing her back. Just like the suicides from the end of the dock.

She supposed there was logic, in that the waves that were pushed by wind up onto the beach in the first place might have been driven back into land again the next time the winds came around, circular. She had thought she was out in the middle of the ocean, but it was equally possible she had never been more than a hundred feet from shore.

Something snagged onto her outstretched fingers, and then in a rush she was pressed against what felt like clawed hands, digging into her skin. Her knees hit muck. She was caught up in the mangroves, what was left of them. They lined the shore all the way to the southern edge of the estate. The branches were cutting her hands but their sturdy bases were thick enough, even in the midst of all this chaos, to support her weight: after all, they were made to survive storms like these. What to humans was a disaster was to them merely an opportunity to propagate.

Magda locked her hands around them and held on, getting her knees underneath her, scrabbling up. The bushy arms seemed to embrace her, drawing her in like a mother would cradle a child tired from playing. Kneeling in the mud, Magda closed her eyes, trying to shut out the terrible racket of the storm, her own fear and pain and exhaustion, tuning out the cold and the wet. She felt certain that if she just kept her eyes closed, she'd be safe. With her eyes closed, she could imagine she was sheltered in a beautiful house—Whimbrel House, but even better, fully restored—full of books and words, where everything was clean and orderly, placed in exactly the right spot. And she could stay there forever, even as the years rolled past, and then decades and then centuries, a noiseless perfect shadow in a brilliant light-filled house.

If she opened her eyes, she'd be plunged back into the world of suffering and ruin, where everything seemed impossible, with only greater struggle and destruction ahead of her: shattered furniture, ocean water soaking through plaster, bricks crumbling away, roofs collapsing, priceless treasures destroyed in front of her eyes. A world of blood and sweat and saltwater.

*I fought,* said Isobel. *I fought for my right to live. I didn't just give up.*

Magda could picture her now, walking in the shade of the garden. Her father, watching from the porch, waiting for her to turn away. The rifle, shiny then and well maintained, resting in the crook of his arms. He lined up his shot, his face wet.

She pictured Isobel falling down to the green grass, her short, exceptional life draining out into the sea and sky.

The fingers of the mangroves tangled in her hair and tugged. Magda opened her eyes.

She was bleeding badly from the wound in her thigh, which had reopened in the water and stung horrifically. The salinity might have decreased from all the rain, but it was still salt in a wound. Magda forced herself to imagine, instead of disease and contamination, that the ocean was burning it clean.

The bullet that had entered the back of Isobel's skull, low and tight—Magda was no physician, but she was guessing it would have been quick, maybe so quick as to be unrecognizable, or maybe it was something like this—a dizziness that came up from the extremities and lodged, throbbing and like canons and drums, in the brain—

*Focus,* thought Magda. Emily. Emily was out there, with Hank.

By some marvel of wind and water, she had been washed back into shore, and Magda wasn't one to waste a miracle. What would Hank do to Emily, believing that Magda was dead? He had only tried to kill her when Magda herself remained ignorant; perhaps, if he believed her drowned, Emily was safe for now. But only for so long as she remained obedient, and none of them—not Magda, not Isobel, and not Emily—could remain obedient for long.

Magda hauled herself up into the tall grass, apologizing to the mangroves that had saved her for pulling out their roots. But she had saved them first. And they were unkillable—even the act of tearing them up only helped them to proliferate.

When she gained the land, she looked up to see Isobel standing in the shallow water, in her long dark dress, watching Magda with solemn eyes.

"Finally," said Magda, with a sigh.

Isobel's hair was tangled and loose, falling to her waist, and she was soaking wet, as though she too had been standing out in the storm. Waiting.

Without a word, she turned, facing away—back to the house, Magda understood, although she couldn't tell where it was in the gloom. Without looking back, Isobel took a step, and then another.

Of course she must be delirious. It was the only thing that made sense. But Magda didn't care.

"I'm coming! Wait—wait for me. I'm right behind you."

Magda staggered to her feet, the water streaming off her like a sheet. Her bad leg was locked up and useless, the wrappings long gone, the wound exposed to everything in the air and sea. She leaned forward on her knees and spat seawater, coughing. *Alive.* She was alive. And she was the only person who could save Emily, the only person who could ever tell the truth about Isobel's life and death. Maybe she was sick and injured and half dead, but her work wasn't finished yet.

When she straightened up, Isobel was gone. But if she kept the sea on her right side, Magda could follow the line of mangroves all the way back to Whimbrel House.

CHAPTER

# 17

Friday, October 11<sup>th</sup>
12:00 PM

THE WALK BACK to the house from the far edge of the
property would have taken less than twenty minutes
on a mild day, following the shoreline. For Magda, in the
gusting rain, sick and dehydrated, with only one good leg,
it took hours. She focused on breathing—two deep breaths
in, one strong blown-out exhale. Pause. Repeat. She had to
pause often to cup her hands under the dripping leaves to
drink what fresh water she could collect. Puffing like a
woman in childbirth, she managed to keep moving.

Although it should be midday, all was gloomy and
dark as dusk.

Finally the house loomed from out of the open water.
The same surge that had pushed Magda back to shore had
surrounded the building. Hank's runabout was still tied to
the porch like a dog on a leash.

She knew every inch of the terrain by feel, so it was
possible to keep to the highest ground, circling around to
the back of the house in the half light. Was she being
watched from within? Perhaps, if Hank was standing in

the right window at the right time. But the house was dark and silent. With so few windows uncovered, it wouldn't be impossible to stay out of sight, and even easier once she got in close.

At the moment, she needed strength, and she had at least an idea of where to get it.

She waded to the side garden. Her mouth was still dry with the salt of the ocean, so she cupped a few palmfuls in the rainwater that was overflowing from the birdbath, swished and spat. A second scoop she swallowed.

In the shadow of the house, Magda felt impossibly strong. She'd had almost nothing to eat in days, but the cold water felt like all she could ever need. Even her injuries, her illness, seemed to be healing, unattended, with near-supernatural speed.

It was also possible she might be delirious.

She felt for the bobbing flag of the fish trap. Perhaps it had been swept out to sea too—but no, there it was, wedged where she had left it.

She pulled it up. The woven pieces were broken, and her heart sank—but lifting it higher, there was something of weight inside it. A dead crab. Perhaps it had been trapped and then bashed to death on the rocks, poor thing.

Magda tore it apart with her fingers and ate it raw in a few bites. She didn't think it was recommended, health-wise, but at least it probably wouldn't kill her right away.

She picked shell out of her teeth with the tip of the claw.

She had no way to defeat Hank, and he had all the advantage; safe inside the house with dry clothes, all the food she had gathered the day before, clean water, and medicine. Magda had crawled out of the ocean with nothing but what she could scavenge or forage; even her clothes were torn. And she was trapped outside in a storm that could shift again at any second.

She needed to even the odds a little. She climbed up carefully onto the porch to get out of the rain, but fell back with a cry as something—something wet and slimy—curled around her ankle in the water.

This was it, finally, she thought. She had been waiting so long for that snake or octopus or some slithery sea creature unknown to man to find her, and here it was at last, and she wasn't even afraid.

*You're being an idiot,* said Isobel.

Magda looked down and found that it was long a coil of blue rope, which must have washed into the garden and gotten tangled. From the pickup, she remembered now—holding the plywood on the back of Hank's truck. Bastard must have let it blow away as trash.

*Please concentrate, Magda.*

It was a strong, thick line, and it occurred to her that it might be useful. She shook herself and climbed back down to retrieve it. As she shook it loose, she paused, then had to laugh: she was standing in what had been a bed of pigeonberry and low-growing Florida silver palm. Although she had planted it herself, it seemed miraculous: pigeonberry was used as a poultice in swamp medicine, to reduce pain and promote healing.

She pulled it up with the rest of the rope and crushed the roots and garlic-scented leaves. She packed it around her wound, then wrapped the whole thing in the long leaves of the silver palm, for waterproofing.

There was a good twenty feet of rope, all told, so she doubled that up, making a coil, and slung it over her shoulder like a jaunty bandolier. Or like her father's guitar strap, maybe.

The house seemed silent, but they must be inside. There was nowhere else to go. She braced against the wall and shuddered at the feel of it grinding under her hand. Was this what it felt like when a building shifted on its foundation?

Well, there was one way to get their attention. Magda skirted around to the kitchen side door, pulled one of Hank's busted hurricane shutters off its dangling hinges— and swung it full force against the glass window.

The sound was incredible.

Now she just needed to sink back into the shadows to wait. If nobody came, at least she could unlock the window and climb in.

But after a beat there was the sound of heavy footsteps. The door flew open and Hank spilled out, holding Magda's own flashlight above his head, peering out into the darkness.

Magda stepped forward into the light. She stood there, wordless. It seemed to her that Isobel was standing right next to her, or maybe even in front of her, a faintly doubled vision, blurred around the edges.

He stared at her, uncomprehending. "Magda," he said. "My God, you're—you're *dead*."

"I think I just might be," said Magda, coming forward.

Hank stumbled backward, and he turned to grab the damned rifle from behind the door. Holding it by the fore-stock, he swung hard at her head, but Magda anticipated the arc of it, as if she'd known what he would do before he did—she ducked to the side before he connected, and left him staggering, off balance.

She let herself drop down off the porch as he hit the stock, full strength, against one of concrete pillars where she had been standing. Tiny antique fragments of wood and steel rained down over Magda's head and shoulders.

She didn't advance, and when he recovered, he followed her down off the porch with a splash, seized her shoulder and shoved her hard into the wall of the gift shop. "I'll make sure you don't come back again," he said, his eyes wild.

Magda heard movement through the wall behind her, and as Hank grabbed at her, trying to get his hands around her neck, she backed up into the broken door and turned the handle hard, falling inward when it opened.

"What the—"

Hank's cry was cut off as the white bird glided soundlessly through the doorway, almost directly into his face. A heron was a surprisingly large bird up close, and Magda used the element of surprise to rip the broken rifle out of his hands and swing it hard enough to nearly crack his skull as the bird sailed off overhead.

That was all a rusted rifle was good for, to be used as a club. The wood, soaked and dried and soaked again, cracked along the grain.

Hank fell, soundless, and Magda threw the broken gun deep into the gift shop and slammed the door, turning without checking to see if he was alive or dead. She limped back to the kitchen side. The water was already up past the steps, blocking her from opening it until she used all her weight.

"*Emily!* Emily, where are you?"

The water had definitely risen, waist-height through the whole first floor and still climbing. Furniture was sloshing and rolling—she had to dodge a wooden chair that she remembered buying from an estate sale up in Orlando.

"Emily?" Had he killed her anyway, even believing Magda was dead?

"M-Magda?"

It was faint, and coming from the upstairs. Magda waded through the water in the hallway and made her way to the center of the house.

The rotted stairs were half collapsed, spreading out from where she had fallen through them. She leaned on the lower banister—it was starting to shift on its base—and peered up through the gloom. "Emily, are you still up there?"

A pale head appeared over the railing at the top. "I thought you were dead," she said softly. "He said you were dead. He said I got you killed."

Magda had the mad desire to waggle a cigar and say, *"Rumors of my demise have been greatly exaggerated."* Instead, she said, "He was lying. I'm okay, honey. But we have to get out of here."

"Where is he?" asked Emily, shrinking back.

"I think I knocked him out. I don't know how much time we have, though. We have to get to the boat, okay? You don't want to be on the second floor with the way this water's coming up."

"Where are we going to go?" asked Emily.

"I don't know, but it's not too bad out there right now. I was just out in it. The flooding is getting worse, but the wind and rain aren't that strong. We can take the boat and try to get—somewhere."

"I can't get down," said Emily. "He pushed me, I think my ankle is broken."

*Could anything get any worse?* "Okay, honey, I'm coming up. I'm going to help you, alright?"

She scrambled mostly one-footed up the stairs, which were clearly starting to collapse from the bottom; she had always suspected they had been rebuilt during the bed-and-breakfast era, no doubt out of inferior materials. She wondered what the original staircase had looked like. The metal spiral of a ship's stairs? That would have probably withstood the hurricane better.

The plaster of the stairs slipped away every place she set her foot, but she was able to skirt around the broken boards and reach the top. Nothing was left on the landing. All the antiques were gone. She could only send a prayer for the books and the painting in the attic—there was nothing else she could do for them now.

"Emily? I'm here. We need to go."

Emily had a new black eye. She was huddled in the corner, still wearing Magda's raincoat, holding her ankle. Magda bent over to examine it. It was swollen and purple, but she wasn't sure if it was broken or just badly sprained.

"Maybe we should stay here," said Emily. "We're safer inside than out in the storm, right? And we can lock him out. We could—we could go up onto the roof, if we had to."

"The water is coming up too fast," said Magda gently. "It's too—it's too late. There's nothing else we can do here. We have to leave."

"I'm scared," said Emily. "Hank could . . . he could still be out there, right?"

"I'll do it with you," said Magda. "Take my hand; we'll go together."

Emily closed her eyes and reached out her hand. Magda took it and their fingers locked. She helped her to stand and brace herself on her good foot. "Okay?" asked Magda. Emily shrugged.

"Let's go."

"Let me get my jacket."

Emily packed up as Magda stood looking out the double doors from Charles's bedroom. The shutters had broken and were hanging sideways. The glass would be next.

Although she couldn't see it, she knew she was looking at the site of Isobel's grave. The first thing he saw when he woke up, and the last thing before he went to bed. Had he avoided the view or looked at it every day?

He must have poured the gravel himself, later, after the ground had settled. On the early flyover photos, there was a garden there. Had he dropped in the bulbs himself, trumpet lilies and asphodel? He must have, Magda realized—who else would have known the significance? Flowers for funerals, for graves. Isobel would have liked that.

He must have stood in this window, watching the flowers grow in around the old cistern. Brought his new bride here, that one year of their married life they had lived at Whimbrel House. Perhaps she had cut the lilies in the summer and arranged them through the house, that heavy scent of death. He must have shuddered to smell it. However had he stood it?

Well, he hadn't, she supposed—they were gone from the house before another summer blossomed. And then dead in a ship that he should have abandoned when it foundered, taking his wife and son with him. Perhaps the new life he had hoped for had disappointed him. Perhaps he was thinking of her, of Isobel, when the last wave came.

"Okay, I'm ready," said Emily.

Why hadn't he thrown the gun into the sea, buried it in the trunk, or destroyed it? Why hide it in the wall? It was as if he'd wanted to be able to prove what he had done. Wanted someone like Magda to find it and reconstruct the story, piece by piece.

That he had loved his daughter, Magda didn't doubt: there was evidence to prove it in the care he had taken of her early in life, when she was medically fragile and easily overlooked. But she must have also become, in time, an obstacle to him. Her refusal to publish the book, which must have been greater than the recorded letters indicated, must have been a source of frustration for him, wrestling with the household bills. Isobel was strange and backward and stubborn as an ox. And here was a new woman from a family of fortune, with a daughter of her own, the future mother of his looked-for son.

Like contestants in a three-legged race, Magda and Emily made it down the hallway. Isobel's footfalls shadowed them, her bare feet placed in the exact points where Magda stepped. She glanced back and saw the footprints.

"The whole house is filling up with water," said Emily in awe, looking over the railing.

"The stairs are going to be tricky," warned Magda. "Let's just take them nice and slow."

"The water is coming up," said Emily, still looking down.

"Don't worry about that. Just pray they're structurally solid."

It was a struggle to get down the first few steps, until they came to the hole where Magda had fallen through. "Okay. I'm going to step over first, and then I'll help you over, alright?"

"It's too big a step, I can't make it with one foot," said Emily.

"You can do it. We don't have a choice. That makes it easy."

Still Emily hesitated.

Magda brushed her wet hair out of eyes. "Honey, I know it's hard. I know you're scared. But we have to fight. No matter what, we have to keep pushing, okay? We either fight or we die."

"I can't," said Emily. "I can't."

"We can *do it this time*, Isobel."

"Emily," said Emily.

But Magda couldn't hear her. "We'll do it together, okay? I won't let go, I promise. I'm not leaving you here. He'll have to kill us both, Isobel. I'm here now."

"Stop it!" said Emily. "Stop calling me that."

Magda blinked. "Emily," she said. She put a hand on the wall, which was vibrating as though with suppressed excitement. "You're not going to fall, Emily. She won't let you."

"Who? Who are you talking about?"

"Just reach for me. Come on. I'm right here."

Emily shook her head, but she closed her eyes and stepped—too short, damn it, too short—and Magda leaned forward to catch her under the armpits and haul her up over the hole. They hung for one second over the precipice together, and then Magda hooked her bad foot under the lip of the next stair down and pulled them both back to brace against the wall. She thought for one second she was going to pass out from the pain, and then it faded.

"We did it," said Emily in wonder.

Magda looked down the stairwell at the water coming up like a whirlpool. "We have to keep moving," she said. "These stairs aren't going to be passable much longer." In fact, they were barely passable now.

Emily shivered.

"C'mon. We should make for the front the door. I don't want to risk trying to get out through the kitchen." The metal bannisters were coming loose at the base; she pried one free. "Here," said Magda, wading into the water. It buoyed her up, taking the weight off her leg. She turned away and squatted lower. "Climb on. Piggy back."

Emily reached, her arms trembling.

"Don't be afraid," said Magda, waiting. "I won't slip."

Emily wrapped her arms around Magda's shoulders and Magda kept her feet. The girl was heavy but the water lifted them up as they descended. She felt indestructible as she made her way down. "It's okay. I've got you."

It was a slow walk, one foot dragging, the other carefully planted. Emily laid her head down on Magda's shoulder. "I'm sleepy," she whispered.

"Don't fall asleep now. Stay awake and talk to me."

Something underneath her creaked piteously, ready to give away. She froze, closing her eyes, and counted to five. Magda could feel the heat rising from skin where it was pressed against hers. Her heart was pounding, or was that Emily's heart?

Magda remembered suddenly that she had almost died here. Well, they both had. *C'mon, Isobel.*

The floor didn't collapse. She started walking again.

"You know, Isobel once compared the stars to a staircase, in one of her final poems," said Magda, aiming for distraction. "She was probably picturing this very spot—well, the old stairs that were here—when she wrote that line. That's—kind of fun, right?"

"Sure, I guess." Magda knew when she was being humored. Maybe the distraction wasn't working. "You sure know a lot about Isobel," Emily said.

*I don't know anything about Isobel,* thought Magda. *I never did.*

They made it down, but the water was rougher at the base of the stairs. "Hold on tight," said Magda. "How are you at swimming?"

"I grew up in Tampa. Of course I can swim," said Emily.

"I've lived here for years, and I'm still kind of scared of the water," Magda admitted. "At least, I used to be. I don't think I am anymore."

"I don't think you're afraid of anything," said Emily.

The two of them waded on, the waves catching them before they got back to the hallway and buoying them up. Then Emily scrambled off, and they linked hands. The water was up to Magda's chest—Emily, a little shorter, was almost up to her armpits—as they skirted the edge of the hallway and out into the main foyer.

"Wait—I've got a rope," said Magda, unwinding it from around her shoulders. "We can use it to try and keep ourselves from getting separated, okay?" She remembered stories of the Galveston Bay hurricane of 1900, how people had roped themselves together. It hadn't saved them; they'd been hauled out from the sand that way, still connected, one after another. But at least they hadn't been separated.

They doubled the rope—it was long—and each tied a generous loop around their waists, not too tight. They checked and double-checked the knots.

"Okay, hold on to the window frame," said Magda. "Hold tight now." The water behind the door seemed to have built up quite a lot of pressure, based on the way it poured in around the cracks.

She used the sharp tip of the banister spike to peel back the splintering plywood. It came away easily now, sodden from the spray. It wouldn't have held too much longer anyway, Magda judged. It had held out just long enough.

"Hold on," she warned, tossing it aside and gripping tight to the door handle. She turned it and was immediately swept off her feet. She heard Emily shriek but all her concentration was on keeping her grip. "Hold on!" she spluttered, as her legs were lifted off the ground in the rush of water.

It seemed that all of the ocean was trying to pour itself in through the opening of the door. *Well come on in then, you bastard. I'm giving you permission now.*

Finding the art of pulling herself through the stream like a swimmer, Magda used the knob to drag herself out and around to the front porch, reaching wildly to hold tight to one of the sturdy columns. She was lurched by a sudden increase on the pressure of the rope. Thank God it was so sturdy and strong.

"Emily?" She twisted herself around the railing, using the force of it—still cemented to the base of the porch—to take the weight. "Come on, Emily, you can stand out here." Like hauling in a giant marlin, she pulled hand over hand, trying to keep the tension in the rope without breaking it.

Emily must have been caught in the current behind the open door, but finally Magda saw her white fingers gripping the frame and the pressure on the rope lessened. She kept tension so Emily would be able to use the line as a guide and a counterweight.

Like a mountaineer, Emily was standing, heaving herself through the water as if she was on a steep incline. "You're almost here," Magda called. "Just a little farther."

Emily collapsed, panting, as soon as she was safely out of the channel. "We did it!" she said.

"We sure did. Let's get you to the boat."

Hank's runabout was still bobbing anxiously where it had been staked. Magda cast a look around the landscape— her car was long buried, the garden was gone, the dock was twenty feet under the sea—there was nothing left except what they were carrying.

Still roped together, they slipped across the porch to the boat. Magda hauled it in and climbed in carefully first. It was still slightly listing, but it didn't sink. She reached over the side to help Emily follow after.

"We made it," said Emily, letting herself flop into Magda's arms. "I can't believe we made it."

Magda hugged her back, hard. "We're not out of the woods yet," she said. "I don't even know how to drive this thing."

"I do," said Emily. "And I know where he keeps the spare key."

She searched through one of the small compartments under the wheel and produced it.

"Great, start it up." A few minutes of playing with switches and gauges, and the engine rang out, satisfyingly loud and strong.

"The rain really isn't so bad right now," said Emily, looking around. "The wind either."

Magda had heard that being in the eye of a hurricane could be something of an anticlimax; many storms were too disorganized to have a perfectly clear center like on TV, but she wondered if this sudden drop-off of weather was as close as they were going to get.

"Okay, take it around the side of the house," said Magda. "There's just one thing I need to get."

"What? What do we need? We should get out of here now."

"I can't leave," said Magda. "I have to go back for Isobel."

Inside the trunk was the proof of everything she had learned, the way to finally change Isobel's legacy—but only if Magda could save it. Without proof, she would sound like a crazy woman, raving about a murder in a hurricane.

*"What?"* said Emily.

"I have to. I can't—I can leave the house, but I can't leave Isobel. It's not right. I have to save her."

"She's been dead for a hundred years! It's too late to save her! It doesn't matter anymore," said Emily.

"It matters," said Magda, wiping her nose with her wrist. "It matters to me."

"You're insane," said Emily, shaking her head. "I guess I knew that." She tugged on the tangled end of her own hair and sighed. "But I guess—we did this together, and we should finish it together too—one way or another."

Magda couldn't help it—she slung an arm around Emily's shoulders and pulled her in for a quick, hard hug. "Thank you," she whispered into her salt-smelling, sodden hair.

"Sure. You're welcome, and we're both crazy, and we're all going to die," said Emily. "What's the plan?"

So, at Magda's instruction, she steered the boat around to the back of the house and drew up as close as she dared. Magda splashed out into the water and swam to the metal stairs.

Floating in the water was the kayak paddle she had used to free the box. She forgot she had left it on the side porch, where it must have been washed off by the rain. She tossed it into the boat.

"I hope we don't end up having to row," said Emily.

Magda laughed. "I thought you could use it to bring the boat in closer; you can push off something. We'll keep the engine off to save the gas."

Emily complied.

Magda hauled herself up onto the stairs, feeling every second like a heartbeat—they had to get out while the weather held and before the flooding took out the whole house and the boat as well.

The trunk was still wedged where Magda had been forced to leave it last time, snugly wrapped in plastic. "We can do this together," said Magda. "Okay? You can steady the boat while I lower the trunk down."

"Won't it be too heavy for you?" asked Emily.

"I hope not. The bones barely weigh a thing, but the box itself is waterlogged and hard to maneuver." It was strange to think that Isobel, whose presence had dominated Magda's life for the past two decades, now weighed barely enough to sink in the water—a handful of calcium, turning to dust.

"You're sure you don't need help?"

"Just keep the boat level," said Magda. "Do you think you can keep it still?"

"I can do it." Emily was shivering, but her hands were steady, holding the right side of the boat against the column. The water was fairly smooth, but Magda knew how quickly it could kick up again. She needed to make this fast. But the trunk wouldn't survive a trip through the water, and she couldn't get to the boat from the porch.

She untied the rope from around her waist, told Emily to do the same, and then threaded it through the knotted extension cord around the trunk. Then she then threw the long end of the rope over one of the balcony rails above.

It didn't have perfect slide, the frayed edges catching on the metal bar. Grimly Magda jerked it harder, knowing that she didn't have another plan. They were running out of time. If she couldn't retrieve Isobel now, she wasn't sure she could bring herself to leave without her. And this time she'd be damning Emily as well as herself.

"Pull harder!" called Emily, sounding excited. "I think it's working!"

Magda was sore and sick, underfed, dehydrated—but she leaned back against the pressure of the rope and put all her strength into it, feeling the solid metal of the balcony working with her, the house itself, and finally the trunk had to give way to their combined efforts and it lifted free. She held her breath as it spun slowly up into the air— would the rope hold? Would the waterlogged sides break open, spraying bones and leather into the water in all directions?—but it seemed to bear up, although it was visibly caving in around the cord.

As it swung unsteadily, Magda pulled a little more so it would clear the stairs, then guided it down over the open air above the boat, lowering it hand over hand. It took all of her effort to keep it level and not let it tip as she coaxed it down. She prayed that the trunk would hold together just a little bit longer. The skeleton was fragile, and she wasn't willing to risk losing even one bone. But Isobel had been safe in the trunk all these years, and it would protect her for the rest of the journey.

"Okay, we're getting close," said Magda to Emily. "Now I'm going to try to drop it into the center of the boat, okay? Can you guide it down?"

"Ready," said Emily, shivering.

*Come on, Isobel. Time to get out of here.*

Magda tied off the end of the rope, using Hank's own double hitch.

Then, still using the tension to take some of the weight, she could use both hands to steady the trunk for Emily to guide it into place. It was an awkward size for the runabout—too wide to sit between the seats, but turned the other way it took up more than half the boat.

"Are we all going to fit?" asked Emily doubtfully.

"Sure we are. The question is, can we steer without getting flipped over."

They paused thoughtfully.

"I think she should go in the back seat," said Emily. "Instead of the middle."

"You know what? I think you're right." Emily walked the boat backward, the trunk still suspended by the rope, although Magda also kept a hand on it, afraid it would start to spin. The sodden walls of the box were distinctly bowed and she didn't think they'd be able to maintain integrity much longer.

"Okay, there," said Emily. "Put her down there, maybe."

It was a better plan; with Isobel tucked down on the bench seat behind them, they'd probably have more control of the boat. "Are you sure she won't throw off the weight?" asked Magda. "Once we drop her here, it's going to be hard to move her."

"It'll be fine. I can do it," said Emily.

So Magda untied the end of the rope and they slowly lowered the trunk into place, wedged against the sides. "I hope there's not going to be too much water sloshing around back there," Magda fretted.

"Uh, she was literally under water for like a hundred years. I don't think this last part is going to be the deal breaker. Now let's get the hell out of here."

Magda let the rope drop into the boat, then climbed clumsily back down the stairs, splashing into the water and swimming to the ladder at the back of the boat. "Thank you, Emily, I couldn't have done it without you."

"Yeah, great stuff. We got a skeleton into the boat that we're probably going to die in. Can we just go?" But Emily's voice didn't sound as harsh as it could have.

As Magda got in, Emily slowly and deliberately retied the end of the rope around her waist, still threaded through to cord around Isobel's box. Magda thought she should stop her—it didn't seem that unlikely they would tip at some point—but it felt right. Emily held out the other end and Magda sat in the shotgun seat to retie it. Either all three of them would make it, or they wouldn't make it at all.

"Okay, let's do this thing. But we probably need to inch our way out at first, okay? There's a lot of stuff in this water we don't want to hit. Put it in the lowest speed you can until we get through the trees at least."

"*Your* job is hazard lookout," Emily told her. "I'm on propulsion and steering."

"Got it." It wasn't clear who was in charge of the directions. Maybe it didn't matter. They didn't even know how far up the islands the storm had pushed the water. Maybe there was nothing but hundreds of miles of open water.

"What if we can't make it?" said Emily.

"Of course we'll make it," said Magda. "We'll go all the way to Orlando if that's what it takes."

At least they were together. All three of them.

She looked back at the house, her life's work, and thought about her years as a gardener, the endless weddings, the early mornings, even the suicides—thought about all the times she had read Isobel's poems by lamplight, taken school groups out into the back garden, trying to show them the magic of this place, the power of Isobel's words—Isobel, who loved the water and the birds and the garden.

She, Magda, loved them.

"Let's go," said Magda. "Slow and steady."

*Let it go,* she thought. It was already way too late. What had happened could never be patched over.

Even with Isobel centering the weight from the back, it was lucky the runabout was so shallow bottomed and light. They would use the engine for as long as they had gas. If they had to, they could rig up the shower curtain for a sail. Hell, if they ran out of options, they would row until they caught the Gulf Stream to ride it north.

Magda felt as if she could row forever, just then.

"The sea is still coming up," said Emily in wonder, as they made their way cautiously up what had been the driveway.

"Watch that log. Four o'clock."

"It's pretty uneven here." Emily steered the boat in a slow, wide turn.

Magda was looking back over her shoulder at the water climbing up over the shoulders of the house like a shawl.

"I know how much it meant to you, Magda," said Emily, glancing over as they entered a thicket of branches. "It must be hard to leave."

She had always been the caretaker of the house. But this was also caretaking, thought Magda. The way a mother would bury a child, or a woman would hold the hands of a dying parent. That was still an act of care. The final act.

"You *bitch!*"

Hank grabbed the side of the boat and rocked it violently, almost overturning them entirely. Emily screamed. How on earth had he made his way here from the house? He must have realized which way they would go.

"You think you can just sail off and leave me? I'm the one that got us here, kept us alive, and now—what? You think you don't need me anymore? You think you can do this without me? You can't do *shit* without me. You're not worth shit without me."

The engine cut off and died. "Hank, let go of the boat," said Magda, her voice steady. "You'll tip us all."

But Hank, enraged, didn't let go. He had a bloody lump over one eye and was soaked to the skin. His eyes were wild. Magda rushed to grab for the opposite side of the runabout, to lean her weight on it as a counterbalance so they didn't flip.

Three days unshaven, salt bleached, and hungry, he seemed to have been transformed by the storm from the man Magda had first encountered. Standing waist deep in the murky water, he seemed more like a vengeful sea creature than an ordinary man.

"Hank, we're leaving now, so let us go," said Magda calmly. "There's no room for you." Between Magda, Emily and Isobel, the boat was full.

"I'm the one who brought this damn boat," sneered Hank. "You're not taking it. You ain't gonna make it ten feet without getting dragged down in the water to drown."

"Only if you drag us!" said Emily, from behind Magda's shoulder. "Just let go of the boat!"

"Think you know better'n me," he said, shaking his head. "Think you get to make the decisions around here." His grip on the side of the boat tightened, and he made as though to hoist himself up, rocking the little craft precipitously. But he wasn't high enough to be able to get in, he would need to find something to climb up on. "We aren't leaving. We're going back to the house. It's madness, trying to leave now. The wind and rain are going to start right back up again, you'll see."

"It's too late for the house," said Magda. "You can stay if you want, but we're going now."

"You won't do a damn thing without my say-so," said Hank. "None of you. Not you, not her, and not *her*." He pointed to the box and for one moment Magda thought he could see Isobel the way she could. But of course that was insane.

Still gripping the side of the boat, Hank turned, somehow able to plant his feet on the debris-strewn ground below. "We're dumping that damn thing as soon as we get back to the porch," he added over his shoulder. "Y'all are nuts to be carrying that corpse around like some precious baby. Well, you want to kill my baby, I'm going to kill yours."

The kayak paddle was between them on the floor, the same one she had once used to reach for him and save his life. It had a strong, sharp tip. But she would have to reach for it fast, and it would be obvious, and one end was tangled up under the seat.

She needed to get him back into the white-hot rage that had had him ineptly swinging the rifle at her head. "There is no baby," said Magda. "It's gone. It was gone before you ever got here."

"Magda . . ." whispered Emily.

Hank stopped, still gripping the boat tight. "Lies," he said.

"It's true. Emily—Emily tell him."

"I didn't kill it!" said Emily. "I didn't kill it, it just—it just died."

"Where is it then?"

"I—I hid it in the backpack," said Emily. "I—it got taken out to sea, back at the harbor when the water came in."

Hank hissed through his teeth, the same sound he had made when the boat had slammed into his hand.

"I threw it out," said Emily, sobbing.

"That's how it goes in a disaster like this," said Magda. "We lose things. We have to give them up. There's no point in keeping us here, Hank. The baby is already gone. And Emily and I are going to leave now."

Hank wiped his face. Magda couldn't tell if it was tears or sweat. "You can have more babies," he said. Behind her, Emily moaned.

"You won't be able to control her forever," said Magda. "She knows what you are. She's not going to cooperate anymore."

"What the hell are you doing?" whispered Emily.

"There's no point in trying to appease him, Emily. He'll kill us both sooner or later anyway. We need to end this here, now."

"You shut up," said Hank. "You been talking crazy long enough. Don't listen to her, Em. I always took care of you, better than your mother ever did. I took care of us this long, and I'm going to get us through this storm."

"He already tried to kill you once," said Magda, "And me too. He'll do it again. It's only a matter of time."

"Shut *up*," said Hank, rocking the boat wildly. "You *made me* do that." Water was sloshing over the side, filling up the bottom. Emily screamed. "This fucking—this fucking *place* made me do it. No, shut up—you don't know shit."

The paddle slid past Magda and back toward the stern of the boat. She closed her eyes in despair.

"You don't know *shit*," Hank repeated. "I'm the one who makes the decisions here."

*Just like Charles,* thought Magda, numbly. He must have thought the same thing as he lined up to take that final shot.

"Hank, please," said Emily. "Just let us go. We won't tell anyone."

"You have to listen to me," he said, still dragging the boat back towards the house. They would all go over soon. They would hit some of the jagged wreckage under the water. He would kill them all. "I'm the one who takes care of you. Me. I'm the one!" He swung around, and at the same moment Emily stood up with the paddle and slammed it hard into his chest.

Magda kept her seat, holding each side of the boat so Emily could stay standing on her injured ankle. The disintegrating box, water sodden again, provided counterbalance as she reached take the slack of the rope that still connected her to Emily and to Isobel.

Trusting Isobel to keep the boat centered, she leaned out and threw a loop of the rope around his shoulders, praying that Emily would be able to brace herself. Then she pulled. The boat remained steady, unrocking.

Emily brought the oar down on his bad hand, still gripping the side of the boat—once, twice, three times. He let go and swore, lost his footing and slipped, the rope tangling under his armpits—his hands flailed above the water as he was slammed against the side of the boat and slipped down underneath it.

Emily used the end of the paddle to push him down by the back of the neck. She had her feet well planted now. She took hold of the rope around her waist, keeping it from pulling on the box on the other side of her. Numbly, Magda gripped her end tightly too, and held on.

Isobel steadied the boat. The rope tightened like a noose.

They held their breath while the splutters at the surface of the water—slowed—stopped. Until the bubbles stopped coming up and the rope went slack.

*We did it, Isobel,* thought Magda. *He didn't win again. This time we won.*

She leaned out over the water and shook the rope free. It came up after a moment of struggle.

Emily moaned, covering her face.

Magda took in a breath, and let it out. The wind was still slack, and the sky was the lightest it had been in days. This was their chance. She slid Emily into the shotgun seat and reached to turn the key in the ignition. The engine sputtered and started. Just like a car, as it turned out. Magda turned the wheel slowly, trying to navigate around the many obstacles in the surrounding water.

*Let the ocean come,* she thought, keeping them steady with the cumbersome box weighing down the back of the boat. The house was built from coral and shipwrecks. Most of it had been salvaged from the water in the first place—maybe it was right that it should all go back to the sea. Magda remembered the stories of ancient places that had been lost as the peninsula sank. Was it wrong for Whimbrel House to become one more? She had already found what the house needed to give her.

She steered them toward what had been the highway, through the tall trees in the berm south of the airport, where the lemurs were probably climbing in the mahogany. It might be more difficult to navigate through the trunks and branches, especially with the box weighing them down, but at least they wouldn't be swept away. She kept them pointed northeast—the direction of the next Key in the chain, and if that was gone, the next one after that, all the way to Miami. Whatever dry land was left, that was where they were going.

Emily huddled in next to her, still sobbing, and as Magda steered through the branches, she turned her face into Magda's hip. Magda dropped a hand down to stroke her hair.

*Moving, keep me moving, Lord,* she hummed under her breath. She remembered the long nights asleep in the front seat, her father's hand on the wheel, his rough voice in Magda's ear. *Keep me working, Lord, Till the end of the road.*

She turned at a flash of white, to watch the heron make a last slow circle over the house—a thank-you? A goodbye? A warning?—before it headed out over the open water.

Magda kept them pointed toward the horizon. Behind them the ocean, inexorable, continued to advance.

# Isobel Reyes: The Oxford Literary Companion

## Introduction to the New Edition

Prior to the present period, much of the academic discourse around the poetry of Isobel Reyes has focused on its morbid themes. No doubt this is due in part to the dramatic story of Reyes's own suicide, accounts of which have been widely repeated. However, more recent evidence relating to her untimely death (Trudell, 2023; Trudell & Hulbert, 2024), and particularly the forensic evidence of her murder (Pierce et al., 2024), have added new voices to the discourse and re-energized the scholarship surrounding Reyes's life and works. It is now widely accepted that the killer was her own father (Hulbert & Williams, 2022; Duncan & Fleitman, 2023), after the substantiation of a rifle belonging to Charles Reyes.

This collection of essays by notable Reyes scholars provides an overview of current interpretation, particularly of the later poems such as "Antigone" and "Blood-Root," which have been traditionally overlooked. This edition will address the broader historic and thematic questions revealed by the scope of her composition, cementing her place among the most original and powerful voices in American poetry.

It is our humble wish that a new generation of readers will connect with these remarkable works of candor, grief, and genius. The experience of the poems as a whole should be taken not as the tragedy of a life early lost, but as the enduring legacy of an exceptional mind.

Special thanks are due to the Director of the Reyes Archive at the Library of Congress, for the access granted to the newly expanded collection of materials.

# ACKNOWLEDGMENTS

M Y SINCEREST APPRECIATION goes to all those who advised me in writing this book; while the errors are entirely my own, there was a small army of people who tried to steer me right. On hurricanes, the wonderful Dr. Stephan Morey of NOAA Center for Coastal and Marine Ecosystems, Florida A&M University School of the Environment, and the Center for Ocean-Atmospheric Prediction Studies at The Florida State University was so patient in answering my questions. On history, I was blessed to visit The Hemingway Home and Museum and ask about the staff's experiences during Irma. The Key West Historical Society and the Key West Botanic Gardens kindly provided resources and support. My friend Martha Roesler had to answer the strangest questions from a local's perspective but always answered with such good humor. On marine radios, Lawrence Kreitzer did his best to keep me within the realm of the possible. The writer Dr. Heather Clark generously shared her personal experiences studying the life of Sylvia Plath and inspired Magda's more sensible moments. The Emily Dickinson Museum served as additional inspiration. Real-life poet Sandra Beasley graciously reviewed my efforts and served as poetry consultant; her poetry is still a lot better. More personally, without Chris Bucci this book (and my career) would never have happened. Jenny Chen and particularly Melissa Rechter made this project real—thank you so much. To Jeff, Kellie, Sharon, John, Anastasia, Eugene, Katherine, Deana and Monica: I wouldn't know how to do this without you.

DEC 0 7 2021